The Ladies of WACK

A Practicum in Perjury

Book 2

Stephanie K. Clemens

ISBN:

978-1-957508-05-4

To my friend Phillip Gisi, thank you for always believing in my endeavors. I hope you have moved on to a better place with Rufus beside you.

Prologue

Fintan 1852

Standing at the top of the stairs, I knew this was the right decision. I had to disappear if I was going to survive, if we were going to survive. I looked down at my corseted waist, briefly rubbing my hands over my stomach. I grabbed my valise and took a deep breath.

"Lady Augusta, are you planning to go out to the country?" Lord Randolph Taversham asked.

Turning, I looked at the man I married. Early on, I thought we would be happy together. He had swept me off my feet with his aristocratic good looks, what I thought were kind green eyes and his skill at waltzing. But then we said our vows and everything changed.

"Yes, Lord Taversham. I'm headed to the country estate. The air here in Fintan is a bit stifling." I pushed the corners of my mouth into a small smile, knowing he wouldn't look at me close enough to be able to tell if it was real or not.

"I see, my dear." He paused, his hand flexing at his side. "Were you going to let me know or were you just going to leave without a word?" He raised one eyebrow as he questioned me. I hated that eyebrow.

"I left word with Jeffries. I didn't want to take you away from town. You have important business here and I didn't want to disturb you." I knew he would never believe me, but I had to try to convince him. It was so hard to tell if he even wanted to believe me. My eyes darted from his face to his hands. He looked relaxed, but I had been wrong before.

Taversham reached up and grabbed my chin. His green eyes which I once thought were filled with kindness were now hard, cold, and unfeeling. His fingers dug into my skin, the pain indicating that it would leave a mark. I didn't care as long as I got to actually walk out the door. My stomach fluttered, reminding me why I had not yet given up hope.

"My dear, do you really think I believe a single word

that comes out of your mouth right now? Country house indeed." I could smell whiskey and smoke as his hot breath hit my face. It made me want to weep. My tears would only motivate his actions, his violence. He let go of my face. My heel slipped off the top stair, but I managed to keep my balance.

The distraction cost me: I didn't see his right hand come down, so I was completely unprepared for the impact of him backhanding my left cheek, spinning me enough that my heel slipped completely off the top step, and then the next. I slid down stair after stair after stair until I was on the cold marble floor, unable to move.

*   *   *

I opened my eyes to the light breaking through the curtains. Instead of lying on cold marble, I was surrounded by the familiar sights of my room and the comforts of my four-poster bed. I looked down at my waist. At some point, someone had removed my corset. I rested my hands there, and I knew. The babe was gone. Of course, a doctor would confirm it. I knew I was lucky to have survived the fall down the stairs.

"Milady, you're awake. I'll go get the earl." I thought I heard a housemaid say before rushing out of the room. What did it matter, though?

Through the fog that had settled over my mind, I heard

the clicking of men's shoes on the polished wood of the floor.

"Lady Augusta, my dear." Taversham grabbed my hands. "I was so very concerned."

I carefully removed my hands, barely suppressing the shudder I felt every time he touched me.

"The babe?" I asked.

Taversham at least had the decency to look ashamed as I questioned him. Though from my experience, I knew it wouldn't last.

"I'm so sorry, my love. There was so much blood. I'm afraid you miscarried. The slip and fall brought it on."

"I slipped and fell and miscarried," I repeated, like he hadn't backhanded my face, causing me to fall down the stairs. Indeed, like everything that had happened rested solely on my shoulders, like it was all my fault.

"I'm sure trying to carry your valise downstairs on your own didn't help. Why didn't you call Jeffries to help?"

Yes, apparently while I was unconscious, Taversham had already convinced himself this was all my fault.

"How could I ask Jeffries, my dear?" I said through gritted teeth. "He must be ninety if he's a day. The poor man can't even remember to give you messages. He can't assist me with my valise. In fact, my love"—Cue the internal eye roll at the sugary sweetness in my tone—"I think it's time for Jeffries to retire. I have a perfect candidate for a butler."

"Jeffries is fine, my dear."

"No love, he isn't. If he had remembered to give you the message, none of this would have happened. I must insist that we get someone new. Someone actually capable of the job. And as I am the lady of the household. It's something I should be in charge of anyway."

Taversham's eyes glinted hard once again. But I had backed him into a corner. "Of course, my dear, a new butler is the least you can ask for."

Chapter One

Grantabridge 1870

"Come on, little guy," I cooed. "You can do it, just a little bit farther." I stretched my hands out a little more, standing on the very tiptoes of my ivory leather boots, my bustled backside the only thing anyone could see as I stretched over a hedge, trying to rescue the poor creature looking at me with big, scared blue eyes. "This isn't working, little one," I said, leaning even more of my weight onto the greenery. "I can't tell if you're stuck on something or not."

"You're Lady Georgiana Spencer. Are you going to let a bit of nature stop you from achieving your goal? I don't think so," I said to myself as I lay on top of the hedge and stared at the annoying bit of greenery preventing me from saving the animal behind it. "Maybe I should try to go from under the bush?"

I grabbed the wrought-iron fence that stood behind the hedge with one hand, attempting to get some leverage to actually stand back up. Corsets were not all that useful if one needed to bend at the waist, but they created a lovely silhouette with today's fashions. I continued to struggle to shift my weight back, but I had leaned too far forward in that last attempt to reach my muddy friend. Almost throwing myself backward, my heels finally hit the ground, and I was able to maneuver myself into an upright position. I stood there, one hand on my hip as I picked leaves off the front of my lemony-yellow linen dress.

The poor thing was whining again. It had stopped when I was trying to get it over the hedge. The little whimpers were going to break my heart if I didn't figure out a way to save it. I could just cut out the hedge, although I doubt anyone would truly appreciate my efforts. It would be worth it, as the greenery was in desperate need of maintenance.

With that thought, I carefully dropped down to my knees. So much for this dress. I should have known better than to wear the bright color on such a dreary day. But the color had made me happy this morning, much more than the dreary sky had, so sacrifices were made. At least, they were being made now as my knees rested on the damp stone sidewalk situated directly in front of the offensive hedge. I leaned over, my hat nearly brushing the cobblestone sidewalk, and reached out for the poor little guy, trying not to actually touch the dirt beneath the greenery. I really didn't want to ruin a pair of gloves as well.

"Come on, little guy, can you make your way out this way?" I said, shifting my weight so I was leaning into the bush. It was not an easy feat to both lean in and keep my eye on the trapped creature. "That's it, come here, you've almost made it." With a final stretch of my fingers, I was able to get a grip on the little fur ball and pull him out from under the hedge.

I sat up and gave the muddy creature a good look. A puppy. I had rescued a very muddy puppy.

So much for my gloves. Those were ruined as well.

The puppy was probably about three months old, with ears that flopped down at their tips, piercing blue eyes, and big paws for such a tiny little thing. The little guy—I shifted the puppy in my arms—I mean, girl seemed perfectly content in my lap and had wrapped herself up like a sticky bun in the middle of my skirt and fallen asleep. I sat there, amazed at how happy I felt right in that moment. Until I checked my wristwatch.

"Bloody hell, I'm late, again." I moved the muddy fur

ball into the drape of my dress and carefully got off the ground while gently holding onto my new cargo. I had to get back to the new house, and apparently introduce the ladies to our newest resident.

I looked down at myself, deciding whether it was worth trying to wipe myself off or not. The answer: definitely not. I set off to meet the ladies. I walked through town, passing by the hotel the four of us had been staying in since the unfortunate incident at the dormitory. I still found it hard to believe that someone had burnt down the building. The four of us were all so lucky to be out at the time of the fire.

The walk wasn't easy while trying to contain the little mud ball. The entire time I tried to use my drape like a basket, really wishing I had a basket to carry my new friend in. I watched as some of the locals moved to get out of my way until they actually realized it was me. I'm sure my appearance would be the talk of the town until the next gossip-worthy incident occurred. It was unfortunate that a woman's appearance was something everyone found gossip worthy. I hoped someday that would change, but right now it helped me justify my love for clothing and my need to have the right ensemble for every potential life event.

I must have gotten lost in my own thoughts because before I knew it, I was standing in front of my dear friends outside the house I had just purchased for our new dormitory. Actually, my father had purchased it, but I had done all the research to find the home and brought it to my solicitor. I was so incredibly lucky to have both supportive and extremely wealthy parents. Phineas Spencer was a marquess. His land, our family estate, was on the northern border of Brython, out of the sight and minds of most of society. However, my father's head for business and investments never steered him wrong, and it brought him and the rest of the family under the ever-meticulous eye of the aristocracy. Society did not approve of the eldest son getting his hands dirty working in business. His fortune made some earls look like paupers, which only caused more scrutiny. Not that it was ever talked about in polite society. No one would ever be so gauche.

"Georgi! What happened? Are you okay? Were you attacked?" The questions fell from Philippa Stanhope's mouth in rapid succession as she worriedly twisted her red braid around her fingers, her green eyes wide with fear.

"I'm fine, Pippa, just went on a little rescue mission," I said with a smile. None of us called Pippa by her full name; actually, none of us went by our full names. I looked over at her holding up her steamer bike, wearing her leather leggings, per usual.

"I take it that's what's struggling to get out of your

arms right now? And apparently viciously destroyed your dress. I doubt Hannah is going to be able to save it. Although, your lady's maid works miracles, so there might be a sliver of hope," Madeleine Cavendish said, tucking a stray black curl behind her ear as she spoke. I could almost hear her internal sigh. Mads was used to these sorts of shenanigans from her three younger sisters back home. I'm sure she just didn't expect them from me.

"The shrub was really to blame for the destruction of my dress. This little girl only added a little extra damage." I laughed.

I had stayed out of trouble for the first couple of months at university. In fact, I had spent most of my time trying to keep Pippa out of trouble. Especially after someone tried to frame Pippa for the murder of her steam engineering professor. But with Pippa's name cleared and both the murder of the professor and Edmund Fremont solved, there just wasn't that much for me to do in between worthless meetings with my misogynistic professor. Especially now that we had a new home.

"I see you found the place." I turned to the octagonal building where we would live. It was the opposite of everything the dormitory had been. The dormitory was so grey and shabby before anyone set fire to it. We had all made do.

But this eight-sided four-story building was bright and colorful, painted brick red, with deep-green and white accents. It had a beautiful domed roof, a wraparound porch with an ornate railing, and two curving staircases framing the double doors that led to the entryway. It was unique, one-of-a-kind, really, and I had fallen in love with the building as soon as I saw it. I'm so happy my father's solicitor had listened to me when I showed him the house. It seemed out of character for him. But this house was perfection. If I thought clothing was armor, this home took it to the next level. It was going to define who the four of us were in this town. More importantly, it indicated that we were here to stay.

"Georgi, the h-h-h-house is b-b-b-beautiful. It's so ornate. I think it would have been impossible to miss," Wilhelmina Schulz said, looking absolutely lovely in a soft lavender gown. To think, just a few months ago Willa would have been out here wearing some shade of beige, trying desperately to blend into the background.

"Oh, Willa, wait until you see the gardens, and more importantly, the greenhouse." I went to grab her hands and ended up holding out the puppy. I grinned sheepishly before tucking the mud ball back into my arms. "You're going to love it for your plants. I saw the workspace and knew it was for you. Let's go inside so I can put this fur ball down without having to worry about her getting stuck somewhere."

The ladies followed me into the airy entryway. I walked directly to the kitchen before dumping my little monster into the sink.

"How far did you carry that muddy monster?" Mads asked, staring at it, and then at me. The monster in question was busy frolicking in the sink without a care in the world. I could feel the goofy grin on my face just watching her.

"Across town. She's why I was late. Poor thing was trapped under a bush."

"Of course she was. And you couldn't help but get her free," Mads said, rolling her eyes.

"If you had heard her whimpering, you would have helped her out," I said.

"You overestimate my kindness. Get her cleaned up. And then show where each of us is sleeping." Mads turned and almost floated out of the room. I assume she could find the parlor on her own while I cleaned up. I couldn't really do a house tour in my current state, which I had a feeling was about to get even worse.

"I'll g-g-g-go with Mads. I don't think all of us need to ruin our dresses today, do you?" Willa said, before skipping out of the room.

"Are you in or are you out, Pippa? I need the mud gone

so I can see what this girl really looks like." I looked Pippa
square in the eye, as if this was the most serious question that
had ever been posed.

"Might as well. I'm at least better dressed for the
activity." She grinned, looking down at the playful pup.

"See if you can hold her while I try to rinse her off," I
said, grabbing a tankard before turning on the water. I filled
the tankard up as Pippa cooed at the puppy. But it was like the
monster had a sixth sense, predicting the unwanted stream of
water I had intended to dump on her. I managed to get just a
little on her ear. Which led to an incomprehensible amount of
shaking, mud flying everywhere, and an even more playful
pup. I gave up on the tankard, and both Pippa and I worked on
pushing the monster under the spigot. That strategy worked
better, even as the fur ball slipped out of our hands, drenching
Pippa and me every time she shook. Finally, we were able to
rinse the puppy off and soap her up before she escaped and the
shaking started again. I swear the entire room smelled of wet
dog and fresh citrus oil thanks to the puppy's aversion to
water. It was only one more brief rinsing battle before we
were done. I looked around the kitchen, calculating what the
appropriate bonus was for the staff to have to clean this mess
up. Cook was going to have my head when she saw the
disaster I had created in her kitchen.

Clean, the puppy was a pale gold color with icy blue eyes that looked like they were outlined in kohl. She had a white blaze on her forehead, cute little black eyebrows, and adorable mismatched white socks.

"You're in trouble. This dog is too cute for its own good, and you are already smitten," Pippa said.

"How could you not be smitten with that little face? I don't think I've ever seen a dog quite like her." I held up the monster and wrapped her in a towel before indicating with a nod that Pippa should follow me. "Let's get changed so I can show you around the house."

I showed Pippa to the backstairs. Thankfully, I had thought ahead and had all of our things brought over from the hotel. I entered my room. Pippa and I had shared one at the dormitory after someone set her room on fire. It was such fun sharing, but now it was time to have our own spaces. I dumped the puppy on my bed. She ran around like a maniacal fool until she fell asleep. I swear she was midrun when it happened.

Laughing, I went back to the door. "Hannah, can you please help us change? There was a bit of an incident in the kitchen, and earlier today."

I turned back into the room. Pippa had made herself comfortable, so I sat on my bed petting the puppy, looking around at how perfectly the room had come together, with white wainscotting on the bottom of the walls and a deep blue wallpaper on the top that made me think of mountain views and foreign countries. There was an enormous four-poster bed with luxurious bedding that complemented the walls, adding bits of coral and navy to the design. And the silk Latikan rug brought everything together. I even had a wall of bookshelves and a writing desk set up so I would have a place to work on my studies in peace.

"Well, what do you think? I know it's not your room. But isn't it so much nicer than the old dormitory?" I asked.

"I honestly don't know how you got it all done, with classes and everything. It feels like the old building burnt down just the other day."

"True, but it has been over six weeks. And I wanted us to have a place to stay for the holidays if we didn't want to go back home." Even though Pippa was engaged to the next Duke of Nordaoine, her parents, especially her mother, still hadn't relented in their silly disowning of her. She would come around eventually; after all, Pippa's mother had always wanted to have a duke in the family.

"You . . ." Hannah knocked on the door briefly before walking into the room and taking in my appearance. "Nevermind, miss, I see what needs to be done. Would you like to stick with spring colors, or are you ready to admit that it's winter?" Hannah asked.

"Fine, Hannah, I'll wear something more winter appropriate. Maybe the blue velvet." I let Hannah get to work on fixing me while Pippa kept me company.

"Have you decided what to name her, Georgi?" Pippa asked, referring to my four-legged friend.

"I think so." Even though until that moment I was probably just going to call her a monster. But as Pippa asked, it just clicked into place. "Justice would be a good name for her to grow into."

Chapter Two

"I can't believe I made it through another one of Professor Smythe's classes," I said, throwing my burgundy leather-clad hands into the air. I turned back around to face Lord Kaiden Fremont, the future duke of Nordaoine and Pippa's fiancé. It felt like his tall frame towered over me. It was an unusual feeling for me as I was as tall if not taller than most men. "Did you see how he ignored everything I had to say? It's like this every single time we meet. I don't know if I can take much more of it."

"There are people that hear what you are saying, even if Professor Smythe doesn't," Kaiden said. "They have to be to repeat your theories back almost verbatim to the professor. Even Lord Bradbury is repeating your ideas, and he used to follow Simon around like a lost puppy."

"I know you're technically right, Kaiden. But I also

want recognition for my ideas, my theories. If you were to speak in class, or at your club, or even in parliament, people would not only listen to what you have to say but give you credit for your ideas as well. The only place I'm allowed to speak is our class, and even there I'm never given credit for any of my ideas." I flounced onto the bench in the courtyard outside of our class-meeting spot. The grey-and-burgundy pinstriped wool of my bustle dress artfully fell into waterfall pleats as I sat. I tapped the toe of my burgundy boot on the cobblestones underneath my wool skirts.

"Georgi, you are one of the most brilliant minds at this university, and one of the most impatient. It's like you haven't noticed that we actually have class twice a week now. Why do you think that is?" Kaiden looked over at me. "And no, it's not because we all love listening to Professor Smythe at ten a.m. on a Tuesday morning."

I perked up, just a little. "You think so many of us meet because of me?"

"Of course, most of us would have been perfectly happy continuing the process of self-study that's been happening here forever." Kaiden stood there, his tall frame towering over me for a moment. He then sat next to me on the bench, his warm amber eyes imploring me to believe him. "But you came in and started these interesting and meaningful discussions. Not to mention making a mockery of Lord Bradbury. But even he seems to be listening now, and there's a group of aristocratic men that come every week to hear what you are going to say. And some of them even agree with you."

Kaiden really was too sweet. Pippa was lucky to have found herself such a supportive man, not that I would ever tell him that. "Oh Kaiden, you're just worried that I'll actually follow through and quit. You know that's never going to happen." I pushed myself off the bench. "I'm off; I have to find some small part of this town I can take over before luncheon." With my last words, I turned and walked away, Kaiden's laughter following me in the distance.

Kaiden's logical words had helped to mellow my post-class frustrations. I had gone from fuming to annoyed, but I wasn't ready to go back home. If I did, I would just recount class to Pippa and whoever else was there and work myself up again. What I needed was a brisk walk down by the river to really calm down.

The dreary weather had driven most of the people I would see walking about the town inside. I wasn't about to let it deter me from my goals, though. What was a little mist when you had a sturdy umbrella and a warm wool frock on? Hopefully, the mist didn't turn into an actual rain that might ruin my boots, and I did so love how the burgundy leather matched the striping in my dress so perfectly.

I adored walking through this part of town. I almost had rented one of the townhouses that lined the river, but then I heard about the Octagon House, and I was sold almost sight unseen. My love of our new home didn't stop me from appreciating the stately brick buildings with their wrought-iron fences and green shrubbery. Some of the wealthiest and most influential individuals in Grantabridge lived in these homes.

Out of nowhere, I was knocked, quite literally, out of my revelry.

"I'm so sorry, miss," a young lady sobbed. My hands immediately went out to steady the woman who had run into me. The young lady was wearing the traditional uniform of a household servant, and her brown hair was pulled back into an unforgiving bun. She glanced up at me and then immediately looked back down at her hands and the valise in them. The scuffs and dings on the valise indicated it had seen better days. Her blue eyes were rimmed with red, her face splotchy: it was clear that she had been crying heavily for some time now.

"Oh dear, are you okay?" I asked.

"Yes," she gulped, "miss."

"No need to pretend. It's quite clear something awful has happened. Why don't we go sit somewhere and you can tell me all about it?" I attempted to gather her with one arm and take her with me.

"Oh miss, I couldn't go with you. You don't know me." She sniffed, taking a step back.

"You haven't stolen from me, and you've had plenty of time so far. Leads me to believe you are not a thief. You appear to be in a bit of a spot. Why don't we walk over to Jarrin's, and you can tell me what has you so upset? Having someone to listen to you always makes things a little better." I offered my arm to her once again.

"I guess that will be alright, miss." The young woman went to wipe her eyes with her sleeve, but must have thought better of it, as she lowered her arm rather abruptly.

Reaching into my reticule, I grabbed my handkerchief. "Here you are, dry your eyes, and let's be on our way. There's no need to stand in the rain when chocolate ices await us just around the corner."

I took the maid's arm and steered her down the street. I could see her looking over at me, mouth agape, as we passed the local bookseller. Her reaction wasn't a surprise to me. I tended to get that a lot. It probably had to do with my overwhelming need to take charge and control a situation.

"I'm Georgiana Spencer. What's your name?" I asked once the young maid's crying had subsided.

"Lotte Lane—actually, Charlotte Lane, but only my

mum calls me Charlotte. Everyone else calls me Lotte," she said with a sigh.

"Why the sigh, Lotte?" I asked.

"I don't know what I'm going to do to help my family out now that I've been let go." Lotte sighed again.

"We will have to figure that out, after we have our ices." I stopped in front of Jarrin's, opening the door to the ice parlor. I loved the pink-and-brown decor and the smell of sugar that overtook your senses as you walked into the shop. It always brought a smile to my face. Stopping to get ices was one of my favorite things to do; the sugary goodness was not appreciated enough.

"What can I get for you, Lotte?" I asked, already salivating at the thought of a chocolate ice.

"I don't know, miss. I've never had an ice before. I wouldn't even know where to begin." Lotte's blue eyes were the size of saucers as she looked around the small parlor.

"Never had an ice before! We are going to have to remedy that immediately. My favorite is chocolate, but they have all sorts of flavors, like lemon and lavender," I said.

"I'll try whatever you suggest, miss. I'm sure it will be divine."

"Of course, Lotte. Why don't you grab that table over there in the corner so we can have a little bit of privacy?" I watched Lotte settle into the table before ordering two chocolate ices at the counter. I sat down at the table to wait for the ices and hopefully hear what had happened to Lotte today.

"Why don't you tell me what had you so upset when we met? You looked quite inconsolable."

"It's nothing, miss. I wouldn't want to bother you with it," Lotte said, blushing.

"Clearly, it is not nothing. Anything to make a person cry like that is obviously something. And I'm sure it's something quite horrid."

The waiter arrived and set our ices on the table in front of us before disappearing to wherever the waitstaff hid in the parlor.

"Lady Taversham gave me notice today and refuses to give me references. I'm never going to get another job in Grantabridge, or anywhere else for that matter, without references. And I didn't even do anything to deserve getting sacked." Tears filled Lotte's eyes as she sat there. She blinked over and over again, trying to stop her tears from falling. "I can't move away from here either. My family counts on my wages. And I'm pretty sure Ben is going to propose soon. Unless he thinks less of me now too."

"Oh, you poor thing. That's cold to let you go without references. It causes so much more hardship. Did she give a reason for letting you go at all?"

"She didn't need to. I know exactly why I'm out on the street, miss. Her husband can't keep his hands to himself. He thinks it's his right to have anyone that works for him. And I caught his interest, but I swear I didn't encourage it." Lotte looked frantic at the thought that I might think she had started some sort of flirtation with Lord Taversham.

"Of course you didn't. Everyone in the *ton* knows that he's a lecherous old man that can't keep his hands to himself. There are young ladies who dread seeing him at their annual holiday masquerade for that very reason." I enjoyed a giant spoonful of the chocolate ice.

"Lady Taversham walked in and he had me pinned down. I was so thankful at first. She had saved me from, well, you know." Lotte grew quiet, then shook her head as if she was trying to shake away the memory. "But then she fired me on the spot. Not that I want to be in a house with that man ever again. Whatever am I going to do? I have no job and my family needs my wages to survive. And I don't want to leave Grantabridge. I've been stepping out with Ben Harrison; he works in the Taversham' stables."

"Eat the chocolate ice. It won't solve anything, but you will feel better. I promise. After that, I think I can help you with your other problems as well." I sat back, trying to determine the best place for Lotte in our household.

Chapter Three

As soon as Lotte and I finished our ices, I escorted her to the Octagon House. I just couldn't think of the Octagon House as a dormitory after the abysmal place the four of us were staying before, even though that's exactly what it was. I even hoped to house any other ladies admitted into University in the future.

"Are you sure that the other ladies will let me work in your home? I know I am very good at what I do, but without references, won't they question my ability?" Lotte asked, wringing her hands as we walked. I'd attempted to reassure her that she would be accepted, but after her experiences today, she remained on edge and untrusting. Not that I blamed her. Lady Taversham had dealt her a serious blow.

"Lotte, it's going to be fine. I know you have no reason to trust me, but I'm positive my friends and the few servants we have will welcome you and find a place for you in the household." I patted her shoulder.

"It's just . . .," Lotte began.

"Now, I do so hate interrupting, but there's no sense in working yourself up. I know today is not a day that has inspired trust in others, but I have no intention of setting you up for further disappointment."

My words didn't seem to calm Lotte's nerves. The wringing of her hands was a constant as she walked beside me. She did, however, stop voicing her concerns. I'm not really sure if that was better or worse.

"Where have you been?" Pippa asked, careening into the entryway as soon as I walked in the door. Justice followed right behind her. It looked like Pippa and the puppy had been playing; there were tiny scratch marks on Pippa's leggings. It did not surprise me that Pippa was the first into the entryway. She was used to me coming directly home from Professor Smythe's class, oftentimes with her future duke. Mads and Willa followed her in at a much more sedate pace.

I bent down, picking up the rambunctious puppy and letting her lick my face in an exuberant greeting before turning to my friends.

"Yes, Georgi, you are home rather late today," Mads said. Her dark brown eyes scanned the room. "It seems you met someone on your way home, I'm sure providing a reason for your delay."

Mads's calm demeanor always impressed me, especially since it was a direct contradiction to her nickname. I always expected her to be a bit more emotional. But she took everything in stride for the most part.

"Oh, you brought someone with you. What's your story?" Pippa asked, turning towards Lotte.

"Pippa, this is Lotte Lane. She worked for the Tavershams," I answered for Lotte. Sometimes Pippa could be a bit direct and lacking in expected social graces.

"Not Earl T-T-T-Taversham! I don't even w-w-w-want to go to his masquerade, he's so awful," Willa said. She was the shyest of the four of us and didn't enjoy parties, and the earl had a reputation.

"Yes, I was let go by Lady Taversham today. She won't even give me references. All because her husband tried to—" Lotte gulped. "Well, you know. Miss Spencer heard me crying outside of the Taversham residence and offered to help. But I don't need to stay if it's too much. I can be on my way if you like."

I watched as Lotte tried to head back to the door.

"Of course you must stay," Pippa said, reaching out to grab Lotte, but thinking better of it.

"See, Lotte, I told you it wouldn't be any trouble." I

patted her on the shoulder while pushing her farther into the house. "Let me introduce you to Hannah. She's our lady's maid. And basically runs the household. She'll find a place for you."

After I introduced Lotte to Hannah, I made my way back to the parlor, where the ladies were having afternoon tea. I walked into the room, taking a moment to appreciate the colorful decor. Nothing was drab or grey like the dormitory that had burnt down. Our new parlor was bright and happy. I had made sure of it. There was wainscotting up to the chair rail, a gorgeous blue-and-yellow floral papered the walls above the wainscotting, and buttery yellow curtains accented the multitude of windows in the room.

"I see you've taken in another stray, Georgi," Mads said, her eyes following me as I took a seat on the blue velvet settee.

"Two in one week. I do believe that's a record for you," Pippa chimed in, looking up from her book briefly. It didn't surprise me at all that Pippa was already studying something. Probably figuring out how to build a new machine that would change the world.

"It's not like I had much of a choice. Assaulted by the earl and then fired by the lady of the house? I didn't want her to end up on the street because those in power would rather take advantage of her rather than protect her." I took a plate from the tea tray in front of me and filled it with sandwiches, my favorite red pepper and cream cheese being well represented amongst my choices.

"True, you definitely did the right thing," Mads said, taking a sip of her tea. Tea that lacked both milk and sugar. I truly did not understand how she could drink her tea without, at the very least, a splash of milk.

"It makes me wonder what more we can do. I know we had planned to have more salons with the women that worked in service, but it fell apart after our dormitory burnt to the ground." I stood up, pacing the room as I thought. "There has to be something we can do to help others that end up in the same situation as Lotte."

"We definitely need to keep the Women Adventurers' Consortium of Knowledge alive. After what happened, I don't know where I would be without the ladies of WACK. And I want to be able to help others as well. I wouldn't mind trying more self-defense classes," Pippa said, closing the book she was reading. "We never really finished the first one due to an unpleasant interruption. Do you ever wonder who broke in that day? I don't think it was Lord Middleton. I believe whoever was there would have left with a shiner from my punch, but in my last run-in with Lord Middleton, he was uninjured."

I couldn't stop the chill that raced up my spine as I thought back to that day. Pippa had disappeared, kidnapped right outside our dormitory by Lord Middleton. I had gone to Kaiden for help, along with Willa and Mads, only to find that Pippa had managed to rescue herself and to get Lord Middleton to confess to killing Professor Aneurin and Kaiden's brother Edmund. Lord Middleton had been arrested, and we hadn't heard from him since, but his parting words still worried me. I just couldn't believe that others were out to get us, or I didn't want to believe it. It was hard to ignore, though, after someone burnt down our home.

"There's so much we don't know about yet. I think Lord Middleton was just a small part of a much bigger scheme. I'm hoping that our new home will be much safer than the last one." For a moment, I stopped pacing. "You're right, Pippa, we need to teach more self-defense. I wish there was something we could do to give the serving class more bargaining power. Too bad they can't form a union of sorts," I said, resuming my back-and-forth walk across the room.

"Something like that would be nice, but I think it only really works when there is one employer. Not so much when there are dozens of employers like we have here," Pippa said.

"We also have to be careful with the self-defense. We don't want maids getting fired for defending themselves, but we want to keep them safe. I wonder if we should also work on avoidance techniques?"

"That's a start. But I really think we need to teach them skills that can hopefully get them out of service so they never feel stuck in an untenable situation. I was thinking we can start with Mads teaching them how to budget. Willa can teach first aid as well as cooking. If you're up for it, of course. We can add some engineering to our salons for you, Pippa. And I'll work on writing and reading," I said as the plan formulated in my head. I knew we couldn't actually save everyone from situations like the one Lotte had found herself in, but I wanted to do everything I could to prevent them. And I couldn't punish the Tavershams: society would never support a servant's word over that of an earl or his wife. It seemed the only help I could offer these ladies was to give them options. If they felt they could leave an unpleasant situation, they would be in a better position overall.

"I know you want to save everyone, but it's not possible," Mads said.

"I know; the world is divided into too many camps. If you think about it, there's a set of rulers who believe the only way to rule is out of fear. It's like the treatise about the young prince who was advised that it was better to be feared than loved if you could not be both. This was the main advice to avoid revolt and maintain power." I loved political theory: I could go on and on, and often did. "Now, another camp looks at what the people want and considers ruling more like an obligation. As a ruler, you are obligated to represent the people you rule. This means ensuring their rights are protected, even if it means protecting the people from each other."

"As much as I love your lectures, Georgi, is there a point to this one?" Pippa asked with a smile. I knew she loved me, even if she didn't appreciate my lectures.

"Just that the earl believed his servants should fear him, not love him. Where others, including myself, believe that servants have rights, and as someone with some authority, I should do something to protect them."

"She's basically just giving us reasons to hold more salons," Mads said.

"That's true, I am." I shrugged.

"Let's pick a Sunday afternoon for the next one and have Hannah spread the word," Pippa said. "If I remember correctly, that's when most staff had time off, if their employers gave it to them."

Chapter Four

The days blurred a bit as all of us fell into a routine at our new home. Lotte was fitting in with the small staff we had. The cook absolutely doted on her and had taken Lotte under her wing. Lotte didn't seem to mind as she became the cook's go-to assistant. I cannot even begin to describe how happy I was that Lotte was comfortable here. Almost as happy as I was when Justice jumped into my bed at night and curled up right in the crook of my knees and slept. I felt like I was right in offering both of them a place, even if my friends were always mocking me about taking in strays. I had even taken in our butler, Mr. Pendrake, when he left his position at the Lankershams'. Lord Lankersham had accused Mr. Pendrake, a footman in his household at the time, of stealing a painting. Hannah had solved the mystery of the missing art, proving what had actually happened to the painting.

"Lady Spencer, there is a collection of correspondence for you and the ladies," Mr. Pendrake said as I descended the stairs. Yes, Mr. Pendrake was quite young for the job of butler. He couldn't have been much older than twenty-two, but he was a rather burly fellow. After all that had happened at the dormitory, I felt youth and cunning would serve us better than someone older and statelier. Thankfully, the others went along with my decisions. Most of the time with absolutely no fuss.

"Thank you, Mr. Pendrake," I said, holding my hand out for the correspondence, which he handed me with great aplomb. He may be young for a butler, but he was mimicking the required snobbery quite well.

I thumbed through the letters. One for Pippa from her brother Percy, a missive for Mads from her sisters, or at least one of her sisters, and an invitation.

"Ooh, I wonder what this is for?" I asked myself. "We so rarely get invites to anything here in Grantabridge." I tore open the envelope to find a gilded invitation. It was to the Tavershams' annual winter masquerade ball. Interesting. This could be an opportunity for a bit of revenge on Lotte's behalf. I wanted justice to be served for what happened to her; maybe this party would be just what I needed to make that happen. Of course, if I was going to get revenge—I mean justice—I would need some help.

*   *   *

I had gathered everyone into the parlor for some plotting, one of my favorite things to do. I stood in front of them as they sat around the room, all looking up at me, waiting for me to speak. It was a heady feeling, knowing people wanted to hear what you had to say. Prior to coming to University and meeting my friends, only my parents and those they paid to watch after me had ever taken the time to listen to my ideas.

"I have an idea," I started, pressing my hands to my stomach as if that would calm the butterflies wreaking in there.

"Those are never good words to hear. Whenever one of my sisters started a conversation with 'I have an idea,' it normally meant there was trouble right around the corner," Mads said, looking up at me as she waited for me to continue.

I cleared my throat. "We just received an invitation to the Tavershams' annual winter masquerade."

"Not another party." Pippa sighed. "I hate events like this, and you know Lord Taversham is going to try to grope every woman in attendance. Can't we come up with a different plan? You know, I could just break into his study or other personal space. I am really good at snooping around now. I could even create something to help me scale a wall."

"Why d-d-don't we let Pippa invent and scale walls? I

would rather avoid a party. Especially one at the Tavershams' home."

"Don't you think it will be easier to get into the earl's study if we are invited into his home?" I asked. I wanted to illustrate how practical it was to go to the masquerade, hoping Pippa and Willa would agree with me.

"How? We have to make sure we know where the earl is, in a room where everyone is wearing masks, and sneak off to his study without being seen. Wouldn't that be easier if no one even knew we were there?" Pippa folded her arms across her chest and leaned back in her chair.

"You know, Pippa, Georgi does have a point. If we are already inside, it would be much easier to drift down the hall and even easier to explain why we were there if we did get caught," Mads said.

"Yes, that's exactly what I was thinking, Mads. You just put it into words so much better than I. Thank you." I wanted to hug her. I might love political debates, but I didn't love arguing with my closest friends. This was starting to feel like an argument.

Pippa looked at me, then over at Mads. She threw her arms up in defeat. "Maybe if I have to go, I can dress up like a man."

"Or you could coordinate costumes with Kaiden. I'm

sure he has an invitation and will protect you from roaming hands. At least the earl wouldn't get too far before Kaiden stepped in to stop it. He has training in hand-to-hand combat from his time in the military," I said.

"I see you are dead set on all of us going," Pippa said. "My idea is a good one and could be done without being noticed. But we'll do it your way, this time."

"If I m-m-must, I will make the sacrifice." Willa blushed. I wasn't used to her being sassy, but here she was, definitely adding a little sass to the conversation.

"I appreciate your sacrifice, Willa. Who knows, you may even have fun. While I would want to go to a masquerade no matter what, I actually have a plan. I want to find out more about Lord Taversham. Maybe find something that could be used to control his behavior."

"Georgi, that sounds an awful lot like blackmail," Mads said.

"That's because it is blackmail, but sometimes you have to go around the law to get justice, and we would be seeking justice." I finished my sentence right as my little fur ball charged into the room and catapulted towards me. I reached out just in time to catch the exuberant puppy. "Oh, little one, I guess I should be careful with my words from now on." I snuggled with the pup as I waited for a response.

"It would be nice to put that man in his place. I might even add it to my list of hobbies." Pippa laughed as she responded.

"The question really is, how do I find what I need to convince the earl to change his ways at the party? I'm going to need to get into his study without attracting any attention."

"Sounds like you need a distraction. I'm sure we can help with that," Mads said. "In fact, there are lots of things we can do to provide distractions. Starting with costumes. I have some ideas on what I can wear to help keep the guests' attention."

"That's fantastic, Mads. I can't wait to hear more. I thought it would be best to plan out what we would each wear and then head over to the modiste. The ball is next Friday; that only gives a week to get everything ready. Plus, we have the salon in two days, and it needs to be a success after our last debacle." I paced as my thoughts started racing from masquerade costumes for each of us, to the salon on Sunday, to what sort of distraction we were going to need at the masquerade.

"Will you please sit down, Georgi? Your pacing is making me dizzy." I could tell Mads was exasperated with me. Sometimes I had that effect on people, especially when I didn't quite flesh out my plans fully.

I sat on the edge of a delicate blue-velvet and oak chair, my feet crossed to prevent my foot from tapping incessantly. Justice curled up in my lap and fell asleep. My normal state was one brimming with energy that tried to escape my body in any way possible. Foot tapping, finger drumming, and pacing were my favorite methods of releasing energy while I planned or plotted.

"I'm sorry, Mads, there's just too much circling in my head. It makes it hard for me to sit still."

"You shouldn't worry about the salon. It will be superb. I'm prepared to teach them how to successfully budget. I've even prepared small notebooks for them to keep their budgets in. Willa has prepared the menu so the women will have a snack while we work. And Pippa has some physical exercise for them to do when we break or to help them stay engaged if they struggle with math."

Mads explained all that had been done in planning the salon to me. I was impressed. I was used to all the details being left up to me when it came to carrying out any plans I was a part of. But my friends had a way of taking my ideas and running with them—something I appreciated very much, even if sometimes it left me feeling a little lost. I was very much used to being in control of everything and having all the details left to me to figure out.

"Since that is taken care of, we should come up with ideas for the masquerade. I have some thoughts, but I want to hear yours first. It's always more fun dressing up if you like the costume you are wearing," I said, back to my usual bossy self.

"I would like to do something like a wood sprite." Pippa chimed in. "I can even do it wearing leggings. Everyone will talk about my costume, and me. You know even with a mask, they'll know exactly who I am." Pippa gestured to her hair as she spoke. She was right. It would be impossible to hide her fiery red hair from anyone. "Causing a stir doesn't bother me, though. I do it almost every day."

"You are getting better at causing less of a stir. Professor Gates would probably have a conniption if you wore leggings to study alchemy," I said.

"I know, it's so frustrating. Did I tell you I almost caught my bustle on fire the other day working with him on an experiment? All he did was mutter under his breath that things like that wouldn't happen if he were working with a man. Then continued with the process." Pippa laughed, I'm sure at the ridiculousness of the entire situation. It was truly unfortunate that Professor Aneurin had been murdered. He had been such a great mentor to Pippa. Now she was biding time, studying alchemy while the university searched for another steam engineering professor. Although to listen to her ideas, she could probably teach the course herself. At least it sounded that way to my untrained mind.

"That would be perfect, Pippa. Can you imagine the look on Lady Corinne St. Gramflurri's face when you walk into the ballroom? It's going to cause quite the stir. You should show up after me, with Kaiden, of course. That way I can sneak out while you are being announced." I would normally rub my hands together gleefully as my plan came together, but the addition of Justice made it rather difficult, so I settled on petting her instead.

"I think I should wear the traditional attire of Sindtha. The cut is very different from the fashions here. With the sarida over a shorter skirt and a short blouse and no bustle, it will scandalize people. They will be shocked at seeing the clothed female form without corsets or bustles to hide my natural curves. Brythionites are ridiculous in their views on women's clothing," Mads said as she lounged on the settee. Mads was elegance and grace personified. I could envision her walking into the ballroom in rags, and everyone would turn and look at her. But in something as gorgeous as she described, jaws might break as they hit the floor.

"Aunt Honoria would agree with you. Did you know she was part of a safe clothing movement during her time spent in Eletharis?" Pippa asked.

"That sounds divine, Mads. You are going to turn heads. I can just picture it in the deep red of garnet, with gold trim, sparkling in the lights illuminating the ballroom. And with the mask on, you will be stunning." I clapped my hands in excitement. Justice looked up at me with judgment, then jumped off my lap and curled up on the Latikan rug. "And Pippa, your aunt is inspirational. We should have her come talk at one of our salons, or just visit. I would do almost anything to just sit and listen to her talk about her adventures."

"I hope th-th-that means I can wear something that blends in. I'm not c-c-comfortable standing out like Pippa and Mads are," Willa said, looking at her hands. She always looked at her hands when she was nervous about something. "I don't want to let anyone down. But maybe I can be the lookout or something along those lines."

"You could never let us down, Willa." I took her hands in mine. "And I think a lookout would be a fantastic idea. You can wear a dress you are comfortable in and a lovely mask. I wouldn't want you to be uncomfortable."

She looked up at me, her big blue eyes wide and glistening. "Th-th-thank you. I think I would be much more comfortable filling in that role of the plan."

"Perfect. Now, I think I will dress as a goddess from

Hellias. It's a pretty common costume, but maybe I can have it made without the need of the bustle for a little more maneuverability," I said.

"You're going to go as Themisia, the goddess of law and justice?" Pippa asked, raising an eyebrow at me.

"Of course I am. I couldn't go as anyone else, especially with our mission," I answered with a coy smile.

Chapter Five

The salon came and went, and was a tremendous success. The women who showed up were enthusiastic about learning whatever we threw at them. I was surprised. Even though I appreciated mathematics and the importance of budgeting, I could barely muster any excitement at the thought of spending hours learning about it. To see so many others excited about it made me so happy, and budgeting could help some of these women progress to housekeeper, or if they ever wanted to, they could open their own shop. It seemed like the possibilities were endless. Granted, that was due to my overwhelming optimism. There was still a lot to overcome, depending on what they wanted to become.

The success of the salon bolstered my spirits through the week and helped me make it through another of Professor Smythe's antiquated discussions on Thursday. Lord Bradbury had monopolized the entire time set aside to speak with or listen to the professor. Today, he espoused why married women should not be allowed to maintain ownership of property, even if it had been theirs prior to marriage. I had nearly jumped out of my skin at his arguments, attempting to get in my counterarguments. But Professor Smythe had just clapped Lord Bradbury on the back, telling him what a good job he had done analyzing the nuances of the situation. Nuances my arse, more like repetitive misogynistic drivel.

Really, what else did I expect? One of these days, I was going to stop going to these meetings. It wasn't worth it. I wasn't learning anything, unless you counted learning how far these so-called gentlemen would go to wrest power away from women. It was absurd. Although maybe learning how far they were willing to go was the exact education I needed. It would help me determine just how far I needed to go to make the changes I thought the world needed. I pondered that thought as I walked into the entryway of the Octagon House.

"Georgi, it's about time you are back. What took you so long? The masquerade is tomorrow night, and I'm questioning everything." Pippa accosted me as soon as I closed the door. She had one of her braids in her hands and was twisting it over and over again.

"What's caused all these nerves? You were almost

excited about the ball yesterday," I said, taking her braid out of her hand and placing it behind her shoulder. I steered her towards the parlor.

"The modiste delivered the costumes for tomorrow. I don't think I can do it. The fabric is almost the same color as my skin tone. So I look almost completely undressed in it with vines wrapped around me, covering my unmentionable parts." Pippa stared at me, eyes wide. "I was thinking it would be a darker color, almost like wearing my steamer-bike clothes, just fancier. I enjoy pushing boundaries, but this is too much. It will reflect poorly on all of us and Kaiden. It's too much of a scandal." The words rushed out of Pippa's mouth one atop of the other as she paced. She stopped in front of me when she was finished, expecting an answer of some sort.

"It does sound rather scandalous. What do you think your Aunt Honoria would do? Would she wear it?" I asked. I had met Pippa's Aunt Honoria when Pippa was arrested for hindering a police investigation. Aunt Honoria was a whirlwind. I had never met a woman like her before, and I wanted to be just like her, in my own way, of course.

"It is probably too much, even for her. I'll show you, and then we must decide how to fix it," Pippa said, running off to her room before I could say anything. I followed behind her, hoping my dress was ready as well. I made my way up the stairs at a slightly more sedate pace. At the top of the stairs, I turned to the right. Yes, the dress had arrived. Hannah had hung it on my door. She knew I always wanted to see the new clothing before anything else.

"See, Georgi, it's a bit too much, don't you think?" Pippa stood in the doorway to her room. She was right. The fabric and the draping of the vines made her look naked with vines wrapped around her. I couldn't send her out in it. We wanted a distraction, not a scandal.

"Why don't we see if we can make a toga-like frock to go over the bodysuit? And we can wrap the vines around the toga in a bit more circumspect manner. How does that sound, Pippa?" I hoped I could find something in my closet to help her out. If not, I might be without a costume of my own. I would have to give her my dress with some alterations. I didn't really want to do that, but if I must, I would do what I could to make our plan work.

*   *   *

It was the day of the masquerade. With a little effort and the repurposing of the yellow gown I had inadvertently ruined, Pippa felt comfortable in her wood-sprite costume, and we would not set society on its heels as we would have with the original costume. Now, Pippa looked more like a fairy from a ballet or theatre performance.

I had spent the evening wrapping her hair around papers in the hopes it would stay curled for the event today. This morning, I must have looked ridiculous as I sat taking out the curling papers from Pippa's hair while Hannah curled my hair. I planned on piling the curls on top of my head with a gold laurel leaf headband that complemented my brown hair. I insisted Pippa wear her hair down this evening, with the costume fixed, and curls cascading down her back, she looked like a wood sprite in the best of ways. I hoped I could pull off Themisia half as well.

The toga the modiste designed looked fantastic on me. All the pleats sewn into the pale gold fabric were flattering, but not revealing in any way. Even if it looked like with one good pull it would come tumbling to the floor, leaving me quite exposed, the dress itself was much sturdier, and I thought the deception was almost magical. Mads's beaded crimson sarida was stunning on her, as were the jewels she had put around her eyes. I loved how she had done her hair. She had a beautiful garnet-and-gold chain lying on her part and resting on her forehead. The entire look was both dramatic and exquisite. She was sure to stop everyone in their conversations when she entered the room, which was just what I needed to carry out this plan. And Willa looked absolutely sweet and demure as a sheepherder from a lovely nursery rhyme.

Willa and I left first for the masquerade. The plan would only work if we staggered our entrances to the ball. I donned my cloak, protecting myself from the winter chill that would blow through my attire without the heavy wool protecting me. I shivered as I stepped outside. The carriage was waiting—well, the steam carriage was waiting, and the driver, Mr. Colin Finnigan, looked quite dashing as our chauffeur. It was the cap that really finished off the look. Willa and I got into the steam carriage, immediately bundling up under a wool blanket to stay warm for the short drive.

It wasn't long before Colin pulled up in front of the townhouse where I had first seen Lotte. Just thinking of her tears that day had my hands tightening in fists around the wool blanket. The thought of even more victims steeled my resolve. I would find something about Lord Taversham that could be used against him. The women who worked for him needed that protection.

Willa and I made our way to the door. I handed the butler our invitation and then my cloak before moving up the stairs to the ballroom. Willa dutifully followed behind me. Her hands clasped in front of her. I knew she was nervous, but I wasn't quite sure how to calm her nerves. I paused, looping my arm through hers, and continued up the stairs. Since it was a masquerade, I didn't have to worry about anyone announcing us. Instead, I checked Willa's mask and then mine before entering the ballroom.

I had to admit, even though I hated to, the room was stunning. Two crystal chandeliers lit the room, sparkling above the dance floor. Crystal sconces adorned the outer walls and each alcove. One side of the ballroom opened to the outdoors. While still quite chilly, it cooled the crowded room off nicely.

"Let's grab a refreshment," I said, turning to Willa. "Maybe they have mulled wine. How splendid would that be at a winter event like this? I have heard the Tavershams always spare no expense for their annual winter ball. Some people even come down from Fintan to attend the event."

I looked at Willa as her eyes widened, and she gulped. "That m-m-many people will be here? It's such a crush. I hope we don't have to stay too long."

"You will be fine. In fact, if you would like to, we can sit by the matrons over there. It will let everyone know that we don't feel like dancing tonight. It would make my escape to the study much easier once Pippa and Mads come in." I handed Willa a warm glass of mulled wine.

"That would be l-l-lovely. I would rather not draw much attention to myself tonight if I can avoid it." Willa stared at the glass in her hand.

"I'll do what I can, but Willa, you know you could shine at an event like this. You look absolutely adorable. Any of the men here, and probably some of the ladies, would love to steal a moment of your time." I smiled at Willa. Taking Willa's free arm, I kept to the outside of the room to avoid all the lovely men and women dancing under the sparkling chandeliers. It took most of my focus to maneuver around the room. The dance floor had the most space, but couples were waltzing with an abandon you only see at masked balls. The outside of the room was lined with people waiting to take to the dance floor. Then there was the rest of us just trying to get from one side of the room to the other.

"Maybe until I opened m-m-my mouth. They would lose interest as soon as I couldn't get my words out." She looked down at her hands.

"None of us have ever lost interest in what you have to say."

"B-b-but you and the others are different. You've always been kind. Most people in this world are not kind." Willa looked at me with her wide eyes.

I shook my head. I knew she was right, but I wanted her to be wrong. Everyone should get to know people first before judging them. If they did, they would find Willa to be one of the best of us, while others, like Simon Middleton, to be the absolute worst of us.

"I know, but you are one of the good ones, and I can't help but want others to know your goodness. One day, you'll feel comfortable sharing it with more people."

Willa and I finally made it to the corner where the matrons sat. I had glared at some men pretty pointedly on our walk over. It was clear they wanted a dance, but I didn't have time for dancing tonight. All of them had looked at my face and ran, except for one.

"Excuse me, Themisia, would you give me the privilege, nay, the honor of dancing with me?" I looked up to see Vrondias, the king of gods, beside me. More accurately, I looked up to see a tall, somewhat gangly Brythionite dressed as Vrondias beside me. I glared at him from behind my mask, but he did not retreat. Instead, he raised a single eyebrow. It was like he was daring me to say no, but how could I now, surrounded by some of the worst gossipmongers in Grantabridge? I was trying to stay anonymous tonight, and this, this *man* was drawing attention to me.

"Since you obviously cannot take a hint, it would seem I'm obliged to say yes, Vrondias. Couldn't you go harass one of your other wives or human mistresses and leave me be?" I said under my breath. I glared back at him while offering him my hand.

"I'm afraid not, for tonight it is you, Themisia, who has caught my attention." The soft burr of his voice almost subdued my annoyance. His deep whiskey-colored eyes seemed to sparkle behind his mask as I sparred with him verbally. He took my hand and maneuvered me to the dance floor. His arms did not look strong, but he moved with determined purpose as we took our place. The beginning strains of a waltz played. His hand pressed into my shoulder, the warmth of it seeping through the thin fabric of my dress, sending a tingle up my spine. My pulse raced. I turned to look at him and found myself staring at his lips. My, he was tall. It was quite rare that I was shorter than anyone.

Surprisingly, he did not speak as he led me around the dance floor. His steps were confident and his arms strong leading me through the waltz. Lights blurred with the brightly colored costumes of the other dancers as we twirled and dipped, moving around other couples who were struggling. He pulled me slightly closer than was proper to avoid colliding with another couple. I looked up at him as we stopped, forgetting to breathe for a moment. His face, half hidden by a mask, was unfamiliar to me; his brown hair flopped down across his forehead, hiding even more of his face. I wanted to reach up and move it, but I stopped myself.

"I must be getting back to my friend. I wouldn't want to leave her by herself." Turning, I all but ran back to where Willa was sitting, happily being ignored by others. Or so it seemed by the small smile on her face.

"You l-l-looked lovely out there, Georgi. So interesting that his costume matched yours. It looked like you two were meant for each other."

"Oh posh, we aren't meant for each other any more than you and I are meant for each other. We just happened to both like Helliasion gods." I waved, dismissing the entire incident.

"If y-y-you say so, Georgi." Willa smiled at me before looking down at her hands.

I took a seat next to Willa, wondering who Vrondias actually was. I had met so few men who were actually taller than me here in Grantabridge; it would be more accurate to say I had rarely met someone taller than me ever. And his accent reminded me of up north, where my father's estate sat. We rarely stayed there, my father having a trusted local to take care of the land and our tenants while we stayed in town. My family was titled, but my father had found it imperative to be in Fintan where he could watch over his business investments, the real reason my family was as wealthy as it was.

I shook my head. I didn't have time to ponder just who

the gentleman was or how his accent reminded me of home.
Pippa and Mads would be here soon, and I needed to be ready
to scurry off when they did arrive. Until then, I would wait
patiently. Ha! Like patience was in my skill set. More like, I
would wait on the edge of my seat until they arrived.

"Did you see the house they are in now? It is bordering
on gaudy. But what would you expect from those women?"
The clipped tones of a society matron stood out above the
sounds of the ballroom. It always amazed me how someone
could find the right tone to cut through the noise of a party,
especially if they wanted to express their disdain. I looked
around to see who was speaking, and saw none other than
Lady Corrine St. Gramflurri sitting next to Lady Augusta
Taversham. Lady Corrine's pinched expression spoke volumes
on its own. I turned back in my chair away from the gossiping
women but attempted to hear every word uttered by those two.

"Oh, I did. Apparently, Lady Georgiana Spencer has
leased it for an indefinite amount of time to provide a space
for those women to continue to attend classes at Grantabridge
University. The way she flaunts her wealth is so gauche. It's
as if she was one of those heiresses from Eletharis. No sense
of propriety whatsoever," Lady Taversham sniffed as she
finished her diatribe.

"It's because her father insists on involving himself in

trade. I know he is a marquess, but he refuses to act like one. It's no wonder that his daughter is the way she is," Lady Corrine said. I could picture her shaking her head in disdain, the feathers in her hair swaying.

Do not cause a scene, Georgi. These women and their opinions do not matter. They were stuck in the past, ignorant of what was actually happening in the world around them. I repeated this to myself a few times while taking deep breaths like Mads had suggested I do whenever I wanted to correct someone ever so impolitely.

"It is no wonder the moral character of Grantabridge has deteriorated since those women arrived. You have the one with red hair riding around on that contraption. I heard her parents disowned her when she decided to study here to protect their older daughter's prospects. Then there's the one that isn't even fully Brythionite. Her father made his money trading spices since he was the second son. Then there's the merchant's daughter. She can barely put a sentence together. I don't know what she is doing here. And, of course, Lady Georgiana—did you know she hired that maid you fired? Their staff is even of disreputable character." I looked back and I could tell Lady Corrine was just getting started. "Since they have arrived, there's been a murder, and that building burnt down. It cannot be good for Grantabridge."

Lady Augusta nodded her head in agreement. "And did you see their butler? He is so young. With them hiring the maid I let go and a butler that young, I wouldn't be surprised if all sorts of unspeakable things are happening there. It must be absolute chaos, with not a moral fiber amongst anyone there."

I wasn't going to be able to keep my mouth shut. How dare these, these—ugh, I didn't even have a word for it. Women were their own worst enemies. It was bad enough that men saw the advancement of women as a threat, but when powerful ladies in society felt the same thing, progress became nigh on impossible.

"Can you believe there isn't even a chaperone amongst them? One of them is even working in town with a man," Lady Corrine said. I couldn't tell what she thought was more offensive: the fact that Pippa was working, or that she was working with a man. The gossip about Pippa was surprising. I thought the engagement to the future duke would have stifled much of it, if not all of it.

"With their disrespect for the rules of society, I wouldn't put it past them to be running a house of ill repute. They are doing everything within their power to thumb their nose at good society," Lady Corrine continued.

That was it. I couldn't stay silent anymore. These

women went too far accusing us of being madames and whores!

"Excuse me, did you call for me? I do believe I heard my name," I said, standing as I turned towards the two harpies, pulling myself to my full height so I towered over them as they sat in front of me.

"Oh no, we didn't, well, I didn't," Lady Corrine spluttered in front of me.

"I see, so you were gossiping about my friends and me while I was in position to hear every word you said. Didn't anyone ever tell you it was rude to talk about others? Especially when one of the people you are discussing is less than three feet away and can hear every word you are saying. I would have assumed you had more class." I could have said more; in fact, I wanted to say more. However, I knew these women would not listen to me, so what was the point of an angry diatribe? Instead, I walked away with as much poise and grace as I could manage. I wished I moved as gracefully as Mads.

Speaking of Mads, it was at that moment Pippa and Mads entered the ballroom on the arms of Lord Kaiden Fremont. The entire room went silent, taking in the attire, or the lack of attire, of my friends. Their entrance definitely had the impact we desired.

I hurried out of the room and made my way to the study. I hoped the entrance of Pippa and Mads had distracted Lady Corrine and Lady Augusta from my actions. Since I didn't hear anyone following me, I assumed it had. Willa was already waiting at the door for me, hands clasped in front of her. I could tell she was trying not to fidget. She must have snuck off when I mouthed off to Lady Corrine. I shouldn't have done it. All it did was draw more attention to me, attention I didn't want tonight. But, I couldn't find it in me to regret it.

"Hurry, G-G-Georgi, I don't want us to get caught." Willa looked around, her eyes darting up and down the hall.

"It's okay, Willa. I'll be as quick as I can. Remember, speak loudly if anyone comes down the hall and say you were looking for the ladies' retiring room and somehow got turned around." I knew I didn't need to give her instructions. But telling others what to do actually helped settle my nerves.

I took a deep breath and straightened my spine, rolling my shoulders back before I opened the door. The room was dark, with only one light on by the desk. It smelled of pipe tobacco and whiskey. I considered pouring myself a sip before searching but thought better of it.

The earl's desk was directly in front of me, imposing

because of its size, and made of solid wood, with a large window behind it flanked by heavy velvet curtains. The walls were lined with bookshelves; they even stood on either side of a fireplace with a stunning tile-and-wood surround. Above the mantle was a detailed landscape, with rolling hills and a babbling brook running through them. It was so detailed I could almost hear the water. I made my way to the fireplace, surprised that it was lit on the night of the masquerade. No one should be using this room. I ran my hand down the top of the leather sofa facing the fireplace, almost surprised by how soft the material was. It had clearly cost a fortune.

I was about to make my way to the desk, but something drew me back to just how comfortable the sitting area looked. That was until I looked down at the sofa. Lying there, unmoving, was the Earl of Taversham. I would have guessed he was just sleeping but for the knife sticking out of his chest.

Chapter Six

I stifled my scream, looking in horror at what—I mean who I had just discovered. I hurried to the door, frantically trying to process what I had seen.

"Willa, I need you to come look. I'm sorry. There's a body. You need to see before we alert anyone." I stumbled over my words, grabbing Willa's arm and dragging her into the room and over to the corpse.

"Oh, m-m-my, how interesting. He appears to have been stabbed, but there's no blood." Willa looked at the body, very detached from it all. My heart was pounding, and my palms were sweating. But this was the calmest I had seen Willa all night. Medicine must really be her forte.

"What does that mean? Wait, we can discuss it later. Get back out to the ball. I'm going to scream and run out, alerting everyone."

"Wait, l-l-let me examine him a little more. If we are going to investigate, which I am assuming we will, I won't have to wait for the coroner's report." I watched as she looked at his fingernails and everything else. When she finished, I pushed her out the door and closed it behind me once again.

I counted to ten, and then I screamed, throwing open the doors to the study and screaming again. I raced to the ballroom, gulping for breath. By now, those in attendance had noticed me. The musicians silenced their instruments with a disharmonious, off-key note. The ballroom was so silent when I stopped in the entryway I swear every single person here could hear my heart pounding. I made myself glance around the room wildly as if I was searching for someone I couldn't find. My eyes stopped for a moment when they connected with a set of piercing blue eyes serving champagne.

Was that . . .? It shouldn't be, but I swear it was.

After a brief pause on the maid, my eyes came to rest on her, Lady Augusta Taversham.

"I'm so sorry, but he's dead. Stabbed. In the study. I didn't mean to go there. I was looking for a place to rest and compose myself. My head was pounding after, well, you know. Instead . . ." I shuttered. "I found him. Lord Taversham."

With that statement, I collapsed to the ground. I hoped

everyone believed I had fainted due to the stress of finding the earl. I heard someone (was that the king of gods, my dance partner?) tell the crowd to give me room to breathe. If only he knew how good of an actress I really was.

"Oh my, Georgi, someone get me some smelling salts." Pippa fell to her knees beside me, bending over my body. "You better be faking this. I didn't even faint when Professor Aneurin died, and I liked him."

It was all I could do not to giggle at her statement. Somehow I persevered. I gave a quick nod. There was a loud clicking of heels on the floor that stopped beside my head.

"I will stand guard at the door until the police arrive. It is important that we keep the crime scene clear until a thorough inspection can be done." The clicking of heels moved away from where I lay.

"Kaiden will make sure the crime scene isn't disturbed for now," Pippa whispered as the most obnoxious smell in the world entered my nostrils. The smell was so bad I couldn't even put words together to describe it.

I spluttered and tried to sit up, but Pippa pushed me back down before I got very far. I coughed delicately, allowing her to assist me in maintaining the show of being overwrought and fragile. A part I didn't really enjoy playing.

"Clear the way, please. Is there a retiring room I can

take her to? She clearly needs to sit." Pippa helped me off the ground, her petite frame holding me up as I stood almost a head taller than her. "Miss Cavendish, Miss Schulz, a little assistance if you would." Our friends fell in around me, and we quickly removed from the ballroom, down the hall, into the room next to where the earl lie dead.

"Bloody hell, Georgi, what happened?" Pippa dropped any pretense of helping me as soon as the doors to the room shut.

"I have no idea, Pippa. I was looking around the room, admittedly admiring the masculine decor before I searched the desk, when I looked down at the sofa, and there was the Earl of Taversham, dead." As I sat down on the cream-colored settee, I shivered. This was my first time actually seeing a dead body. It was all I could do to hold myself together. The whole thing was quite distressing. "He had a knife protruding from his chest. Right where I imagine the heart would be." I pointed at my chest, illustrating where the knife was. That's when I noticed the trembling of my hands. I lowered my hands to my lap, then clasped both of them together, trying to do whatever I could to stop them from shaking.

"Georgi, dear, this all must have given you quite a fright. It is rather unexpected. Are you alright?" Mads sat on the settee next to me. She took my hands in hers. "Why, your hands are as cold as ice and your entire body is shaking."

I hadn't noticed until Mads said something, but I was quite cold. I could not stop shivering and my teeth chattered uncontrollably.

"Oh, Georgi, I'm so sorry. I wasn't even thinking how this could be affecting you. Let me see if I can get you a warm drink, tea perhaps." Pippa ran off before I could answer, not that I would say no to a fortifying cup of tea.

"She m-m-must be in shock." I heard Willa whisper to Mads. "I was reading about it in a recent medical journal."

"What should we do?" Mads asked. It was like I heard them talking off in the distance.

Willa and Mads sat next to me while we waited for Pippa to come back in with the tea cart, which seemed to be taking forever, or maybe it was a few moments. I took the time to compose myself as much as I possibly could. I was a little annoyed with myself at the moment. My reaction seemed both extreme and detached. I preferred the detached to the shaking mess, though.

Pippa was back, followed by a maid pushing a tea cart. Mads took it upon herself to pour, adding just a dash of milk and sugar to the one she handed me. I was thankful she was serving. My hands trembled so much I would have sloshed tea all over the place if I had tried to pour. I took a sip of the hot fragrant liquid, and I swear I felt it move through my body, warming me up. After a few sips, my teeth had stopped chattering. I no longer felt like there was ice living inside my body.

"Now, Georgi, can you tell us anything more? Before you have to tell the police," Mads asked.

"Not really. Willa probably could say more than me. She took the time to look over the body. All I remember is the knife in his chest and the lack of blood." I shivered again at the thought of the pearl-handled knife sticking out from his white dress shirt and waistcoat. Hmm, strange, he didn't appear to be wearing a costume, not even the unimaginative domino those that didn't like costumes wore, for the ball at his own home. I don't remember seeing a domino lying around anywhere in the room either. "The lack of blood surprised me. His white shirt was just so white, even with the knife sticking out of it. I would think if a person was stabbed in the chest, blood would be everywhere. Oh, and he wasn't in any sort of costume, just his evening coat. Wait, I said that already, didn't I? I don't know if that matters or not, but it seems odd since he is the host for this event."

"The l-l-lack of blood is an indication that he was already dead when he was stabbed," Willa said. "His fingers, particularly around the nails, were blue, as were his lips. This could be a sign of heart failure or cyanide poisoning."

"Really? That many people wanted the earl dead?" I don't know why I was shocked, but to stab a dead body seemed strange to me. "We all knew he wasn't a good person. In fact, he probably was the worst sort of person. But that doesn't normally lead to one's murder. No matter how much it may have been deserved."

"Georgi, you cannot say that about people. No one deserves to be murdered." Pippa looked at me in shock. She might not know it, but she was a lot nicer than me. There were definitely things I thought needed harsher punishments, and taking advantage of anyone who could not protect themselves was something I could not forgive.

A knock on the door interrupted my vengeful thoughts. I looked up, along with the other ladies of WACK, to see Kaiden standing in the doorway.

"Georgi, Detective Inspector Radcliffe is here. He's examined the crime scene and would like to speak to you." He looked at the others in the room briefly. "Alone."

My heart raced at the thought of being alone with the detective inspector. I knew it had to happen, although I really hoped he didn't arrest me after the interview like he had arrested Pippa the last time one of us had come across a dead body. I can't believe two of us had found dead bodies since arriving at Grantabridge. My hands trembled in my lap.

I took a sip of my tea. When I set the cup down, it chattered against the saucer. "Send him in." I sighed, looking at the others. "I'll be okay. What's the worst that can happen?" I asked, knowing full well each of us was thinking of the night Pippa had spent in a jail cell.

The others got up, each stopping by me to offer some gesture of comfort before exiting the room.

"Okay, Kaiden, let him in or bring me to him, however the detective inspector wants this to go." I stood, once again rolling my shoulders back and straightening my spine to prepare myself for whatever was to come.

"This way, Georgi. The body has been removed, but Radcliffe would prefer to see you in the study." Kaiden offered me his arm as we walked to the next door in the hall. I don't think I had ever met a gentleman as naturally polite as he was in my life. Once again, I thought about how lucky Pippa was to have found him. He opened the door to the study for me before stepping aside.

I thought about my breathing, regulating it to a slow in and out, then I thought about my mother. What would she do in this situation? Not that a police officer would ever interview her. Still, it would not hurt to channel the marchioness. I rolled my shoulders back before speaking.

"My dear Detective Inspector Radcliffe, I had not expected to see you again, especially not under such dire circumstances. I assure you I will do whatever I can to help you find this culprit," I said, trying to sound like my mother.

"Ah yes, Lady Spencer, I just want to go through what happened here tonight. Please take your time." Detective Inspector Radcliffe stood with his notebook and pen in hand.

I went through the very little I knew, not mentioning the fact that Willa was in the room with me. It was not long before Radcliffe was done with me.

*   *   *

After being dismissed by the detective inspector, I gathered my fellow ladies of WACK and made our way back to the ballroom. Most everyone was still there, masks removed, waiting to be told what was to happen next. Milling about the guests was staff in quite elaborate livery serving glasses of champagne. Once again, I thought I saw Lotte amongst them, but that could not be right.

I continued to watch as the detective inspector approached Lady Augusta Taversham. I wondered if she would become a suspect. The conversation was brief, far enough away that I could not hear a word of it. That is, until the look on Lady Taversham's face completely changed. I looked to where she was staring and realized I had actually seen Lotte serving at the party. I moved through the crowd to her. I had to get her out of here as quickly as I could. Before . . .

"You! You dare to show your face here again? Detective Inspector, it must have been her." Lady Augusta pointed at Lotte. Lotte, in turn, stood there, eyes wide, the color draining from her face. Lotte's eyes darted to me, but it was too late. "I fired her after I caught her seducing my husband."

My scoff interrupted Lady Taversham's speech. She looked over at me, clearly displeased with my reaction to her words. But I could not help it. To think she would fire Lotte for her husband's actions and now accuse her of murdering him. I would not stand for it. I took a step forward, only to feel a hand on my shoulder stopping me.

"You cannot help her at the moment," Kaiden said, a tone low enough that only I could hear him. I looked back, scowling. I knew he was right, but I would rather walk up to Lady Taversham and slap her.

"It must have been her. She has no other reason to be here," Lady Augusta continued, glaring at me as she did so.

The detective inspector did as was expected. He approached Lotte and took her off with him. All I could do was stand there and watch it happen.

Chapter Seven

My friends rushed me out of the Tavershams' home after
Lotte was arrested. They knew I was about to tell Lady
Augusta just what I thought of her and her accusations.
Seducing her husband. Ha! Every single lady of any standing
knew that Lord Taversham had been a lecherous old goat.
What was Lotte doing there, anyway? I told her we would
handle the earl.

It wasn't long before my friends and I were standing in
our foyer. I pushed open the pocket doors to our parlor,
marching into the center of the room. I didn't know if I wanted
to sit or stand. Stand, I wanted to stand; there was too much
angry energy coursing through me to sit sedately anywhere.
So I paced. I was sure to wear a hole in the rug with the way
things have been going. But I couldn't think while sitting still
when I had so many emotions circling through me. And I

needed to think.

"We need to fix this. I don't know why Lotte was there tonight. But she wouldn't have been discovered if I hadn't been snooping. We have to get her out of this situation."

"We will, Georgi, but for it to work, we have to be calm. You know as well as I do that none of the officers at the Station House, especially Radcliffe, will listen to us if we are in a state. And Georgi, you are in a state right now," Mads said, sitting herself down calmly on one of the more delicate chairs in the room.

I flopped down on the settee. "You are right. Always the one to speak reason, while the rest of us are in a snit. What I need is a plan and information."

"There you go. Getting your wits together will only benefit Lotte in the end." Mads looked at me with her knowing gaze. She knew that the gears in my head were already turning. Which they, of course, were turning fast and furious as I thought about all that had happened and what steps needed to be taken next.

"We need to get Lotte out of jail. I will not have her lingering there as we work to solve the case. I will have to post bail for her."

"You do not have to do it all on your own, Georgi. I have some extra funds to contribute to the cause," Pippa said. I went to interrupt her, but before I could, she continued. "No, don't. I've been working with Colin for a while now and have put some aside."

"We will all c-c-contribute, Georgi," Willa chimed in.

"The three of you are the absolute best friends a lady can have." I clapped my hands together, excited that plans were coming together. "I do need to figure out why Lotte was at the party. It does make her look rather suspicious."

"It does, but it would be good to hear why she was there before coming to conclusions. I'm sure she has her reasons, even though those reasons lack thought," Mads said.

"I'm so pleased that you don't think I'm ridiculous for not suspecting her," I said.

"Honestly, I haven't written her off completely. But she really had no reason to kill him. She's working here, making more than she was at the Tavershams without having to worry about a lecherous old man. She's actually in a better situation now than she was in before. What would murdering him get her, other than revenge? And she knew we were working on it," Pippa said. "But she does have some explaining to do."

The four of us continued to plot. I made a list of legal treatises I might need to help Lotte with her case. Then we turned to the manner of the body. It was clear I needed more information to help in the pursuit of determining the cause of death. The blue fingers and lips pointed to too many things. Then there were the reasons someone would want to murder the earl. At this point, the only one I knew with a motive was, in fact, Lotte. But if any of Willa's theories were correct, there was a chance that the poisoning had been going on for some time, if the earl was indeed poisoned.

"There is nothing to it," I said. "I need more evidence just to be able to make a list of suspects. You know they will not turn away from Lotte unless there is someone else to take the blame."

"Isn't that the truth?" Pippa sighed. I was sure she was thinking of what happened to her and her unpleasant night in jail.

"I'm going to have to break in: that's all there is to it," I said. "My search wasn't successful at the ball. The only thing to do is plan to go back in. Now the question I have for you ladies is what should I be looking for while I'm there?"

I stood back up and started pacing, thoughts whirling in my head as I did so. I could never plan while sitting. There was something about moving back and forth that sparked creativity in my brain. Or in this case, a list of things to look for to find suspects for this murder, or double murder of the same man. I shook my head. That made no sense. Why would someone stab a dead man unless they didn't know he was already dead?

"I would look for financial records. Money is always a motive for killing someone. The earl must have kept records of his expenses and his profits," Mads said. Our numbers lady was always thinking about, well, numbers.

"I would start there, too, Georgi. I doubt the earl was involved in anything engineering related, but you could always see if he was stealing ideas or designs from someone. It may seem petty, but when you've worked as hard as most designers have to come up with an idea, someone stealing it is the worst thing ever. Especially if they make a success out of it," Pippa said.

"I w-w-would love to see health records, or if the earl was on any medications. Determining the actual cause of death could be useful," Willa chimed in.

"Oh, these are all such great ideas. I wonder if there's a list of recently fired maids like Lotte. Or their families. I can imagine a father or a brother would want to murder someone who treated the female staff like workers in his own personal brothel. Or illegitimate children from one of these incidents. I'm sure there are many."

"Oh yes, those are some superb ideas. I'm sure you

will find something there," Pippa said. "Now you just have to figure out how to get into his study again. I think it will be rather more difficult than the last time."

"No Pippa, it will not. It's not like I'm going to be able to walk through the front door this time. I'm sure I will need your help in figuring out how to scale the wall." I laughed as I spoke. Pippa was our resident troublemaker. Less so now, since she was someplace where she could focus her energy, but her work with Professor Gates didn't excite her like her studies with Processor Aneurin did.

"I could definitely figure out something to help. Of course, that would mean you taking the time to listen to my instructions. Listening to others isn't exactly one of your stronger talents," Pippa said.

"Oh Pippa, it's not the listening I have problems with. It's the following of orders."

Chapter Eight

The next morning I arrived at the Station House as early as possible. I hadn't been there since Aunt Honoria, Kaiden, and I had tried to get Detective Inspector Radcliffe to release Pippa from jail. Kaiden and I had stayed after Honoria and Pippa had left. I had done my best to smooth over the injured pride of Detective Inspector Radcliffe while also sneaking away to talk to the coroner and convince a younger officer to let me look into the file on Professor Aneurin's case. The file was almost empty at the time. It is a good thing the detective inspector had had us on the case, or it never would have been resolved.

The last time I had stepped foot in the Station House, I tried my hand at looking like the most patriotic miss in the county seat. Today I was dressed much more conservatively in a deep grey walking suit with a matching hat. I was attempting to give the impression of men's day wear with the femininity of still being a woman. I had even packed my glasses. They gave me a right smart look, or at least that's what I thought. The funny thing was, I had no medical need for the spectacles, but they made others think I was more intelligent than they would normally give me credit for. Little did they know, I was still smarter than I looked.

The Station House itself surprised me every time I walked through the door. It had warm wood-paneled walls and these large desks that reminded me of my father's study. It didn't fit in my mind as a place where they solved crimes and held criminals.

"Good morning, I was wondering if Detective Inspector Radcliffe was here. If he is, would you be so kind as to let him know Lady Georgiana Spencer is here to see him?" I said to a young officer who had kind eyes. He looked too nice to just ignore me.

I watched the officer walk towards the detective inspector's office as I stood in the front room. I was doing all I could to appear to belong. But it was difficult to do so; a woman wasn't supposed to be here. I managed to keep my back ramrod straight and my shoulders back, looking down my nose at anyone who passed.

"Bloody hell, what does that interfering woman want

this time?" I heard Detective Inspector Radcliffe yell. I doubt he knew just how well his voice traveled inside these walls.

"Sir, I believe she is here about Miss Charlotte Lane," the young officer said.

"Another one, isn't that just dandy?" I don't think I had ever heard sarcasm in a person's voice quite as clearly as I heard it in the detective inspector's. "Well, show her back here. I'm sure if we leave her up there much longer, she will create quite the stir. Which is the last thing that we need right now."

Within moments, the young officer was back, escorting me to one of the interviewing rooms. I was surprised but wasn't about to correct him. This would give me time to speak to Lotte, let her know what was happening, and determine her actual innocence.

The officer held the door open for me, and I swished past him right into the room. "Oh Lotte, I hope you were alright during the night. I came as soon as I had gathered the funds to post your bail. I . . ." Lotte's eyes were darting back and forth between me and something else, which brought me up short.

It turns out we were not the only two people in the room. There was also a young gentleman. He must have stood when I entered because he stood now, taller than me by a good six inches. He had dark brown hair that appeared to flop down over his forehead. His eyes were the color of whiskey. As for the rest of him, he almost looked scrawny—that wasn't quite accurate. His frock showed off broad shoulders, but everything else looked gangly. With the training Pippa had done, I thought I could probably take him out if necessary.

"Declan Bailey, at your service. I am going to be representing Lotte in this matter."

I looked at Mr. Bailey, trying to discern why he felt familiar, like I had met him somewhere before, but I could not quite figure out how or where.

"If you are representing her, have you arranged for bail yet? I am here to post it for her and take her back to our home, the Octagon House. Any meetings you need to conduct with Lotte can be done there," I said, channeling my mother the marchioness.

"Miss, do you mean I won't have to stay here another night? It was positively dreadful," Lotte sniffed.

"Of course not, Lotte. I would have had you out last night, but I wasn't sure I would have enough pin money to see to your release. I am so very sorry for leaving you here overnight. Just a little while ago, the same thing happened to Pippa. She has told me it was an awful experience." I tried to soothe Lotte, holding her hands as I spoke. Mr. Bailey seemed to have failed at comforting her. "So, Mr. Bailey, have you discussed bail with anyone here? If so, can you please direct me towards the person to whom I should speak?"

Declan Bailey cleared his throat, his whiskey-colored eyes boring into me. Once again, I had the thought that he seemed familiar, something about those eyes. "Ah miss, I don't believe I got your name, or why you would concern yourself with this case."

"That's because I have not offered it. And I'm not sure if it is any of your business why I am 'concerning myself with this case,' as you put it. I could ask you the same thing. I know Lotte cannot afford to pay you, and yet here you are offering your services as a solicitor or barrister?"

"Miss, he said I did not have to pay him, something like he was taking the case pro bono," Lotte said.

"Not getting paid. Why would you do such a thing, Mr. Bailey? What is in this for you?" Maybe it was wrong to judge him so harshly, but gentlemen lately have proven to be anything but actual gentlemen. I paced in the small interview room. It was not nearly as satisfying as pacing in the parlor, but it would have to do.

"I saw a young lady . . ." Mr. Bailey watched me walk back and forth. He pursed his lips. "That is to say, last night . . ." He glared at me more intently. Out of the blue, he slammed his hands down on the table. "Dear god woman, will you not sit still? It is impossible to concentrate with you fluttering about."

I stopped, placing my hands on the table opposite him. Anyone who knew me would have known to back away. However, Mr. Declan Bailey did not know me yet.

"Fluttering about," I said, my voice low and even. "Mr. Bailey, I do not flutter. I move with a purpose. And the purpose right now is to help me think."

"Whatever do you need to be thinking about?" Mr. Bailey said as we glared at each other over the table.

"Whatever do I need to think about? What, you assume just because I am a lady, clearly my head must be filled with lace, ribbons, and other fripperies? In fact, I'm here to get Lotte out of here and help her with her case."

"Help her with her case? Help her with her case," Mr. Bailey looked down at his hands on the table, straightening himself out so that he stood at his full height. Which was shockingly tall. "And how exactly do you plan on doing that? Are you going to go to court, stand in front of the judge, and plead for mercy? Hoping your good looks and pleasant tones carry the argument? Oh wait, you cannot stand in front of a judge. You are not licensed in any way, and you are not licensed because you are a *woman*."

I stood up to my considerable height, my spine ramrod straight and my shoulders back. "I hope you are not implying that I am incapable of doing the job because I am a woman. If that is your belief on the subject, I'm sure I can find a solicitor who is more open-minded, which I do not mind paying for. My dear Lotte deserves the best, and I'm afraid your words have led me to believe that you are not the best." I turned to Lotte. "This will take but a moment. I am going to arrange bail and get you out of here at once."

I turned to Mr. Bailey, giving him a brief nod, and made my way out of the room. As I was leaving, I heard him say, "That is not what I meant at all . . ." But the door shut before I could hear any more of what that insufferable man had to say.

I looked around the station, spotting the detective inspector. Once again, I thought of my mother, who was a tempest finding land, and made my way towards his desk. He looked up at me as I was still a few desks away. His eyes darted from me to the door as if he was calculating if he could make it there before I stood in front of his desk. He reached for his hat, planning his escape.

"I wouldn't try it, Detective Inspector Radcliffe. This will be so much easier if you stay."

I watched as he sighed and settled back into his chair. "What can I do for you, Lady Spencer?"

"I'm here to post Charlotte Lane's bail. She is a maid in my household, and I find we do not run efficiently without her. I can assure you she will not run from the house. Her family is local, as is her beau," I said, shooting down the arguments that I knew were coming.

"Shouldn't you talk to her lawyer? He is in with her right now. Maybe he has already arranged for her bail." Detective Inspector Radcliffe tried his best to dismiss me, but I wasn't having any of it.

"Has he? I spoke to him shortly, and it seemed he had not arranged for anything. In addition, I am contemplating hiring her an attorney from the firm my family frequents. She needs fair representation if she is going to prove these charges are false. I'm not sure Mr. Bailey is the best choice at the moment."

"You're going to have to do a lot to prove they are false. She was serving at an event after Lady Taversham fired her and told her to leave the place. Why in all that is holy would she do that? Unless she had a nefarious purpose."

"Nefarious purpose or not, Detective Inspector, I intend to prove that Lotte did not commit the crime. Haven't you learned anything from your last murder investigation?" I placed some money on his desk. "There. That should cover her bail. I'm going to go get her. She will be staying at the Octagon House if you need either one of us."

I walked away, leaving Detective Inspector Radcliffe wondering what had happened. At least he nodded to his underling when I went back to the interview room and collected Lotte. She looked at me, shocked, as she followed me out the door, thanking Mr. Bailey as she did so.

I felt rather than saw Mr. Bailey follow us out of the Station House. I continued walking with my arm around Lotte until we were far away.

"Are you okay, Lotte?" I asked.

"Yes, miss, I survived. I'm sure it is my fault I ended up there overnight. If only I had listened to you."

"None of that, I'm sure you had your reasons for being there, as foolish as they may be. And we will discuss them once we are back at the Octagon House. For now, I just want to make sure you are okay and nothing untoward happened while you were there."

"I'm fine, miss, thankful to be away from that place but worried it is just a brief respite, and I'll be back before long. Who is going to believe me over Lady Augusta? Nobody, that's who."

"I believe you, Miss Lane," Declan Bailey said,

interrupting the conversation between Lotte and me.

"Is your belief enough to convince others of her innocence?" I said, turning towards him. "Are you so important that people will believe her at your say so?" I glared at him, shaking my head as I did so. "I did not think so."

I continued walking back to the Octagon House with Lotte, Declan Bailey still following us. I swear I could feel his anger rolling off him, all of it directed at me.

"And am I to assume that you have a plan? You know each and every thing you are going to do to prove Lotte's innocence?"

"As a matter of fact, I do. My only actual dilemma is if it makes it to trial. Because, as you so kindly pointed out, I am not allowed to become a solicitor or a barrister because I am a woman, despite the fact that I've been studying court rules, testimonial exceptions, and so much more. I could probably conduct the trial in Latin if it was required. But I'm not even allowed to enter the room and speak to the judge because I was born the wrong sex." I threw my arms in the air and continued walking.

"You need me," Mr. Bailey said from behind me. I stopped, turning very slowly to face him. None of my friends were around to hold me back, so I must do it myself. I wasn't sure I had the strength to hold myself back. Needing a man to do something I wanted to do on my own made me so angry.

"I need you? Mr. Bailey, I believe you have it all wrong. Lawyers like you are all over the city. I do not need you at all. I need someone with the requisite licensing to be allowed in court to present a case. What I do not need is an arrogant, self-absorbed man telling me what I do and do not need. In fact, sir, I would even go as far as to say, you need *me*. I'm the one with the plan, the team of people to help, and the resources to get anything else I may need. Can you say the same?" I turned away from him once again and continued on my way back to the others so we could sit down and discuss the matter.

"Lady Georgiana, I feel you are going to be most displeased when you find out that I'm the only attorney in the area who was willing to take the case. While your title and name are impressive, there are very few who are willing to go up against the combined power of Lady Augusta and Lady Corrine. I am the only one potentially in all of Grantabridge."

"Is that so? If that is the case, then I will offer you my assistance."

"What makes you think I'm going to need your assistance? I have been managing cases on my own for a few years now. I'm sure I can handle this on my own as well."

"I can see that you believe that. I look forward to

proving you wrong."

Chapter Nine

"I was almost certain Mr. Bailey was going to follow us all the way into our home," I said, removing my hat and gloves and handing them to the butler. "He is the most insufferable man that I have ever met."

"I don't know, miss, he was quite pleasant before you arrived. He had some ideas about how to proceed with my case. It wasn't until you got there that things became rather tense," Lotte said.

I stared at her for a moment, trying to discern if she was blaming me for Mr. Bailey's behavior or just making an observation. I decided to believe it was just an observation and nothing more.

"We do need to speak, though. I want to help you out, but I cannot do so unless you are open and honest with me." Taking her by the hands, I looked at her. "I truly do want to help you, but only if you want me to."

"I do, miss. Your help would mean the world to me. I'm in so much trouble now and I do not know what to do," Lotte said, tears filling her eyes.

I made my way to the parlor since Lotte and I had a lot to discuss. But before we started, I wanted my fellow Ladies of WACK with me. If the four of us were going to take the time to work to clear Lotte's name, they should be in the room when Lotte and I talk.

"Mr. Pendrake, are the others here?" I asked.

"Yes, they are, miss. Would you like me to send for them?"

"That would be wonderful."

I entered the parlor behind Lotte and took a seat on the settee. I gestured for Lotte to sit. Moments later, the others walked into the room and took a seat, Justice following behind them and joined me on the settee.

"Lotte, I really just want to know what you were doing at the Tavershams' last night." I asked, sitting back and petting Justice.

I watched as each of the ladies leaned forward, concentrating on what Lotte was going to say.

"I know it was foolish, but I wanted to see Ben. We hadn't been able to talk since Lady Taversham let me go. I thought the ball would be the perfect time to see him, especially after all the guests had arrived," Lotte said.

"How did you end up serving at the ball?" I asked.

"I arrived right before Miss Stanhope and Miss Cavendish were set to arrive. When I got there, I made my way to the stables, but out of nowhere, this woman was yelling at me for being late. And how if Lady Taversham found out, they would never get hired again. Apparently, one of the new girls they hire for events didn't show. All of a sudden, I was given a uniform for the area and pushed towards the changing room. I didn't know what to do, so I just went along with it, taking a tray whenever one was handed to me. Before I knew it, you were screaming, miss, the police were there, and Lady Augusta was accusing me of murder."

"Were you able to see Ben at all?" Mads asked.

"No, and now I can't go back to that house. If I'm anywhere near there, it will cause more accusations." Lotte quickly wiped the tears from her eyes.

"I'm just going to come right out and ask the question that I'm sure we are all thinking, but it feels inappropriate to ask," Pippa said, leaning forward. "Did you stab the earl? Honestly, I would understand if you did."

"Pippa," I admonished her. Pippa had a very abrupt manner about her sometimes. I'm pretty sure she picked that up from her Aunt Honoria.

"Of course not," Lotte said. "I was out in the ballroom all evening long. I'm sure someone can vouch for me."

"Don't be offended, Lotte. We had to ask, even if we didn't want to. Yesterday we all discussed how you really didn't have a motive. Well, that's not exactly true. Just that it wouldn't do you any good to kill the earl. Even if there was a reason, it wasn't like it made much sense," I said.

"You are right; I did not kill the earl. It had never even crossed my mind. Most people wouldn't even care about what the earl had done. Some might even say that he was entitled to do whatever he wanted. After all, I'm nobody."

"None of us here believe that. And next time you decide you want to walk right into trouble, let us know first. We might be able to help," I said.

"Why would you want to help? Why do any of you want to help?" Lotte asked. Her eyes darted from me to the others and back again. "I've never met a toff that's given two shakes about a servant. They're more likely to just use and abuse us, then throw us away. Just like Lady Taversham." Lotte covered her mouth, her eyes wide.

"We want to help because you deserve help. If you'll let us," I said, watching as a myriad of emotions flashed across Lotte's face.

Eventually, she looked at me. "You still want to help me?"

"Of course we still want to help, why wouldn't we?" I asked.

"Because I was rude. No one wants to help, especially if I'm not nice all the time." Lotte clasped her hands. It was like she had never spoken so honestly to her boss before.

"Here we prefer you to speak your mind. It won't get you fired, and it won't prevent us from helping you out of this horrible situation," I said.

*   *   *

"I need to break into the earl's study." I sat on Pippa's bed as she worked on some invention at her workbench.

"Sounds like something I suggested before, but someone wanted to play dress-up."

"Pippa, that's not what it was about. Breaking in before was dangerous. There was no way to know when the room would be empty. How would we avoid getting caught?"

She turned towards me. "But now it's okay?"

"The earl is dead; we know he's not going to be in there." I shrugged.

"Do you have to have an answer for everything?" Pippa sighed.

"I don't mean to; I just want to keep everyone safe.

And it would have worked if the earl hadn't been murdered. Or what if we hadn't been there, and he was still killed? We wouldn't even know that Lotte was in trouble." I looked down to see my hands twisting the corner of one of Pippa's blankets. "I would have hated myself if that had happened. I already feel like I've failed her."

Pippa turned back to whatever project she was working on. She immersed herself in her work whenever she had a second to spare, which, between going to class and working as a steam mechanic, wasn't often. She was focused on the project in front of her.

"What are you working on?"

"It's something we can use to break into the earl's study. You can use this to shoot a hook that will latch onto the window ledge. The rope will be secured to a harness so you can keep the rope tight as I climb the wall and break in through the window." Pippa held out her invention, rotating it so I could see it from all angles.

"That's fascinating. I would never have thought to make something like that. But I should be the one to break in," I said.

"Georgi, you don't have to do everything yourself. I can do this."

"I know you can. But I should be the one to do it. We

wouldn't be involved in this if it weren't for me." I felt like I was being quite reasonable.

"You don't have to take on everything yourself. You have friends who can help, including me." She set down her invention, then turned her chair to look at me.

"You are helping, Pippa. You're creating a tool to keep me safe. That is helping. Please, let me do this." I made eye contact with her, pleading with my eyes. I wanted her to understand why this was so important to me, but I didn't have the words at the moment.

"Fine, Georgi, I'll help you do it your way. But it doesn't always have to be your way."

"Thank you, I know my way isn't the only way. But right now, it's important to me that I'm the one that breaks in. I can't explain why, but as soon as I can put it into words, I'll let you know. I'm sorry I don't have the words now."

*   *   *

Pippa and I stood outside the Taversham home. It was late at night, and the only light to be had was from the moon. It just so happened to be a full moon, a very bright full moon that illuminated the entire city. But that was neither here nor there. I had a mission, and I was going to succeed. Getting on to the property itself was easy. Thankfully, the family had never been in the habit of keeping dogs, so there was no one to alert the staff, or anyone else, of our presence. The problem was actually getting into the study. Really, the first problem was figuring out which window led to the study, then actually getting into the study.

"I am pretty sure it's that one, Pippa." Pointing to the next-to-last window on the second floor. "If the ballroom is in the front of the house where the balcony is, I would guess it would take up those first three windows on the side. Then there was the room that we waited to be interviewed in, which was next door to the study, and maybe another room after that. Or two windows in one room. I'm not sure."

"If you're sure, we can use this to get you up to the second floor. You have been keeping up with the physical training we started, haven't you?" Pippa looked at me, trying to assess if I had been doing the workouts she wanted all of us to do. "It's going to take quite a bit of strength to get up there."

"I have been doing everything that you assigned to us. Hopefully, it's enough," I said, straightening my back once again. I rolled my shoulders a few times, attempting to loosen them up.

Pippa pulled the strange contraption she had been working on out of her bag. It almost looked like a crossbow, but it had a multipronged hook as the projectile attached to a rope. Pippa laced one end of the rope through this metal contraption and then she hooked the thing to a belt she had around her waist. She checked to make sure the rope was looped through the eyelet at the end of the hook. On either side of the hook contraption were two piles of rope. It looked like the hook was about halfway down the length of the long rope.

"Did you make this just for our little escapade tonight?" I asked. Pippa's ingenuity constantly amazed me. Her mind worked so differently than mine, and I loved it.

"I did. I wanted you to be safe scaling the side of a building, so if all goes well, the hook should catch on that ledge. It would be better if the window was open, but we are not that lucky. I just hope it will find purchase on the ledge. Anyway, we will tie one end of the rope to you, and the other, as you can see, is attached to me with this belay lock, the hook itself is in the center."

"Belay what?" I asked.

"As you're climbing, I'll make sure the rope stays tight. As I pull it through this device, it will lock around the rope. Basically, the rope slides in one direction and will stop the rope from going if it pulls in the other direction. So if you were to slip and fall, my weight and the slack in the rope will prevent you from actually falling. At least that's how it's supposed to work," Pippa explained.

"I trust you, Pippa. I'm sure it will work." I clasped my hands together. Pippa didn't need to see how much my hands were shaking.

"You know, you could have worn something a little more suitable for scaling walls." Pippa looked me up and down, rolling her eyes in exasperation. "I thought you believed in wearing the appropriate clothes for every scenario."

I looked down at my black wool bustle dress and shrugged. Pippa was probably right; all this dress had going for it was that it was a bit short. Hopefully, I wouldn't trip over the skirt climbing up.

Pippa shot her hook contraption, and it clanged around a bit before it found purchase. I held my breath, standing as still as a statue, worried someone might look out a window or come outside and find us. After an eternity, or at least that's what it felt like, Pippa tested her handiwork. I watched as she yanked on both sides of the rope with all her might. It didn't look like the hook was going anywhere. She tied me to the opposite end of the rope from the one attached to her.

Suddenly, it was time for me to climb a wall, and if my insides had any say about it, I was not ready. My stomach flip-flopped, and I drew in a shaky breath. My nerves refused to be calm. Now my knees were weak, my hands shaky, and my breath shallow. I wasn't sure I could do this. Not that I had a choice at the moment. I had to be ready and able to perform the task. This was my idea, and I was going to be the one taking the risks. I checked to ensure I still had the cotton tote Hannah had crafted for me. There was no way I was going to be able to carry anything down in my hands, if I was lucky enough to actually find something.

I walked up to the wall, focusing on a decorative column next to all the fine brickwork. The column at least had some scrolls and such I could grab onto, more so than the brick facing. I tugged on the rope. It felt secure. If only my palms would stop sweating. I put one foot on a toehold, reached up for the handhold above my head, and pulled myself up. I continued like this for a bit, inching my way up, irritated that the Taversham house had such high ceilings. It made the climb an unnecessary distance. All was going well until I was about three feet from my goal. That's when my foot slipped. There I was, hanging off the side of the building, almost to my goal, my arms stretched out above my head, my feet dangling below me. I heard Pippa gasp as she helped me stay in place.

"Georgi, get your feet on the wall. And get to that ledge," Pippa said.

I tried to do what she said, my feet struggling under

me. Finally, my right foot found a sturdy spot, then my left. I was able to reach up and grab the ledge and pull myself onto it. For a brief moment, I sat there, gasping for breath. I eased myself along the ledge to the window I needed to open. Thankfully, the gods of breaking and entering were by my side, and the window was easy enough to open. I went to climb through it and couldn't. The window was not big enough to fit my bustle through. What was I going to do? I was up here now and I had to get what I came for.

I stood on the ledge, clinging to the wall and trying to decide what to do. I went back to the window and tried to go in head first. Which was a terrible idea. I was stuck half in the room, half out of the room. There was nothing for it. I was going to have to lose my skirts. But I refused to be happy about it. I wiggled until I could hold myself up with one arm and use the other hand to reach for the hooks holding my skirts and bustle together. Why are ladies' clothes so difficult? It's like they wanted to make us dependent on others for the simplest of things. I felt like I was fishing around forever before I found the hooks.

As I pulled myself through the window, I removed my skirts. I thought I heard Pippa mutter, "Bloody hell." I'm sure my skirts fell on her. I picked myself up off the floor, wiping my hands down the front of my bodice. God, I looked ridiculous in only a bodice, bloomers, and boots. I hoped no one walked in now, for a multitude of reasons.

I quickly made my way to a rather imposing wood desk with ornate carvings on the front. The desk screamed of the importance of the person sitting behind it, implying that those on the other side were inconsequential. The earl probably kept everything important in the ostentatious desk. I turned the desk light on low, providing me just enough light that I could see what I was doing, but hopefully not enough to make anyone suspicious. I stood there looking at the desk, not really sure where to start, knowing that I needed to start somewhere.

I started going through the drawers one by one. The top drawer had an assortment of odds and ends in it. Like it was a storage space for all the things the earl used most often. To the back of the drawer, I found a bottle from the local apothecary. It seemed the earl had been prescribed a tonic of some sort. The ailment was not listed on the bottle, just how often a person should take the tonic. I tucked the tonic bottle into my corset. I'm sure Willa would understand what it was for based on the ingredients.

I moved to the next drawer and found a set of books, the interesting kind if you were Mads. Here were the earl's finances. I skimmed through them quickly, nothing of interest jumping out, but I knew if there was something there, Mads would find it. In the drawer, there was also a business contract. It looked like the earl was in business with a Lord Frankland. The business itself was long-distance travel by dirigible. If Pippa was up here, she would go nuts. Just look at the use of steam technology! One of her current projects with Colin was working on a dirigible, and she was studying the luminous aether. She goes on and on about it like she does about anything having to do with steam engineering. It was actually exciting to listen to her, even if I didn't really understand what she was talking about completely. I had always been the type of person who liked new technology for what it offered but was never really interested in how it worked. However, if you got me talking about ancient philosophers and theories on social contracts, I would talk your ear off, as my friends have experienced more than a few times.

I shook my head in an attempt to refocus. There was no time for me to get distracted. I expected to find more in the drawer. The outside facing of it made it look so much deeper. I wonder, could it have a false bottom like in some of the novels I read? How intriguing would that be? It would definitely mean that the earl was hiding something. My hands felt around for something that would cause the bottom to open: a latch, lever, maybe a button. I really had no idea what I should be looking for, but after what felt like an eternity, I felt something. I tried pulling, pushing, pretty much everything I could imagine to make it work. But nothing. That's when I accidentally bumped it about a quarter of a turn up and all of a sudden, I could hear gears turning and whirling. Like magic, the bottom of the drawer seemed to fold up into the drawer, exposing an entirely new portion. In this hidden compartment was another set of ledgers. Like that wasn't suspicious at all. Who needed two sets of ledgers unless one was hiding the fact they were stealing money from someone? The question really was, who was the earl stealing money from?

I was almost certain Mads would confirm my theory. And probably be able to figure out even more about it just from these two sets of books. Inside the second ledger was a very thick stack of receipts. They did not look like receipts a person would get from any type of shop. My best guess was the receipts were all gambling debts the earl had racked up using a line of credit at his club. At this point, it was just supposition. I wanted to inspect the receipts closer, but it felt like I had taken up way too much time in the room.

I made one more pass around the room. The leather couch was there in front of the fireplace. It was surreal that the earl's dead body had been lying there the last time I was in the room. I walked over towards the couch, not sure what I was looking for, or if I was actually looking for anything. Scootching around to the front, careful to disturb as little as I could, I saw something glimmer on the floor. Dropping to my knees, I searched for whatever had caught the light. There it was, another bottle of the tonic, almost completely empty. I felt around on the floor until I found the stopper. Finding it, I closed the bottle and returned to the window. An overwhelming need to leave the room right now came over me.

I pulled the cotton tote Hannah had made for me out from my corset. Corsets were annoying, but they could be useful for holding things in a pinch. I put the two sets of ledgers, the tonic, contract, and gambling receipts into the bag, then tied it to the rope. I made sure that the rope was tied tightly around my waist, then climbed through the window.

"Okay, Pippa, I'm coming back down now." Going down was always worse than climbing up. The fear of falling just seemed so much closer and more intense. Pippa helped me rappel down the wall in a slow and controlled measure. I was thankful to have my feet on solid ground without a mishap in no time at all.

"I told you to borrow a pair of my leggings, that

wearing your bustle was not only somewhat foolish, but also potentially dangerous," Pippa hissed, trying to be quiet so we weren't caught while also being rather annoyed with me.

"I know. Just give me a moment to put all my skirts on so we can walk back. I clearly can't go about how I am now. Someone will figure it out. Oh, and did you ever figure out how to get the hook thing down from there?"

The look Pippa gave me when I asked her that question basically said, why would you ask that? Do you think I'm incompetent?

"Of course I did. Leaving it there would just get us caught. I'll take care of it while you get dressed." Her tone implied the same thing her look had.

"Thank you. I know you wanted to come in with me or maybe do the whole thing yourself. Your help was invaluable today with your inventions."

"It's true I would rather scale the walls myself, especially since you didn't even think of wearing something more practical. You, the person who always dresses for the occasion, did not dress for this one."

"I wore all black," I attempted to defend myself.

"Who thinks it's a good idea to climb a wall in today's fashions?" Pippa had finished gathering her invention.

"Apparently, me," I said, shrugging dismissively. "It

may not have been the best idea, but it worked. And just think how many people you will be able to tell this story to one day! Not too soon, because I would prefer not to be arrested for breaking and entering." I stopped Pippa midstride and gave her a hug. "You kept me safe tonight, and that's what matters most. Just like you were wary about involving us in your schemes last time. This time, I am concerned. I feel like Lotte is my responsibility because I brought her into our lives. I know I need help, but if anyone is going to get caught doing something, I need it to be me."

"Oh Georgi, you know none of us look at this situation or Lotte that way." Pippa grabbed my arm, pulling me down the street with her.

I stopped midstride, forcing Pippa to look at me. "I know, but if you had gone in there and been caught and hauled off to jail again, I would be beside myself."

"I would happily do it to help any of you out. Plus, I'm an old hat at spending time in jail." Pippa turned and continued walking down the street like she was out for an evening stroll at midnight.

Chapter Ten

By the time Pippa and I were home, Mads and Willa were already in bed. The impatient part of me wanted to go bang on their doors until they woke up so we could discuss what I had discovered. But that was neither fair nor logical. Instead of doing what I wanted, I followed Pippa upstairs, wished her a good night, and went to my room.

As I prepared for bed, which meant taking off half a dozen layers of clothing, at least it seemed that way, I pondered what I had found in the study. I wanted to compare the two ledgers, but while I understood the basics of mathematics, I really didn't have a head for it, no matter how much Mads said learning math was just like learning a foreign language. I had attempted to improve my skills with numbers after that, especially since I spoke four languages fluently and could read and write in three of the ancient languages. I figured it would be a breeze. It, however, was not a breeze. I somehow always ended up getting different results, even when I did all the same steps. Math always left me feeling frustrated.

That was neither here nor there, though. Mads would definitely be able to determine what was going on in those ledgers. Meanwhile, I could start writing down a list of potential suspects. Hmm, suspects might be too strong of a word at this point. I could at least determine who was involved in the earl's life according to the papers that I found in his office.

Instead of laying everything out on my desk like a reasonable person, I climbed into bed. Justice followed me and curled up in her spot, head lying on one of my many pillows. I spread everything I had grabbed out in front of me. It was quite a bit and somehow seemed like next to nothing. I really hoped it helped clear Lotte's name, especially after the ordeal it was to get it. I mean, when my foot slipped, and I was just hanging there, I thought it was all over for me. Thankfully, everything Pippa built actually worked.

Shaking my head, I opened my notebook and started writing. My first thought was of Benjamin Harrison, Lotte's beau. While I hoped he hadn't killed the earl, he would be a prime suspect. I mean, I just met Lotte, and I wasn't sad the earl was dead. I could only imagine how I would feel if I were in love with her. Assuming he was, in fact, in love with her. Then there was the apothecary, Mr. Benson. At least that was the name on the tonic bottle. I couldn't think of a reason he would be bothered by the earl, but one never knew. A more interesting prospect could be Lord Frankland, Lord Taversham's business partner in the dirigible company. If I was right, Lord Taversham was stealing from the company, and money was always an excellent motive. I couldn't forget about the earl's gambling debts. There was no name on any of the receipts, just a location, Milford's. Although, killing someone was not a very good way to collect a debt. And finally, I had to add Lady Augusta. She seemed to keep to herself most of the time, rarely interacting with her husband, not even at the events she hosted. It was with those thoughts that I drifted off to sleep without ever realizing it.

* * *

Bang! Bang! Bang!

I jerked awake, completely discombobulated for a moment. First off, what was that incessant noise? Second, why did I have ink stains all over my hand and arm? And third, well, I didn't have a third yet, but I'm sure I would come up with one. I reached around the bed where Justice normally slept. Ah, there was my third question. And third, where was Justice?

I finally registered the noise as the distinct sound of banging on wood, and it was actually someone knocking on my door repeatedly. It must not have been Hannah. She normally would come in and open the blinds and let the light wake me up before drawing a bath. It was either earlier than Hannah would normally come in, or I had refused to wake up this morning. Probably the latter, as the curtains were open. However, my clothing from last night was still strewn about the room. Not to mention the mess of papers on my bed.

"Georgi, we all know what a mess you are without the help of Hannah, and we sent her on an errand this morning. So just let us in," Pippa said through the door. She knew better than anyone what a mess I was without the help of Hannah because she shared a room with me for a few months after someone had set a fire in her room. We may have solved the murder, but we never did figure out who was sabotaging us.

"Fine, I'm coming. Let me just find my dressing gown," I said loud enough for them to hear me.

"It's probably hanging up over your dressing screen. You leave it there whenever you get dressed." Pippa hollered through the door.

I looked over to where Pippa was describing, and, sure enough, my midnight-blue velvet dressing gown was hanging over the top of my Latikan dressing screen. I loved how the stained wood had been carved to look like lace. Pippa had learned a lot about my habits. I pulled the gown down, careful not to pull the screen with it, and threw it on. Buttoning it up, I walked to the door.

"What can I do for you this morning?" I said as I opened the door.

"It's almost noon, Georgi. We've been waiting for you to get up forever. I see you looked through everything last night, which is most certainly why you are not up already. You couldn't just go to sleep like a normal person would after a night of cat burglary." Pippa was always teasing me. If she ever stopped, I would be worried. Pippa's teasing was her way of showing she cared.

"Where is everyone else?" I asked. I had expected Mads and Willa to follow Pippa into my room. Prior to the move, my room had been our staging area, and the only way to avoid the prying eyes of Miss Pierce, the headmistress of the burnt-down dormitory. She had disappeared before the dormitory was lost. Disappeared might be too strong of a word; she seemed to have left without a word. Pippa thought Miss Pierce had been spying on us the entire time and caused the fire.

"They are waiting in the parlor. We figured it would be more comfortable to use that room as our war room, especially since there's not anyone here to spy on us," Pippa said, all but dragging me out of the room and down the stairs.

"Pippa, I'm a mess. I can't be seen like this out of my room." I reached up to feel my hair, only confirming that I must be quite a sight.

"You know none of us care. And it's not like you can really get ready until Hannah gets back from her errands. You may be able to perform magic on someone else's hair, but I have seen you try to do your own, and it's not a pretty sight."

"Fine," I said, not that I had much of a choice since we were standing in front of the parlor already. I knew I'd been described as a force of nature before. But here in this house, all four of us were, in our own way, forces of nature. It was fairly obvious when you watched Pippa and even Mads. Willa didn't seem as likely, but I'd seen her talk when she knew what she wanted. Honestly, no one should get in her way, or really any of our ways.

"It's about time, Georgi. I thought we were going to have to wait all day before you were ready to get to work on solving this," Mads said, her dark eyes twinkling, and her smile let me know she was teasing.

"I'm ever so sorry, hanging off the side of a building was a bit more exhausting than I was counting on," I said, smiling.

"Wait, what? N-n-n-no one said anything about hanging off the side of a building." Willa's eyes darted between Pippa and me.

"It was for but a second. I had control the entire time. No need to worry, Willa," Pippa said, looking at me pointedly.

"Pippa is quite right. There's no need to worry, especially since I'm clearly safe and sound now. If not tired." I laid out everything I had taken last night on the table: the apothecary bottle, the ledgers, the contract, and the gambling receipts. Mads pounced on the ledgers immediately. I looked around the room—ah, there was Justice curled up in the bed Lotte and Hannah had made for her.

"Oh, this is going to be fun. He had two business ledgers. I'm going to guess that he was embezzling from someone, and we have the proof of it right here." Mads might as well have been rubbing her hands together and laughing maniacally. Her excitement was palpable. I don't think I had ever seen anyone get so excited over business ledgers. She had, in fact, already started to pour over them. The rest of us might as well have left the room with as much attention as she was paying to any of us.

"Willa, I thought you could help us understand what was the purpose of the tonic bottles. There's only a name, half gone, on both of them, but maybe you can figure it out. Maybe you could talk to Mr. Benson about it, in a roundabout way, of course." I was meddling. I knew Willa wanted to open her own apothecary shop, and what better way for that to happen than for her to work with the local apothecary now? Especially since the professor she was supposed to be working with wasn't thrilled to have a female student.

"I d-d-don't know. I doubt that I'm the best to question anyone." Willa looked at her hands as she twisted them back and forth.

"Trust me, you are perfect for it. You are the only one here that will know what Mr. Benson's talking about. The rest of us don't know the first thing about remedies or medicines. But you do. It is only logical," I asserted.

"When y-y-you put it that way, it does make sense. Even if it won't be a simple task for me." Willa was still looking at her hands, but she had made a conscious effort to stop twisting them and had set them down on the top of her legs.

"Bring someone along. They can be your moral support," I suggested, hoping to make the task more accessible for her.

"Did you see all these gambling receipts, Georgi, all from the same men's club, Milford's? How are we going to find out anything in there? Those clubs make it impossible for women to get in," Pippa asked.

"I was hoping Kaiden could help, if he wouldn't mind. It would be so easy for him to get in and scope the place out. Much easier than us trying to force our way into the last bastion of men's superiority."

"I'm sure he will. He's probably already a member. However, I think it would be way more fun to go in ourselves. Just think of the commotion we would cause. It would be a riot." Pippa laughed. Just the thought of all those stuffy old men losing their minds as two well-bred ladies entered had me joining her despite myself. I was quite single-minded when I started planning and doling out tasks. Not everyone enjoyed that side of my personality.

"Are you done ordering everyone around, Georgi?" Mads asked with a small smile and a raised eyebrow.

"Maybe for now, but I'm sure I will find more tasks in the near future," I said, trying to look serious. Mads raised her eyebrow even higher, which caused a broad grin to break out across my face. "I don't know how you do it, but your seriousness always makes me laugh."

"While that was not my intention, a little laughter is always needed. Especially when you fall into your general mode. We do all adore you for your efficiency at planning. But it's okay to take a breath here and there. You know, so you don't pass out," Mads said, her hair pulled up in a messy topknot that was held together only by a pencil. To call it precarious might be an understatement. The others and I knew that hairstyle, if one could call it that, meant Mads was deep in thought over numbers, or at least had been.

"Since you've joined us in conversation, am I to assume you are done looking at the ledgers, at least for now?" I asked. I had watched Mads lose herself for hours on end working on a math problem, or even longer when trying to break a code. It was unlikely she would have acknowledged any of us at all if she hadn't found something out.

"You are quite right. I've actually found a few things, and while I haven't made my way through the books completely, I think I've seen enough to discuss it. Here you can see entries for Lord Taversham's nephew. The nephew didn't get much from his uncle, but there was money sent quarterly." Mads laid out the books in front of us on the table, pointing to the relevant entries.

"I didn't realize the earl had a nephew," Pippa said.

"If I'm not mistaken Lord Taversham's nephew is his only heir. The Tavershams never had any children," I added.

"Interesting, did you learn anything else from the ledgers?" asked Pippa.

"Not that it is surprising, but Georgi was right. There's

no reason to have two ledgers unless one is involved in unscrupulous dealings. And the earl had his hand in a lot of pockets, or so it would seem. First, in this book, there is a record of all the proceeds the earl made from smuggling in various spirits and cigars. You can see the same entry in his other ledger under gambling wins. However, according to the first ledger, Lord Taversham rarely, if ever, won while gambling. Maybe by luck every now and then on a horse race, but definitely not playing any other games of chance."

"The earl was running a smuggling ring? That's what you're telling us. It just goes to show you that fiction is just that—fiction. The smugglers in my novels are always dashing, and the earl, he was anything but dashing." I sighed, flopping onto the settee.

"It is disappointing, but that is what the books imply. His estate is actually located near your parents, Pippa. He must have been using a small cove or something to get the goods to Brythion, then distributing from there. Some ended up at Milford's for sure. The earl basically lost every penny Milford paid him for spirits and cigars gambling there, whether it was card games or betting on a fight.

"Which takes us to the next shady aspect of the earl's finances. He was embezzling money from the dirigible company. The one in this contract here. I believe his partner was Lord Frankland. If you look in the ledger that shows the smuggling, you can see the actual amount the company is earning, but in the other ledger, it is considerably less, just barely making out a profit. Where, in fact, the company is extremely profitable. The difference matches with the payment of gambling debts listed here in the fraudulent ledger. And finally, which just further proves what a poor gambler the earl was, the amount of profits he should have been getting from Milford is written out here as the expense of being a member of the club. It all points to the fact that the earl was losing money much faster than he was making or stealing it."

"What all this tells me, ladies, is that there is finally a suspect list in the making," I said, rubbing my hands together as I mapped out my next course of action.

Chapter Eleven

I thought I heard a faint knock on the door, but I was enthralled with the ledgers, gambling notes, and contract. There were so many overlapping connections and yet so many loose ends.

There it was again. Someone was definitely knocking on the door. I turned towards the door, and saw Hannah standing in the doorway. She'd taken to knocking on the door whenever one of us, or all of us, were involved in our studies, in this case, our investigation, which was becoming almost as regular an event as studying. One time she didn't knock while Pippa was working, Pippa's hand had slipped . . . and there might have been a tiny explosion.

"Miss, I've just returned from my errands," Hannah said, clearly uncomfortable with whatever she had to share. "And, well, miss, I don't really know how to say this, but there are some awful rumors going on about the four of you and this house."

"Hannah, come in, come in. You must tell us all about the rumors so we can figure out how best to combat them. Is there any basis in the rumors? I know we aren't your average ladies, and we do things a bit differently than expected," I said, patting the settee next to me, hoping Hannah would come and take a seat. Even though I knew she would probably insist on standing.

"Oh no, these are the most baseless rumors I have ever heard about any of you. And that's including the rumors that were going around about Miss Pippa murdering the professor." Hannah sat next to me, wringing her hands. She must be truly distraught to sit down.

"It is easier to prove the rumors wrong when they are not based on truth," Mads said.

"That is tr-tr-true. If there was truth to them, we would have a much harder time." Willa chimed in.

"I don't know. I just don't know how you are going to convince anyone that the rumors aren't true. People are going to believe whatever they want to believe." Hannah sighed, glancing up at me. "I didn't mean to fail you, miss; I should have known about these before they had spread this far."

"Hannah, you did not fail us. I know you are always

listening and asking your friends to listen when you can't be somewhere. You have my best interest, and now all of our best interests in the forefront at all times. You couldn't fail us if you tried." I patted her hand and smiled at her, even though my mind was racing and my stomach was tied in knots. Whatever could these rumors be to have Hannah so upset? Was I seen breaking into Lord Taversham's study in nothing but my undergarments? That must be it, what else could it be?

"Today, while I was picking up new yellow gloves for you—after you ruined those lovely ones saving Justice—I ran into one of the maids that work at the Tavershams," Hannah said.

I knew it! Someone must have seen me there. Why do I have this tendency to mess things up? It's like I plan everything out, but forget one variable, and it all crumbles around me. Although finding a dead body at the masquerade was a rather unexpected variable. Should I actually be blaming myself for that one?

"They had just run into Lady Corinne St. Gramflurri's lady's maid. She was most excited to tell my friend all about what she had overheard during Lady Corinne's tea the day before. Apparently, it is going about town that this home is a house of ill repute and that you are all ladies of the night, with you, miss, as the madame." Hannah looked up at me, her face distraught.

I burst out laughing. I couldn't help myself. Pippa and Mads soon joined me, all of us laughing rather indelicately. Willa was not one to burst out in laughter, but she was quietly giggling behind her hand.

"Oh Hannah, that is quite the story that woman has come up with. It's so very outrageous. I'm certain we can stop it in its tracks. I mean, no one here knows why my last tutor was fired." Oops, I hadn't meant to say that aloud. I was going to have to explain that statement at some point, I am sure. "And the only other gentleman who shows up here is Lord Fremont, and he's engaged to Pippa. How can the two of them seeing each other cause such a stir?"

"The maid said Lady Corinne believes Miss Pippa is carrying on with Lord Fremont and that boy at the steam mechanic shop. I'm sorry, Miss Pippa, you know I don't believe such a thing at all."

"It's fine. You're just doing part of your job coming back here with this information. You know you're the leader of the Ladies of WACK spies. We really need a better name for you. Spies is a little bit on the nose, don't you think?" Pippa said.

Pippa's antics forced a giggle out of Hannah. At least that was something. There was only so much a person could worry about at one time. And us being a house of ill repute, well, that was not on the top of the list at all. But it seemed one of us was going to have to take steps to rectify it.

"Ahem," Lord Pendrake stood in the doorway, making quite the show of clearing his throat, even though it was clear he was only trying to get our attention.

"Yes, Mr. Pendrake, what is it?" Mads said, still pouring over the ledgers, looking for more signs of corruption.

"Mr. Declan Bailey is here to see Miss Lotte Lane. He says he is her attorney." Pendrake sounded stiff and very much like a butler, even if he didn't look it.

"Bloody hell, couldn't he have sent over a card or something first? Maybe made an actual appointment. Hannah, upstairs with me. I need you to make me look presentable in record time. Mads, Pippa, gather up everything I stole from the study and hide it. I don't want this insufferable man to know what I did. Willa, can you go to the kitchen and see if Cook can get a tea tray ready? I'm sure this won't be a brief visit, as much as I would like it to be."

With my last command (cause really, I don't think you could look at it any other way), Hannah and I made our way to the set of doors at the far side of the room. They led to a hall that would allow me to use the servants' stairs to get to the second floor. There was no way I was going to let Declan

Bailey see me in my dressing gown with disastrous hair, especially not at this time of day.

Once in my room, the chaos started. I put Justice on the bed before I went to my wardrobe and started throwing dress after dress out of it. None of them portrayed the look I wanted. You know something that said, 'I may pretend to respect your intelligence, but you and I both know that I'm actually smarter than you.' None of what I owned was right.

"Sit down, miss. It will be much quicker if you let me go through things. Why don't you brush out your hair so I have less to do once I find the perfect ensemble?" I brushed my hair out while Hannah shifted the piles of clothing around. I really did have an obsession. It's just that the right outfit made everything seem possible. "Here it is."

Hannah had pulled out my blue velvet ensemble. Well, one of them. This one was a royal blue trimmed with gold accents, which included two rows of vertical buttons going up the front of the bodice, tasteful epaulets, and gold fringe at the bottom of the apron bustle and skirt, right where the ruffle attached to it. Hannah was, of course, right. This outfit was perfect for today. It was powerful but still feminine because of the soft, velvety fabric. I was really lucky to have such an excellent lady's maid. It was like she could read my mind when it came to what I wanted the other person to feel based on my attire. Plus, she could lace me into a corset in record time. She was braiding and twisting my hair into something intricate and complicated before I knew it.

"Hannah, you are simply amazing. I don't know what I would do without you."

"Right now, miss, you better get downstairs. You wouldn't want to keep Mr. Bailey waiting too long. He might cause some trouble," Hannah said, shooing me out of the room.

Justice followed my every step as I took the main staircase down to the foyer. I decided I should make an entrance since Hannah had done such a good job of making me look presentable. I walked into the parlor. Mads and Pippa glanced up at me as if nothing was out of the ordinary.

I stepped into the parlor, my ever-present sidekick beside me. Everyone stopped talking. Declan Bailey turned towards me, and I saw his hand clench and unclench. I assumed it was because he would like to punch me after our last meeting, but he was a gentleman and would always remember that first and foremost. He looked down at my feet, taking in my sassy puppy.

"Mr. Bailey, what an unexpected surprise. What can we do for you today?" I asked.

He cleared his throat. "I was just telling the others that

I would like to speak to Miss Lotte Lane. You bailed her out, and I need to be able to talk to her about the case," Mr. Bailey said, looking down his nose at me. It was so rare that happened, especially with men.

"Ah yes, I will send for her right away. I hope you didn't have to wait too long." I wasn't sure what would happen here, but I was going to make sure it ended quickly.

"Of course not. I also hope the time spent waiting will be worth it in the end," Mr. Bailey said with a slight nod, taking a seat in one of the chairs facing the settee. "In that vein, I was hoping I could speak to Miss Lane alone."

"I'm afraid you will be disappointed. I know to some she's just a maid, but it isn't right for her to be left alone with a man, no matter how well bred he is. In some ways, that's the reason we are all here in the first place. A young lady getting caught with a lecherous old man," I said, waiting for Mr. Bailey to respond to me, assuming it would be an argument.

"I would never. I am just here to do my job." The offense he took at my implications was obvious. His spine had stiffened, his shoulders were back and his chest puffed. He clearly wanted to defend himself further.

"Mr. Bailey, I didn't mean to imply that you were either lecherous or an old man. The other ladies and I had just been told some rather unfortunate news when you arrived unannounced and without an appointment." I sat down on the settee, my skirts cascading down to the floor. "There are some disagreeable rumors going around town about our moral character and what is done in this house. So I fear all of us must play by society's rules a bit more closely than we normally would because of these disgusting rumors."

"Rumors. I fear I have not heard the rumors. Pray tell what is being said, and is there anything I can do?" Mr. Bailey leaned forward in his chair. It was almost like he actually cared what was being said about us.

"It is neither here nor there. My friends and I will put a stop to them as soon as we are able. Until then, it would be nice to know when you are planning on being here, so I can arrange a proper chaperone for Lotte." I looked at him, my hands folded in my lap, my legs crossed at the ankle, giving off every sign of being the well-bred lady that was expected. I actually was that lady most of the time.

"I see. I hope my arrival here today does not make whatever the rumors are escalate. It is not my intention to cause harm to anyone living in this house." Mr. Bailey sounded different from how he had at the Station House. It was almost like he didn't mind us being here, and therefore ladies attending University. Which seemed contrary to our last meeting.

"I'll admit it probably won't help. But I can't see you concerning yourself with it. You made yourself pretty clear how you felt about women in certain professions when we last met."

"I think you . . ."

"Miss, you asked for me?" Lotte said, bursting through the door, out of breath. She halted her movement immediately upon seeing Mr. Bailey. "Oh sir, I'm sorry. I didn't see you there. I guess you'll be wanting to speak to me. That's why Lady Spencer called."

"Now, Lotte, I told you to dispense with the Lady Spencer stuff. I may be the daughter of a marquess, and a fair one at that, but I don't think the title is necessary when you refer to me. Besides, it makes me think my mother is here." I faked a shudder, but I was actually quite close to both my parents and was hoping to see them at some point this winter.

"I'm sorry, miss. Lady Taversham would have never forgiven us if we didn't use her title. It's a habit I haven't been able to break yet. But I am working on it."

I patted the seat next to me. "Come, take a seat so Mr. Bailey can ask his questions."

"Thank you, Lady Spencer," Mr. Bailey said.

"No need to thank me. I may be thoroughly irritated that you get to represent Miss Lane and I don't. And you wouldn't even hear me out when I said that I could help you out. It did not leave me with the best impression of you."

"I hope you did not think I was questioning your capability?"

"Oh, not any more than you thought I was questioning *your capability*. I'm assuming it was pride that held you back from responding with a firm yes to my assistance. Who would want to risk looking like they needed a woman's help in their business?" I was working myself up into a splendid dissertation on the capabilities of women.

"I never s—" Mr. Bailey tried to interrupt me, but I was having none of it.

Somebody cleared their throat in the entryway, diverting my attention for a moment. Willa stood there next to the tea cart.

"Lovely, Willa has seen to it that we will not miss afternoon tea," I said as Lotte leapt off the settee, shooed Willa away from the cart, and pushed it into the room. "I assume, Mr. Bailey, you are quite capable of pouring yourself a cup of tea, or is this one area where you allow a woman to serve? I mean, help you." Maybe I went too far with that. Seeing Mr. Bailey's jaw clench, his fingers tense, and his eyes narrow, I prepared myself for a comeback. I shouldn't have been as offended as I was that he wouldn't even consider letting me help with Lotte's case. But I was severely bothered by it, and the sentiment had only increased since he had walked into the parlor.

"Lotte, why don't we begin? I want to be able to help you as much as possible. However, my knowledge of the earl is rather limited. I need some avenues I can explore. Potential enemies, or others the earl had wronged. Anything you might know, or even something that you might have pondered at one point, might help." Mr. Bailey had turned completely away from me. It was clear he intended to pretend I was not in the room. Little did he know I had more information for him. If only he would accept my help in the matter.

"I'm not sure, Mr. Bailey. I didn't pay attention to too much of the going ons in that house. I was hoping to find another position soon since the earl was such a leech." Lotte wrung her hands until they were red.

I patted her shoulder. "It's okay, Lotte, remember you don't owe either one of them your silence. It's not like Lady Taversham helped you out when her husband accosted you. No references. Whatever was she thinking?"

"That's just it, miss. I think the only reason anything came close to happening is that the butler was gone for the afternoon. Prior to that, he had interesting timing. Every time the earl managed to corner me or one of the other girls, Mr.

Butler would show up and ask the earl something quite complicated. He had a knack for saving us. If only he had been around that afternoon, none of this would be happening." Lotte sniffed, her eyes glossed over with a sheen of tears. She was about to break down.

"That is most interesting. I will be sure to speak to Mr. Butler. Do you know his real name?" Mr. Bailey asked.

"I don't want to cause him any trouble, sir. He's always treated me nicely," Lotte said.

"I'm sure Mr. Bailey is just trying to help. He will be circumspect in any of his investigations. Correct, Mr. Bailey?" I said.

"Of course, I don't want to cause anyone any trouble. Unless they murdered Lord Taversham," Mr. Bailey said.

Mr. Bailey had a point. It wouldn't do Lotte any good to limit the investigation because she had a soft heart for someone.

"Have you thought about looking into his business partners at all? I believe he had both legitimate and illegitimate interests. Plus, there was the matter of his gambling debts. He spent an indecent amount of time at his club, or so I heard. His debts were so bad it was starting to affect the household budget. I'm sure Lady Taversham was not happy about that." I rattled off the information the Ladies of WACK had deciphered this morning. Well, most of it, anyway. "I believe searching down who the earl's business partners were will keep you busy for a while." I stood, indicating that it was time Mr. Bailey took his leave.

"Yes, it appears I've taken up enough of your time. And that I have some individuals to think about. Good day, Lotte, Lady Spencer."

"Next time, please let us know ahead of time that you are stopping by. It will help us prepare so we can stop any more rumors from starting," I said, walking him to the door. Mr. Pendrake was there with his hat and cane.

Mr. Bailey crossed the threshold to our lovely porch right as Lady Corinne and Lady Augusta were walking by; the timing was not good. He turned to say something, but Mr. Pendrake, the delightful butler that he was, shut the door in his face.

Chapter Twelve

I wanted to talk to Lotte's beau, Benjamin, before she found
out I even half thought of him as a suspect. What I'd noticed
from working with Pippa on Professor Aneurin's murder
investigation, and now this one, was how hard it was to
suspect the individuals you really didn't want to suspect. Case
in point, Benjamin. If he turned out to be the killer, it would
just be another blow to Lotte's life. And I don't even know if I
would blame the guy if he had killed the earl, especially after
everything the earl had attempted with Lotte. It wasn't a nice
thought, but the earl had it coming. Especially when you
thought about all the other maids he had harmed. I shook those
thoughts away as I tried to prepare myself to talk to Lotte's
beau.

      Hannah helped me dress in one of my simpler
ensembles. It was a lovely mauve bustled apron and skirt. My

favorite part was the silvery grey wool coat that opened in the back and fell to either side of the bustle, showing off all the lovely pleats and ruffles. She then braided my hair, twisting and pinning it up so it looked both intricate and elegant. Hannah was a treasure. I did not know if I could survive without her. She was the perfect lady's maid, really to all of us here, and her information-gathering skills were top-notch. She should probably be working for the government instead of me, but I was loath to give her up. She had been with me so long that she felt like part of the family.

Dressed and ready to take on the day, I bounded down the stairs and began my walk to the Tavershams. It was a typical morning in Grantabridge. By that, I mean it was foggy and cold. Most of the time, the sun did not come out until midafternoon, if at all. It did mean that the parks and down by the river weren't crowded in the mornings this time of year. I enjoyed taking a book and reading outside, at least I did at home. It would be nice to set aside time for that here as well. I hadn't taken any time to read for fun since starting university. I missed the gothic novels I used to sneak past my tutors.

With all my musings and the meandering of my mind, it wasn't long before I was outside of the Tavershams' townhome. I snuck around to the side where the stables were located. There in front of me was a handsome young man with sandy brown hair and light brown eyes. He wasn't as tall as I had pictured in my head. I doubt he was as tall as me. He looked kind, though, and while looks could be deceiving, I figured looking kind was a good start.

I made my way to the stables but came to a halt when I heard the not-so-dulcet tones of Lady Corinne. I swear that woman was turning up everywhere as of late. It was grating on my nerves.

"Four women in one house and not a single one of them has a chaperone. It is beyond scandalous, I tell you. What was the University thinking allowing such a thing?" I listened as Lady Corinne spoke. Her voice was one anyone would recognize once they met her.

"And if you recall, they entertained another gentleman in their home yesterday. It was bad enough with Lord Fremont and that steam mechanic showing up all the time, but at least one of them is engaged to Lord Fremont. It lessens the offense somewhat, although not by much, if I do say so." That must have been Lady Augusta speaking. I didn't recognize her as easily as Lady Corinne, but it was a logical conclusion, as it was her home.

I wanted to burst through the door and let Lady Augusta know that we wouldn't have had a gentleman over if it wasn't for her accusing Lotte of murder. However, I chose not to burst into the room. Instead, I stood listening to the horrendous things they were implying.

"I swear the moral character of Grantabridge has gone down since they were allowed to attend classes at the university. I mean, two murders in the last few months! All after they arrived," Lady Corinne said.

It's not like we had actually killed anyone. Lady Corinne needed to learn the difference between causation and correlation. Of course, her opposition to women's learning meant she didn't know the words or their meaning. The Ladies of WACK had nothing to do with the increased crime level of the town. Unless you blamed us for those who were sabotaging us. Nothing was as fun as blaming the victim for someone else's offensive actions.

"So true, Lady Corinne. And we can't forget how many fires they had at the old dormitory of theirs."

"Again, not our fault," I said to myself.

"It's so much worse now. They have their own home, and they are entertaining men there. They are headed down a terrible road, having men in their home unchaperoned. We must do something about it. I think a meeting is in order with the University and some of the upper echelons here in Grantabridge," Lady Corinne said, her voice like nails on a chalkboard to my ears. I should just stop listening and continue with my plan. But then Lady Corinne continued, "We must have those girls removed from University and out of that house. We don't need any place here in Grantabridge like the scandalous activities happening there. I'm sure intimate relations are occurring in that building. Most likely for coin. How else could those women afford such a grand house?"

It wasn't enough that she was spreading these vicious rumors? Now she was suggesting we should be kicked out of University and because of our low moral characters. Even though the Ladies of WACK had more moral character than most of the men here at University. I was going to set that harridan straight. Evil, conniving, rumor mongering . . . suddenly, my feet were dangling, the air knocked out of me as my midsection hit someone's shoulder, and I was now looking at a decently clad derriere.

"Put me down," I gritted out through my teeth, aware enough of my surroundings not to scream or yell.

"I'll put you down, but you have to promise not to go charging into the parlor. I know who you are, and I'm pretty sure you're here to talk to me. Lotte had mentioned the ladies attending University were helping her out."

"You spoke to her, when? She can't be around here. It will get her into even more trouble."

Benjamin put me down. Apparently, he thought I was

distracted enough not to run into the home and defend all of us.

"She did not come here. I sent her a note, and we met in downtown Grantabridge. It was after you bailed her out. Thank you so much for helping her out like that. She doesn't have very many people in her life that would do anything for her, much less risk losing money on her." Benjamin pushed his hair out of his eyes and shook his head. "I keep begging her to leave Grantabridge, but she won't do it. She sends money home every chance she gets, and her family doesn't even appreciate it."

"Oh, I had no idea. That's so disappointing. Lotte has been such an asset to us. How can anyone not appreciate how hard she works?" Standing still became impossible. The back-and-forth movement of my pacing drove my friends to their wit's end. "I hope you don't mind if I ask you some questions." I looked at Benjamin, attempting to interpret his reaction.

"I'll answer, but it will have to be while I work. Come along."

I followed Benjamin to the stables. He stopped at the second stall. Inside was a beautiful chestnut mare. I wished I had a carrot or some apple slices. She looked like such a sweetie, and so much like my horse back home. It had been forever since I had gone riding. Maybe I needed to fill the stables that came with the house and hire someone to work there. Benjamin walked into the stall. The mare headbutted his shoulder, and he petted her blaze in response. Clearly, they shared an affection for each other. I was probably biased because I loved animals, and I liked to assume if animals loved a person, the person was good. Animals were better at judging character than most people. I was aware I could be wrong, but it was a lovely theory.

Benjamin started brushing the mare with long, gentle strokes. It looked relaxing. I missed my mare from home. Taking care of her was always something I did to calm my mind.

"I know you have questions, Lady Spencer. You might as well ask them." Benjamin looked at me as he kept brushing.

"Yes, I guess I don't need to be circumspect in my questions: you know why I'm here and don't seem offended that I would want to question you. So . . ." I cleared my throat. I was nervous because I didn't want him to be the killer. "Do you know what happened to Lotte?"

"Are you asking if I knew that the earl had tried to force her? Yes, I knew. Did I want to make him suffer? Of course I did. He hurt the woman I love. But death is too good for a man like that. He should have to feel all the pain and misery that he caused in his life." Benjamin said this as he continued to brush the mare calmly. In fact, he spoke calmly. Everything about him was calm at this point.

"I've had some time to think about what happened to Lotte. And I blame myself for not being able to protect her. And now the earl is dead, and she's in even worse trouble. I would like to tell the police I did it. And I would, if I thought that would make her happy. But she would kill me if I did something like that."

"It seems like you're telling me you didn't kill the earl," I said.

"I didn't, but if I had been there when he hurt Lotte, I would have." Benjamin stopped brushing the mare, resting his head against the mare's.

"I would have, too, and I didn't even know Lotte at the time. I hate how titled men think the servants are their own personal playthings." Petting the mare was calming; it was either do that or start pacing incessantly. "Where were you when he was killed?" I asked. I might not think Benjamin had committed the murder, but I had to ask all the questions to ensure my conclusions were based on facts and not emotions.

"I was taking care of the horses the gentlemen rode to the party. I made sure the horses cooled down appropriately, then brushed them, covered them with blankets, and ensured that the stables were warm the entire time. It was a chilly evening, and I didn't want any animal injured because of neglect." Benjamin looked up at me, gauging whether or not I believed him. At least that's what it looked like from my perspective. "I didn't even know anything had happened until the detective inspector arrived. In fact, I was so busy I didn't even know Lotte was trying to see me. If only I had taken a moment, then she wouldn't have been stuck serving."

"You know you can't blame yourself. The only one that's at fault is the actual murderer, and possibly the person who stabbed a dead body. Now—" I paused, trying to figure out where to go next with my questions. "What else can you tell me about the Tavershams?"

"What do you want to know? I'm not privy to much because I'm in the stables, but the others still talk around me," Benjamin said.

"Was there any talk about the earl and his wife? Did they get along? How did he treat her?"

"There wasn't much talk about them at all. I know they have had separate rooms for some time now. In fact, the earl and his wife did not spend much time together at all. Or so I've been told. They rarely went out together, but that's not strange for the toffs."

"And the earl's nephew, does he spend much time

here?" I asked.

"Almost never. He prefers to spend his time in Fintan."

"Has he been around lately?"

"No miss, it's my understanding his uncle kicked him out of the house here in Grantabridge. They were not on the best of terms at all, but the nephew was doing quite well on his own."

There wasn't anything left to ask. At least not for now. Maybe I would have more questions later. "I hope I didn't keep you for too long, and if I have more questions, I would love to be able to stop by again."

"I'll do anything to help Lotte," Benjamin said before he went back to brushing down the horses.

I made my way back to the Octagon House, mulling over everything I had learned, which wasn't very much. First, I needed to figure out what to do about Lady Corinne. She was out to hurt my friends and me, and she needed to be stopped. Second, I didn't think Benjamin killed the earl; he was too busy during the ball. And finally, I had really wanted the nephew to be a viable suspect, but he wasn't even in town. I sighed, helping Lotte was taking up so much of my time, I felt like I was letting my friends down by not even having a plan to fix the damage Lady Corinne was trying to create.

Chapter Thirteen

I continued to work on the logic problem that was Lotte's case. Nothing really came of it, other than jumbled thoughts and ideas swirling around in my head, giving me a slight headache. I managed to set up an office space for the Ladies of WACK to work on the case if they wanted peace and quiet. Mads and Willa would make use of the space as they analyzed the budget books and the tonic bottles. I had just been in there, working away at the board I had put together, trying to find any common threads at all. It was not helping, yet I'm sure it would soon. I just needed to plod along until I knew who committed the crime.

What I needed to do was work on interviewing more people, but lately, I was having trouble getting access to anyone. It was beyond frustrating. I had stopped by Lord Frankland's office a couple of times in the past few days only to be turned away without a second glance. I wanted to speak with Mr. Milford, but I knew I would never be allowed into the men's club, which just so happened to be where Mr. Milford lived. On top of the whole men's club limitation, Mr. Milford was known as a very private, if not somewhat secretive, man.

I needed to check in with Willa about the apothecary. Hopefully, she was having more success than I was.

I felt like I was failing Lotte, and that was really not an option at all. She could not go to jail for someone else's crime. It was time for me to sit down with the others and reevaluate the plan to clear Lotte's name. I was spinning my wheels. In addition, the four of us needed to figure out how to squelch these rumors. They were spreading fast. Enough people were talking that it was affecting our lives. Some of the women attending our salons had stopped coming. They didn't believe the rumors, but they couldn't risk being seen coming and going from such a scandalous house. I was so tired of judgmental individuals creating problems for people I cared for or who needed my help.

And now it was time for the weekly meeting with Professor Smythe. I should be impressed that anything this regular had started since my friends and I arrived at Grantabridge University, when we discovered everything was basically self-study except around exam time. This was outrageous to all of us, especially poor Pippa, whose parents disowned her for deciding to attend university. Kaiden was constantly telling me I was the reason for the change, but it didn't make going to the meeting any easier. Every week I got my hopes up that it would be different. And every week, the same thing happened. The professor ignored me while praising anyone else who spoke, even the men who just repeated my theories.

I took a deep breath and rolled my shoulders back. It was time to battle once again. I opened the door to Professor Smythe's work room and stepped in.

"Ah, Lady Spencer, I'm rather surprised to see you here today," Professor Smythe said.

"I don't see why you would be surprised. Every week I am here. I have yet to miss one of these . . . interesting sessions since they started," I responded coolly. One of the things I was trying to accomplish is maintaining my calm in the face of those who wanted to see me fail. Something I had never really succeeded at in life. I was fantastic at convincing people I should have my way. But anyone who directly tried to undermine my intelligence, or, even worse, sought to anger me by picking at things I had no way of knowing about yet always made me lose my composure.

"I assume you haven't heard the rumors then?"

"I have heard the rumors, Mr. Smythe. However, since what is being said is a blatantly false statement, there is no need to let what people are saying stop me from achieving my goals." I felt the calm I was attempting to maintain slip away. It was not slipping away slowly, more like running away like a thief caught in the act, doing anything it could to get away.

"As it happens, Lady Spencer, you should have listened to what was being said and taken steps to divert the narrative. As it stands now, I have no choice but to ban you from my class."

I swear, Professor Smythe's smile was gleeful as he attempted to burst all my hopes and aspirations.

"And why am I being banned from class? As far as I know, there has been no conclave of University and city officials. They have not met. They have not made a pronouncement of any sort. If that had happened, if a meeting was called, I would have been there, standing up for myself and my friends. I would have demanded that they let us speak on our behalf." The door slamming reverberated in my mind as the calm demeanor I was desperately trying to maintain gave out, leaving me with nothing but righteous anger. My words were not going to get me back into class, but they would be heard, and by more than Professor Smythe, I noted.

"It would seem, Professor, that your banning of my person from your so-called class is premature. In fact, it illustrates to me, and my fellow students around me, that your treatment of me in this class was because you have been attempting to get me to leave from the beginning. I would love for you to articulate why exactly you would have me banned now?"

"I'm not sure you want me to expound on it in front of the others." Professor Smythe looked taken aback at what he would consider my audacity. The audacity to call anything he said into question.

"I'm sure all of these gentlemen have heard the rumors. They may even be part of them. It seems these rumors have made their way around town." I looked around to see Kaiden, a few other gentlemen that always listened to what I had to say, and, of course, Lord Bradbury.

"I'm sorry, Lady Spencer, you just don't have the moral character to attend Grantabridge University. The thought of letting a woman who has been entertaining men for money sit in my workspace is abhorrent. And I will not stand for it," Professor Smythe blustered. Or at least that was now what I would picture whenever I read blustered in a book. His face was bright red, and specks of foamy spittle flew from his mouth as he spoke. He gesticulated with a vengeance. And he was going to be apoplectic when he heard what I said next.

"My moral character? That is what is in question here. I don't have the moral character to attend this University because there are unsubstantiated rumors that I have been entertaining gentlemen for money. In case you don't know what unsubstantiated means, let me explain it to you. It means that there is no basis, no proof that these rumors are true. Since you didn't express yourself plainly, let me clear it up for those that don't understand yet. I am being banned from class because the professor believes that I'm a lady of the night, or to put it even more succinctly, a whore." I stood up on a small desk so I could see everyone in the room. "But if my character that is at fault, what about the gentlemen that are visiting? Do you have a list of their names, Professor Smythe? Are you going to ban them from your class?" I stood there, pointing at the professor, out of breath with anger.

"Don't be ridiculous. Why would I do that?" he said, sputtering like a man losing control of his temper.

"Why? Because there would not be women of low morals if the men did not visit them. The crimes you are accusing me of do not happen with just one person. It takes two willing participants. So why does one get a pass for putting a woman in that situation, but not for being in the situation?" I looked around. Some of the gentlemen looked at their feet, shuffling back and forth aimlessly, others looked at me with something that appeared to be admiration, and then there were those whom I could tell despised me. Professor Smythe fit into that category.

"I . . ." the professor started to speak, but I interrupted him.

"So gentlemen, how many of you here have visited a madame before? I bet our esteemed professor has, as well as the majority, if not all, of you standing here. Maybe your father took you once to help you learn what it was like to be a man. How many of you have a mistress either here or in town? How many of you have ever paid a woman to be, shall we say, entertained? And yes, I do mean to imply every euphemism you can think of when I say 'entertained.' Don't be shy, I won't judge."

The men shuffled around me, very few looking at me. None of them raised their hands.

Kaiden stepped between the professor and me, ready to defend me, and Pippa by extension. "Even if you won't admit it out loud, think about it. Why do we hold women to this standard that makes them lack moral character for acting on biological imperatives? Yet congratulate men for their conquests? And you know what I mean when I say 'conquest.' The actresses, singers, and dancers that somehow don't deserve the same thought and protection as the ladies we grew up around receive. If Lady Spencer is in trouble, and these rumors are going around, I'm part of the problem. While nothing untoward has happened, I have spent time inside their home with my fiancée and the others. Are you calling my morals into question? And if not, ask yourself why. Why does the future duke get a pass? But the daughter of a marquess has to prove the rumors false. Do you know hard it is to prove a negative?" Kaiden finished.

I looked around to see the other gentlemen, excluding Lord Bradbury, murmuring in agreement. Something I had never, in my wildest dreams, expected to happen. It was eye opening, to say the least. Here were men, titled and entitled men, supporting what I had to say, even though it took the words coming out of the mouth of a man for them to show their support. Quietly supporting, but supporting nonetheless.

"Ahem, it does not matter how many of these gentlemen support you. I will not let you into my class. Your behavior today shows such violent emotions that I can only assume you do not have the constitution for the subject matter. In addition, if you had the moral standard expected of a young lady, you would never have put on such a vulgar display of emotions. Now go. The rest of you may enter." Professor Smythe turned, walking into his workspace, Lord Bradbury and a couple of others following the professor.

The rest, I believed around seven of us, stood outside. I was astounded at what had just occurred. I could not fathom being kicked out of class, especially one studying political theory. It was one of my specialties. I was even more surprised at how many gentlemen stood with me on the cobblestones outside the building.

"Gentlemen, I'm afraid it appears I must be off. I underestimated the harm these rumors might cause, and I need to see what I can do about stopping them." I nodded to the group, turning on my heel to walk away.

"Lady Spencer, what are you going to do now? What are we to do? Your interpretations have been fascinating, and while I don't always agree, you make me think about what could be. I believe I have become a better steward for my people because of it," one gentleman said. I really should have paid attention to who was who, but it hadn't seemed important at the time.

"Yes, Lady Spencer, you must help us with our studies. All these theories would be stodgy without you and your wild interpretations. Sometimes it sounds like you would do well over in Eletharis," another gentleman said. He looked very much like the first, but his frock coat was a navy blue instead of grey. I would have thought I would at least have some idea of who they were. I did have one rather disastrous season before being accepted to University. They did not look familiar, though.

"Ah, gentlemen. I must do nothing. You see, at this point, the only man who can demand anything of me is my father, and he is not here right now, which means there are no current demands on my time." I turned once again, a chorus of protest following me. "Next week, I might be able to put together something for next week. I will have Lord Fremont arrange for a location, one that does not further damage my reputation. Remember, those rumors are false. Lord Fremont, Mr. Finnigan, and Mr. Bailey can attest to that if you need it to come from a man to be believable. Come, Lord Fremont, I believe we have a lot to discuss."

Chapter Fourteen

Kaiden escorted me back to the Octagon House. The two of us didn't spend much time talking. I was too in my head about the fact that over half the students Professor Smythe taught today walked out with me. It didn't feel like it had actually happened. While I don't know what Kaiden was thinking, I'm sure he was concerned with these rumors. I had no idea how to stop them at this point, but I knew it was going to start with a confrontation with Lady Corinne. Just the thought of it made me straighten my spine and roll my shoulders back. I knew it was going to be a battle that would not be easily won. A battle I didn't have the time for. Why was this woman trying to destroy our lives? Why did four women getting an education bother her so much?

As I thought of the rumors, I sighed. I hoped they weren't affecting my friends like they were affecting me. I'm sure I would find out, though, as soon as I walked through the door.

"Are you okay?" Kaiden asked.

"As okay as I'm going to be. I'm worried I caused the rumors to spread faster. I had some words with Lady Corinne at the masquerade. What if all of this is my fault because I didn't keep my mouth shut?"

"Georgi, standing up for yourself and your friends was the right thing to do. If I had heard her say the things Pippa has said you've heard, I don't know if I would still be able to call myself a gentleman. She deserves to be taken down a notch or two."

"But if I hadn't said anything . . ." I sighed, crossing my arms over my chest as if the motion would protect me from everything happening right now.

"She was already starting the rumors before you said anything. Do you think she would have stopped because you stayed silent? She has it in her mind that the four of you are a threat to her. And she's trying to push you out of the way. Little does she know just how hard it's going to be." Kaiden stood to the side as Mr. Pendrake opened the door for me.

"When you have a chance, Mr. Pendrake, can you bring Justice into the parlor?" I asked as I removed my gloves and hat, handing them to the butler.

"Georgi, the rumors are spreading like wildfire." Pippa accosted me as I crossed the foyer. "Willa was turned away from her botany class today. As if Willa would ever do anything like what's being said about the four of us! Poor moral character, my arse. What are we going to do? I hate seeing Willa upset like this. It's such a hit to her confidence." Pippa stopped as Kaiden followed me into the house. "Oh Kaiden, I wasn't expecting you to drop by so soon. Wait, don't the two of you have class? Why are you back so early? What happened?"

"Today, Professor Smythe—wait, I'll let Georgi tell it. It is her story after all," Kaiden said. It may not seem like much, but I appreciated how Kaiden understood it was important for me to have a voice, to tell my story.

"The brief version is, Professor Smythe banned me from class because I do not have the moral character to be attending University. Much to his chagrin, I hope, over half of his students followed me out, including your fiancé, and now I think I promised to discuss political theory with them all next Thursday. He also called me overly emotional. Standing up for myself was apparently a vulgar display of violent emotions, which was a sure sign of my lack of moral character and ability to understand complex political theory."

"That's horrible, and also not. You would make a

wonderful professor, Georgi, better than Professor Smythe, for sure. Well, I'm sorry you had to go through that ordeal today. It just means we really have to handle Lady Corinne. So I'll ask again. What are we going to do about that harridan?"

"We are not going to do anything. I'm going to talk to Lady Corinne to see if there's anything that can be done to get her to stop spreading these vicious lies. Other than leaving University, that is. Because that resolution is clearly unacceptable. I don't know if that's going to change any of the professors' minds. But if we can get the assault on our character to stop, it would be a start," I said, walking into the parlor. "At least that's my plan for now. But I fear it won't stop her. She clearly wants us gone. This is just one way to attack us. And we will want to be prepared for the next attack, whatever it is."

Mads looked up from where she was sitting, the ledgers spread out in front of her. "I'm afraid you're right, Georgi. We may get a brief hiatus from this mess, but I doubt the war is over. So we will want to be prepared for whatever she does next."

Without a word, Mr. Pendrake carried in Justice. He handed her off to me with a slight bow and then disappeared without a word. I don't know what I had done to deserve such amazing members of my staff. I hoped it meant he was happy here and liked it better than where he worked before. At least none of us would accuse him of stealing a painting.

"Do you think she is who Middleton was talking about when he gave us his dire warning, or would you call it a threat? Do you think he was just a lackey to a powerful woman?" Pippa asked. There was a gleam in her eye as she pointed out the irony in the great Lord Middleton obeying a woman. Normally it would have us laughing, but too much had gone wrong today to appreciate the irony.

"Let us turn our minds to other subjects—I would say, more pleasant, but the murder of the earl isn't much better than the rumors Lady Corinne has spread about us. I can't believe how fast they took off," Mads said, and for the first time since I've known her, she rambled. Her normal composure seemed shaken. These rumors were getting to all of us. "Where was I?" She looked at the ledgers in her lap. "Ah, yes. The embezzlement. Lord Taversham was in debt. I'm surprised they weren't selling the silver, he was so deep in debt. The masquerade must have been paid for on credit, or should I say not paid for. The Tavershams' didn't have the money to throw lavish parties. At least not with the help of his title."

"Yes, you've implied that he had a gambling addiction," I said.

"From the numbers, it would seem he could not control himself. If he won big, he would lose all his winnings and more by the end of the night. If he was losing, he just kept playing, digging a hole so deep there was no way out. I would say this is definitely the behavior of an addict. You called it, Georgi." Mads ran her hands over the filled pages of the book. "This is where it gets interesting. He was skimming quite a bit from the dirigible company he owned with Lord Frankland. All of the original losses at the club coincided with the money skimmed off the top. It was like they knew the exact amount he had embezzled. Once that number was hit, it looked like Taversham's luck would get a little better. And then his addiction would rear its ugly head. And Taversham would play, I'm guessing, until someone escorted him home," Mads explained as she pulled her hair back and wrapped it around her pencil.

"That's interesting. It seems to imply some relationship between Mr. Milford and Lord Frankland." I glanced over at Kaiden, raising an eyebrow. "Is there anything else, Mads?"

"I'm still struggling to figure out how he was so unsuccessful financially while smuggling in spirits and cigars. It should have been enough to keep him going for quite some time. But the money disappeared as soon as it was deposited.

And while I can track most of what is spent by comparing the ledgers, there's a portion of the smugglers' profits that's just gone."

"What? Are you saying someone was embezzling from the earl?" Pippa asked.

"That's exactly what appears to be happening. The earl was meticulous in his ledgers. I don't know how he would have missed it. He tracks every household expense, pin money he gave to Lady Taversham, the smuggling, and so on. He had an accurate tally of his debts, expenses, profits, and what he embezzled, except for this one category. It makes no sense at all. The amounts aren't large, but his math was always spot on. He should have caught it."

"I wonder if he managed to determine who was stealing from him. Whoever that is could be the killer," I said. "It would definitely be a motive."

"I think I can help with some of this," Kaiden said.

*   *   *

"I take it you were able to make it into Milford's without any trouble?" I asked Kaiden.

"No, it was not any trouble. My brother was a member, and I have kept the membership going."

"Have you now?" Pippa asked. "Are you going to find a way to sneak us in at some point? I want to know what happens at one of these gentlemen's clubs."

"I hadn't planned on it. I don't think you'll find it all that interesting. Just a bunch of men drinking, mostly."

"That's okay, Kaiden. I'll just get Percy to get me in when he starts school here," Pippa said with a shrug.

"Just ignore her for now. Did you find out anything interesting?" I said, interrupting Pippa's attempt at flirting.

"I did. First, Milford had no reason to kill the earl." Kaiden glanced around the room. I raised an eyebrow and nodded for him to continue. "At least, not as far as I can tell. The earl supplied the spirits and cigars that everyone in the club partook of. One of the principal ways Milford makes money is by selling drinks to his patrons. The earl smuggled in some unique spirits as well, making Milford's popular amongst even the Fintan set. Another reason Milford had no reason to kill the earl is that the earl always paid off his gambling debts. No one complained about the earl. He didn't cause any problems, paid what he owed, and brought in the things Milford needed to stay popular."

"I bet Milford is scrambling to find another supplier now that the earl is dead. Or at least figure out a way to contact that smuggling crew?" These were just a few of the thoughts that were flitting through my mind.

"I think he already has a person there, one that's

connected to the smugglers," Kaiden said. "I'm pretty sure that Milford has a silent partner. Milford was a former boxer. Even with his fight winnings, he would never have had enough funds to open the place and keep it going through those first lean months while trying to gain the necessary reputation. The earl helped Milford establish the reputation of the club, but someone else has to be financially backing it along with Milford."

"That is interesting. Do you have any idea who it could be?" Pippa asked.

"Unfortunately, no. But I'm working on Milford and gaining his trust. He needed a boxer for the fight next weekend, so I volunteered. He's making me wear a mask because no one will fight me if they know who I am. I swear that just had him more excited to have me enter the ring. It's going to be something of a spectacle, if you ask me."

"What? You're going to be fighting next weekend. Not attending a fight, but taking part? Now you have to get us in to see this. Have you been practicing with the mask on? Does it block your peripheral vision at all?" Pippa rattled off her questions.

"We can talk about this later. But just so you don't worry, I have been training and practicing with the mask on," Kaiden said directly to Pippa. He sat down next to her and pulled her in closer to him.

"Hopefully, you can find out more after the fight. Just remember to keep your guard up and protect that handsome face of yours. We wouldn't want anyone to mess it up," Pippa said with a wink.

"With Mr. Milford interviewed, for now, that leaves us with the apothecary, Mr. Benson, and the earl's business partner, Lord Frankland," I said, my mind running through the potential remaining suspects.

"I do believe Willa met with Mr. Benson today before the debacle at her botany class. When she got back from class, she went upstairs. I think she's taking a nap. I know you know how she must have felt, all those things being said about her. And she's not one to really speak up for herself," Mads said.

"Hopefully she'll be up to talking tomorrow. And I'll take care of the rumors." I was determined to wage war with Lady Corinne and win. She couldn't do this to us, especially to someone who was just learning how not to break under the pressure. Pain radiated through my hands, pulling my attention away from the conversation. I unclenched my fists, noticing that my nails had left indents on both of my palms. I flexed my fingers, trying to find a calm mindset as we continued talking. It was difficult, though. I was so angry that someone would hurt Willa, the sweetest of all of us here.

"Are you okay, Georgi?" Pippa asked.

"Yes, well, no, not really, but I will be. I'm just so angry someone hurt Willa. I would be angry if either one of you were hurt as well, but both of you are more likely to haul off and punch them in the face and then think about what was said later. Willa, you know she took all of that hate in, and it's been running through her mind over and over again, exhausting her and tearing away at her confidence." I started pacing, Justice behind me, turning with me, following behind me again and again as I walked and thought. I'm sure the scene was comical. But no one laughed, at least not this time. None of us liked the thought of anyone in our small circle being hurt.

I stopped pacing. Justice plopped down beside me. "The best way to talk to Lord Frankland will be to go up in a dirigible. Not that I want to go up in one of those things." The thought of it made me shiver. I was not a huge fan of heights, but I could handle them. But the thought of floating in the air hundreds of feet above the ground seemed incredibly unnatural to me. "I believe he's doing an exhibition ride sometime soon, maybe even tomorrow. If we can get on that one, he's sure to be on it. With any luck, one of us can corner him and ask our questions. Of course, cornering him alone is probably a bad idea. He could be a murderer."

*   *   *

I knew Willa wanted time to herself, but I needed to check on her. I felt like Lady Corinne's rumors were my fault, and I hadn't done anything to stop them yet. I stood in front of her door, my heart pounding and my palms clammy. I knocked softly.

"Willa, can I come in?" I asked.

"If you w-w-want to," she said through the door.

I opened the door to find Willa lying on her bed, back to the door, curled up in a little ball. I was gutted.

"Wh-wh-what do you want, Georgi?" Willa sniffed. I could hear the tears in her voice.

"I wanted to see how you were doing after today?" I stood just inside the doorway, unsure what I should do next.

"Not g-g-good."

I had never seen Willa like this. She was timid but always challenging herself. I was used to her always being upfront and honest about how she felt about things, all while pushing herself out of her comfort zone. It did not feel like she was in that space at the moment.

"What can I do to help?" I asked.

Willa turned towards me, sitting up on her bed. "I c-c-can't stay in Grantabridge if this c-c-continues. I'm here to learn, and it was hard before. But now, these awful rumors. It needs to stop."

I sat on the bed next to Willa. "I'm going to take care of it. I promise."

"How G-G-Georgi?"

Her question brought tears to my eyes. I'd lost her trust and it gutted me. "I don't know, but I will fix it. There's no way any of us are going to let you leave."

Willa lay back down, letting me know it was time to leave. I hated leaving things like this, but I didn't know what else to do at the moment.

Chapter Fifteen

The next morning, Pippa and I headed out to reserve our ride on the dirigible. I wanted some company as I took to the sky, an adventure I was not looking forward to. There was no way Pippa was going to let anyone else go up in a dirigible with me. She and Colin had been working on building a dirigible at his workshop for the last few weeks. I looked over at her, and I swear she was going to burst from excitement. I, on the other hand, was going to expire from fear. Humans were meant to have their feet firmly planted on the ground, not floating in the air hundreds of feet above it.

Pippa and I made our way to the cashier. My palms were damp inside my navy leather gloves. I had tried to dress for the occasion, hoping it would give me confidence. So I was in a golden-yellow pleated skirt with a matching jacket. The ensemble was trimmed in navy, and so were my boots, gloves, and leather cap. It reminded me of what Pippa wore when she was riding on her steamer bike. I even had my own set of goggles. Instead of giving me confidence, I wanted to turn and run. Pippa, however, bounced next to me.

"Two please, we've been looking forward to this exhibition for such a long time. I actually have been working on a dirigible with Colin Finnigan. He owns a steam engineering shop in town. Maybe you know him," Pippa said to the cashier, looking at me as I stood there silent, clenching my sweaty palms, eyes wide. How was I one step closer to going up on a dirigible?

"Here you are, miss, passage for two for the Grantabridge Dirigible Exhibition. I hope you enjoy your time here."

Pippa grabbed my arm and pulled me into the corner. "Georgi, you have to breathe. I've told you, these are perfectly safe. You're going to be fine."

"I am not fine. If we were meant to take to the air, we would have wings. Do I have wings? No. Does that thing have wings? Also no. I have a very terrible feeling about this." I was in a state, every nerve in my body standing on end. It felt like my corset was so tight I couldn't breathe. I felt my eyes dart around wildly, but I didn't really see anything. Pippa pulled me towards a bench, gently pushing me down onto it.

"Georgi, look at me," Pippa said. I needed direction, so I tried to do what she told me, fighting the urge to look away. "Good, now I need you to breathe in through your nose and out through your mouth."

"I can't breathe. There's no air. My corset." I could barely get the words out as I gasped for air.

"Your corset isn't any tighter than normal. Georgi, watch me. Breathe in." Pippa took a deep breath in. "Breathe out." She slowly let the air out. I mimicked Pippa, focusing on her words and actions until the band around my chest loosened and I could breathe again.

"How did you know what to do? I haven't felt this way for years."

"My sister was prone to panic attacks when she was younger. I used to help her through them once upon a time, when we were still friends. Now, my question. Why didn't you tell anyone you were afraid of heights or flying, whatever has you in such a state?" Pippa asked.

"I didn't really think about it until today. I had never planned on going up in a dirigible. Suddenly we were here, and it was happening, and the thought was overwhelming. But I'm okay now. Thanks to you." I looped Pippa's arm through mine and, with a show of bravado, I made our way towards the boarding ramp. I looked at the entrance to the dirigible to see Mr. Declan Bailey standing there.

"Ugh, what is he doing here?" I asked.

"Who?"

"Mr. Bailey, Lotte's lawyer."

"He's probably investigating, the same as us. Or he has an interest in dirigibles," Pippa said. She was being perfectly reasonable, but for whatever reason, just seeing him here annoyed me.

"You're right, I know. However, I reserve the right to be annoyed that he's here. Maybe it will distract me from the fact I'm not walking on the ground but on some contraption hundreds of feet in the sky." I shuddered at the thought, but I managed to continue moving up the ramp and step onto the dirigible just by putting one foot in front of the other. Mr. Bailey was no longer standing there. Any interaction we were to have would have to happen later.

"If it helps, I say go for it. Mr. Bailey won't even know you're annoyed." Pippa shrugged.

"Where's the fun in that? Let's go find Lord Frankland. Hopefully, we can talk to him before Mr. Bailey does." If I stayed distracted, maybe my fear would dissipate. Or, at least, I could forget that I wasn't standing firmly on the ground.

Despite my words, I stopped. The interior of the

airship was astonishing. Floor-to-ceiling windows provided a panoramic view of the world below, polished wood tables surrounded by gilded chairs, and a multitude of gorgeous chandeliers above our heads. On the far end of the dirigible was a bar, polished to a high sheen, the details gilded, and every spirit imagined available to try. Around the building, or should I say ship, there was a balcony that passengers could walk around, enjoying the fresh sights they would never have seen if it weren't for some crazy inventor like Pippa. I looked around, past the windows and the railing, just breathing in the air. To my own astonishment, I forgot to be afraid. It was like a fancy home floating through the sky. It should be impossible, but somehow it wasn't. And I was going to experience it.

A smile broke out across my face as I took it all in. I looked over at Pippa. Her eyes were wide. I could only assume she was thinking thoughts similar to mine.

"It's breathtaking," she said so softly I could barely hear her.

"It is. It's like we are in another world, where the impossible is possible." I was in awe at the opulence around me sailing in the sky. Well, it would be sailing in the sky at some point. I believed we were still tethered to the ground right now.

Pippa shook her head. Looking at me, she said, "We better find Lord Frankland before we get too distracted. I don't want us to lose our purpose for the trip. Well, lose our main purpose, that is." I could tell she wanted to just explore the airship, but she was focused on our mission.

Arm in arm, we went in search of Lord Frankland, trying our best to stay on task and not be distracted by the surrounding scene. Which was impressive indeed. Men in their frock coats and hats were milling about the room, almost all of them with a lady on their arm. The ladies were like petals on a flower, all bright, colorful, and delicate looking as they meandered about the ship, taking in all of the scenery. Both the gorgeous views of the countryside, and anything that would make for interesting gossip later in the evening. It was as crowded as the most popular ballroom during the season.

"Over there, that large gathering. Do you think Lord Frankland is in the middle of the crowd?" Pippa asked.

"I do believe you are right," I answered. "Although how you picked out a large gathering in this crush is rather impressive."

Pippa and I made our way through the crowd on the airship until we were part of the group standing around Lord Frankland. The man had drawn a crowd as he expounded on the possibilities of air travel: the luxury and comfort of floating over the countryside to get you to your next destination. Watching him talk, it was obvious this was a passion project of his. He pointed out every little detail, and when he described something he couldn't point to, he tried to draw it in the air, as if we mere mortals could understand what he was trying to illustrate. Lord Frankland was slightly shorter than me, with brown hair and brown eyes, and a mustache that was quite impressive; it even twitched as he spoke. He did not appear to be much more than thirty years old, rather young to have been the mastermind behind this enterprise. Nowadays, with all the advancements in technology being made, it seemed young people did have an advantage in shaping what would become the future. Individuals like Pippa, Colin, and Lord Frankland were changing the world while we were living in it. They impressed me with their passion and ingenuity.

After an interminable amount of time, for me at least, Lord Frankland was alone. Lord Frankland's speech had enthralled Pippa; she hung on his every word. I tried to listen as intently and failed epically. At least he was alone now.

"Lord Frankland. Hello, I'm Lady Georgiana Spencer, and this is Miss Philippa Stanhope. I was hoping we could ask you a few questions," I said.

"Of course, is it about the dirigible?" Lord Frankland asked.

"Not exactly, but it is somewhat related." I looked at him, eyes wide, hands folded together in front, the personification of sweet and innocent. That's at least what I was going for.

"If it's not related, what could you possibly have to talk to me about?"

"It's regarding Lord Taversham, we are helping look into his murder."

"Why would you be asking me questions? Are you the girls that solved the last murder?"

"We are."

"Ask away then. I may not have the answers you want, but I will try. Let's walk and talk. Shall we?" Lord Frankland offered each of us one of his arms. He appeared to be escorting us towards the decorated bar at the other end of the airship.

"Did you know that Lord Taversham was embezzling from your business venture?" Pippa blurted out, covering her mouth as soon as she spoke. She was always one to get to the point, mostly because she had the subtlety of a freight train.

"Yes," Lord Frankland said, raising one eyebrow.

"You knew?" I asked. "And you let it continue. Why?"

"I had other ways of getting the money back. Another business venture I have here in Grantabridge," he said. Lord

Frankland hadn't given a single detail, but something Mads said clicked in my mind.

"Milford's club. You are his silent partner," I said, more to myself than to anyone else. "Milford must give you a portion of Taversham's gambling losses, or he had while the earl was still alive."

"How? What gave it away?" Confusion and something like awe were etched on his face.

"You just did. I've also had someone looking over the earl's financials. There are some numbers that weren't quite adding up that now make sense to me. So how did it work? Were you cheating him?" I asked without judgment. Can you really be mad at someone for cheating a cheat?

"Of course we were. But only until I got the money he stole from me back. Once that amount was reached, the dealer stopped any form of fixing the game. After that, Lord Taversham lost all on his own. He was a rather pathetic gambler." We had arrived at Lord Frankland's destination for us, the bar. If questions were going to be asked, they needed to be asked now.

"Where were you the night of the masquerade?" Pippa asked.

"At the masquerade, of course, along with almost everyone else in Grantabridge. As the earl's partner in business, I couldn't miss the party," Lord Frankland said. He made eye contact with the bartender and tapped the bar. An amber drink appeared within moments. Lord Frankland took a sip, all the while staring at me. "Would you like a drink?"

I shook my head. "Did you conduct any business with the earl that night? Perhaps discuss his smuggling operations?" I asked, another potential motive flitting through my head.

"I did, and Lady Spencer, I must say, you are too smart for your own good," Lord Frankland said, taking another sip of his drink.

"I have been told that before. Many times, in fact. Were you the last person to see the earl alive?" I held my breath, waiting for an answer.

Chapter Sixteen

"I suppose I could have been, other than the person who murdered the earl. That's the last person who actually saw him alive. When I left his study, he was definitely alive and not happy. He did mention he was having some chest pain. Last I saw, he was trying to find his tonic," Lord Frankland said.

"Did he find it?" I asked.

"I believe he did. He pulled an apothecary bottle out of his desk. I left him in his study to recuperate and made my way back to the ball. I was enjoying myself immensely. This heiress from Eletharis was dancing with me. She was definitely on the hunt for a title. That is, until you came out screaming."

"One last question, are you taking over the smuggling the earl was running?" I asked.

"How did you . . . You really are going to get yourself

in trouble. Yes, the earl had already set up the paths for me to get involved. I had met the captain of the ship and the delivery crew. I must say, it is quite convenient smuggling in the spirits for two of my businesses. Now, I have to entertain my guests. Do let me know if I can do anything else." With that, Lord Frankland set down his empty glass and walked away.

I watched him. He had answered all of our questions. But I wasn't satisfied. I still felt like Lord Frankland was a viable suspect for the murder. Lord Frankland may not have murdered the earl because of the embezzlement. He had found his own way to right that wrong. But to now have personal smuggling connections and be part owner of a club and now the fancy airship—that seemed awfully convenient. And like motive to me.

"That was an interesting interaction. Don't you think?" I glanced over to Pippa.

She was still watching Lord Frankland walk away. "He was . . . abrasive. But at the same time, it felt like he was trying to be debonair."

"Do you think he's trustworthy?"

Pippa looked at me like my question was absurd. "I wouldn't trust him one bit."

I glanced to see Lord Frankland stopped on the other side of the airship. He was right outside the steam engine room, where he saw the presence of someone he must have known. He waved that person over. I looked over to see Lord Bradbury making his way to Lord Frankland. How did Lord Bradbury and Lord Frankland know each other? They didn't seem like they would run in the same circles. Their heads met close to each other as they held a brief meeting. I wondered what that was about. Lord Frankland had his hand in everything, it would seem.

"Let's walk outside. I need to get some air, see if I can process all the information that was just disclosed, and all that was left undisclosed." I took Pippa's arm, and we walked onto what I can only describe as a wraparound balcony attached to the airship portion of the dirigible. The balcony was almost as crowded as the inside of the airship. There were so many people on the dirigible and it was still floating.

I looked out, and we were high in the air but tethered to the ground. The demonstration was more about the opulence of traveling in this manner. Pippa was taking it all in beside me, probably trying to take mental notes on every little thing to tell Colin later.

"Did you see that, Pippa?" I asked.

"See what?" Everything about the airship still enthralled Pippa. She looked at each thing around her, every screw and bolt. I bet she was trying to figure out how she could get into the engine room.

"I swear he looked like the Tavershams' butler. But that doesn't make any sense. Why would he be here?" It was a glimpse out of the corner of my eye. But I swear I saw the man who had looked down at us before letting us into the masquerade.

"Lady Taversham must be here. Maybe she brought her butler as a bodyguard type; he is rather imposing. This was a business venture her husband was involved in, after all. I wonder if she now has an interest in it herself? More likely, it's whoever the next earl is going to be. Do you know if they had a son or not?" Pippa rattled off her usual bout of questions, not waiting for the answers. She probably wouldn't hear them if I had the answers, since she was inspecting every aspect of this flying contraption.

"Taversham has a nephew. He's going to inherit everything. He's never around, though. There was a falling out of some sort a long time ago. Anyway, I'm going to see if I can find Lord Frankland again. I want to find out if the new earl, or Lady Taversham, is in business with him now." In search of more answers, I left Pippa after she nodded her understanding.

I walked around the balcony, trying not to run into people as I searched for Lord Frankland, noticing certain spots in Grantabridge that I never would have thought was possible to see from this vantage point. It was strange to be eye level with the University's clock tower and so high above the river I walked by every day. Oh, and there was the Octagon House.

"I see you've spotted your house, Lady Spencer," Mr. Bailey said, interrupting my thoughts. He stood next to me, leaning on the rail. He wore a grey pinstriped frock, with matching pants that contrasted wonderfully with a magenta waistcoat and cravat, somehow both bold and understated in his choices. Excellent armor for a barrister. Not to mention, he looked quite handsome today. The coat emphasized his shoulders, making them look broader than I remembered.

"Yes, it is quite unusual to look down on the world, is it not? Quite magnificent as well," I said, trying to be civil. There was something about this man. Civility left my mind, and I just wanted to be contrary.

"It is quite magnificent," Mr. Bailey said, looking directly at me.

"I, that is, I must be going. I'm hoping to ask Lord Frankland a few more questions." Turning away from the scenery, I took a step to walk away. Mr. Bailey stopped me before I went very far.

"Lord Frankland has gone back inside to the bar. Having another drink. If you want to question him, I would do so now," Mr. Bailey warned. Concern showed in his amber eyes.

"Are you implying Lord Frankland has issues with the alcohol? The man I spoke to was incredibly cunning. I can't imagine him being a sot." Imagining Lord Frankland overindulging was difficult to do. It went against everything I thought I had learned about him.

"Yes, he seems to become quite gregarious, or it could be an act to bring his investors in. Make them more comfortable and willing to depart with their money, because he is just like they are," Mr. Bailey said.

"That would be genius. I bet that is exactly what he does from having just talked to him. He seemed incredibly savvy and manipulative."

"I bet he is," Mr. Bailey muttered under his breath.

I leaned towards him. "What did you say?" I took a breath and suddenly smelled mint and eucalyptus. It was an unexpected scent. I wouldn't have even recognized the eucalyptus, but Willa had some in her lab.

"Nothing of importance," he said, much louder this time. It was Mr. Bailey. His scent was that refreshing combination of mint and eucalyptus. How peculiar to have noticed such a thing about him.

"And if it was important, would you tell me?" I asked,

returning to the comfort of antagonistic questioning.

"What would I know that is important to you? You seem to be the one that has all the information," Mr. Bailey folded his arms across his chest and glared at me.

I leaned on the railing engrossed in our conversation, momentarily forgetting the distance between where I stood and the ground. "If I have information that you want or need, you should let me work with you on Lotte's case. But you have excluded me from the start, not even giving me a chance. It's your loss, you know," I pushed myself to my full height, my hands on my hips, my face inches from his. I was not able to tower over him, but there was no way I was backing down.

"You can't represent her. That was the only point I was trying to make. The courts will not allow it. The laws are inane, but I still must abide by them as a representative of such laws." He had bent over so we were eye to eye, our faces inches from each other. I glanced down at his lips for a second, then stepped away. I made a show of looking out over Grantabridge before turning my head towards him.

"Wait . . . do you mean to say . . ." I felt two hands on my back. I went to turn to see who dared to touch me. Instead, those two hands shoved me. I felt myself tumbling headfirst over the railing. It was in that moment I knew I was going to die.

Chapter Seventeen

As quickly as I had tumbled over the edge of the railing, I felt my entire body jerk to a stop. Pain ricocheted through my right leg and hip, causing all the air in my lungs to rush out. I felt my hat and goggles slip off my head and plummet to the ground below me. I was so thankful it was only my headgear that fell to the ground and not me.

There I was, hanging upside down from a dirigible, unable to see anything around me as my yellow skirts were covering my head. Oh my, that meant an entire airship and anyone below could now see my pantaloons. Well, drat. So much for squelching rumors today; I was like a walking advertisement for our so-called house of ill repute. At least my pantaloons matched my dress. The yellow ribbon through the lace was a really pleasant touch.

I pushed my skirts above my head, trying to see

anything. That was a bad idea. All I could see was open air and the ground below me. I really wanted to loop my left foot through whatever I could. There were a lot of ropes on the outside of the airship that might help save me from imminent death. While I was quite thankful, my right foot was trapped and holding me in place. I very much wanted to be back inside the airship. Or better yet, on the solid ground via the airship. I attempted to look up to see if anything was happening. Surely Mr. Bailey would have called for help or something by now. It was impossible for me to see, though. The only thing I could do was hang there, helpless. I felt gravity take the pins from my hair. It all came loose and fell out. I hoped no one was below me.

"Hold on, Lady Spencer!" I heard Mr. Bailey yell.

"What else do you think I'm going to do? Wiggle my foot free so I can crush my skull like a watermelon falling from this height? I don't think so," I yelled back. Really, telling me to hold on. Like I wasn't the one about to plummet to my death.

I felt someone grab my left foot and loop something around it, tightening it so I could not bend my ankle much. At least I was a little more secure.

"Lady Spencer, I need you to try to reach my hand." Mr. Bailey's voice was much closer this time. I pushed my skirts back down, up, whatever, and saw him hanging off the side of the dirigible, like some kind of hero from a romance novel.

"What do you think you're doing? You're going to get yourself killed, and probably me as well, in the process. What are you doing not on the airship?"

"Same as you, I suppose, just taking in the sights. The view is so much better hanging from the side of the ship."

Even imminent death couldn't keep me from scoffing and rolling my eyes at his sarcasm.

"Or maybe, just maybe, I'm trying to save your life. Do not worry, I'm secured to the railing. Your friend Miss Stanhope helped with that. We just need you to try and reach for my hand. Miss Stanhope says you have been exercising for fencing and boxing. The best way to do this is to try to lift your body with your abdominals as high as you can. Can you do that?" His calm tone should have reassured me. Instead, it enraged me. At least my anger kept me distracted from my reality.

"Of course I can. Why wouldn't I be able to?" So I did exactly what he said to do, and I felt my right foot slip as my weight shifted. I did not get up enough to reach him, and now I was losing connection to what was holding me up. "I changed my mind. I can't do it. Can't we just lower this thing to the ground?"

"We can't get you close enough. The fall would still hurt you, or worse. So I need you to try again," Mr. Bailey tried to coax me into action.

"Nope, my foot slipped when I tried. You're going to have to find another way," I cried. Tears spilt out of my eyes and I was having trouble breathing.

"There is no other way. You can do this, let's do it on the count of three. Ready . . . ," Mr. Bailey tried to encourage me.

"One," we said in unison. "Two."

With all my might, I did that weird crunch motion Pippa had me repeat over and over again during our boxing lessons, throwing my hands out in front of me. My foot slipped farther. I felt Mr. Bailey's hand grasp my arm and pull me in. My right foot came loose, then my left. His other arm snaked around my waist and he pulled me close. And then he rolled on top of me so my back was up against the airship and my front was, well, it was pressed up against the length of Mr. Bailey.

"I need you to wrap your arms around my neck and hold onto me like your life depended on it. Because it does."

Terrified of falling now, especially with all this time to think about it, I did exactly what he said, not saying a word.

He looped a rope under my arms and tightened it around my chest. I did not let go as he climbed the rope netting until we reached the railing. He somehow pushed me over. A multitude of other hands grabbed me, pulling me over onto the airship. I lay on the floor of the balcony, the entire world spinning. In the next instance, Declan Bailey was over the railing, lying on the floor with me.

All I could hear was our panting. I tried to sit up, but it was too much effort. So I lay there longer. Shocked that I was alive. Thrilled to still be alive. I had no words—I should have words, but I really thought my last moments in this world were going to be hanging from the side of a dirigible right before I plummeted to the ground. It was like my worst fears had come to life. I knew flying was a bad idea. I was never going up in an airship again.

"Somebody pushed me," I said, each word broken up as I tried to fill my lungs with air.

"What did you say?" Mr. Bailey asked.

"I felt two hands on my back right before I went over. Somebody pushed me." I sat up, my eyes darting around. I saw Pippa staring at me, wide eyed. She understood what I was saying, having survived an attempt on her life not that long ago.

"Georgi, did you see them? Can you remember

anything else?" Pippa asked.

"Are you sure someone pushed you?" Mr. Bailey asked.

"Of course I'm sure. What do you think I am, some impulsive woman that wants her life to be a gothic novel?" I snapped and instantly felt remorse. "I'm sorry. I should be thanking you for risking your life to save me. Not yelling at you."

"Could someone have bumped into you accidentally?" Mr. Bailey asked. It was a perfectly reasonable question, but it still felt like him pouring salt on an open wound, a wound caused by the general distrust I had been facing as of late.

I shook my head. "I felt two hands on my back. It was distinctive. I was going to dress them down for touching me without permission. Instead, they shoved me and I toppled over the rail."

Mr. Bailey just looked at me, brow furrowed. I wished I knew what he was thinking. Was he looking at me with concern, or like I was ridiculous? I continued to stare at him, trying to deduce what was going on behind those whiskey-colored eyes.

"Georgi," Pippa said. My head jerked towards her, breaking whatever had me staring at Mr. Bailey. "Someone just tried to kill you." Pippa wrapped her arms around me, her eyes filling with tears and darting from one person to another.

Chapter Eighteen

To say I was thankful when the dirigible was back on the ground would be an understatement. I limped off the flying contraption, my leg protesting every step I took. It was not happy at being used to stop me from certain death. I heard its protest and wanted to listen as soon as possible. I felt like my current choices were to sit down or pass out from the pain.

"Pippa, is there some way we can avoid walking home? I know it's not far, but my leg hurts with every step I take." Even though I hated admitting defeat, the pain was overwhelming. I was actually afraid I would faint from it if I tried to walk all the way to the Octagon House.

"Of course, let's go over to that bench and sit, and I'll think about who is closest to where we are right now." Pippa and I meandered—more like she meandered and I limped along, almost hopping at some points.

"Can I offer my assistance?" Mr. Declan Bailey asked, interrupting the pity party I was throwing in my head for myself. He held out his arm and waited, looking at me expectantly.

I really didn't know what to think of Mr. Bailey anymore. At our first meeting, he seemed so against me having anything to do with Lotte's case. Today he had sounded different, like I might have misunderstood him completely that day at the station. Could I have misjudged his character that much?

"Don't just stand there staring, Georgi. Make up your mind and do something," Pippa said under her breath. She was loud enough to snap me out of my thoughts, but hopefully not loud enough to be heard by anyone other than me.

I looked over at her quickly, feeling my cheeks heat. My cheeks had to be bright red. She nodded back to me like, what are you waiting for? I raised an eyebrow at her. Did she not know about our interactions up until now? She just shrugged and walked away, off to find us a ride home.

I looked back at Mr. Bailey, making direct eye contact with his whiskey-colored eyes, and immediately dropped my gaze down to my hands. I wasn't normally shy, but today had thrown me completely off-kilter. In addition, my last interaction with a supposed gentleman hadn't ended terribly well. My interactions with my last tutor made me question my judgment when it came to men in my life. There's nothing quite like learning you were taken in by a handsome face who wanted nothing more than access to your fortune. I might have lost faith in my ability to judge a man's character and now instantly judged them all as misogynistic fools or scoundrels. Except, of course, when it came to gentlemen interested in my friends, then I just wanted them to be together and happy, and I became quite the matchmaker. I didn't even make sense to myself sometimes.

I took Mr. Bailey's proffered arm, careful to only lightly touch him and not to use him as a crutch.

"You can lean on me. I know your leg hurts." Mr. Bailey leaned over and whispered in my ear. "I won't think you are any less capable if you do decide to actually accept my help."

My head swiveled to look at him. Why was he being so nice to me? "Thank you, Mr. Bailey. I appreciate the offer. My leg is, indeed, quite unhappy. I had just asked Miss Stanhope to find us a way home that did not involve walking. I'm rather afraid if I had to walk home, I would faint, which would not do at all."

"We could not let that happen. I believe you've caused quite enough gossip for today. Unfortunately, I also walked here, but I could see if the carriage my brothers leave in town is available. I don't believe either is in town at the moment, but I can't be sure," Mr. Bailey said. I felt myself lean on him even more. The pain kept getting worse. It was making my head hurt.

"Thank you, but I'm sure Miss Stanhope has already arranged something with Lord Fremont or Mr. Finnigan," I said, looking ahead. "See there, she's waving at us. She must have figured out something."

"Then I will escort you over there and be on my way," Mr. Bailey said, somewhat stiffly.

"Georgi, Kaiden is coming around with his steam carriage. He should be here in no time at all," Pippa said, clearly excited to have an excuse to see her fiancé.

I turned to Mr. Bailey. "Can we drop you off somewhere? Or if you are interested, you could come to the Octagon House. I might have some information that you don't have yet."

"Unfortunately, I have another pressing matter to take care of. However, if the offer still stands, I would love to take you up on it in the future. Maybe we can compare notes." I don't think anyone had ever looked at me like Mr. Bailey did just now.

"Of course," I said. I hadn't expected him to say no. It

left me feeling unsure of myself. A feeling I did not particularly like. "Just let me know a good time and we can plan something."

"Yes. That would be quite nice." Mr. Bailey bowed his head towards Pippa and took my hand that was resting on his arm, leaned over it, and placed a kiss on the back. My skin tingled underneath my glove. I closed my hand and dropped it to my side as I watched Mr. Bailey walk away.

"Whatever was that all about?" Pippa asked. "If I didn't know better, I would think he actually liked you, and you might, in fact, like him back."

"Don't be silly, Pippa," I said while wondering if she was actually right, and I was the one being silly.

*   *   *

I was incredibly thankful for the ride back to the Octagon House. Even the short distance I had walked had left my leg throbbing and my head pounding. I wanted to lie down and cry, but there wasn't time for that, at least not yet.

I hobbled into the parlor with Kaiden and Pippa's help. There was no way I would have made it on my own. The pain had just escalated exponentially since Mr. Bailey had rescued me, or at least that's what it felt like. Willa jumped up from the settee and helped make a way for the three of us, so they could sit me down, more like lay me down in actuality. Pippa and Kaiden helped me lower myself to the seat, and Pippa moved my legs up onto the settee while Willa arranged my skirts so I remained covered. Little did she know, the majority of Grantabridge had already seen my underthings today. As soon as I was settled, Justice moved from her pillow bed in the corner of the room, jumping up on the settee with me. She was careful around my leg, making sure not to touch it as she made herself comfortable. Willa went to move Justice off the settee, but I waved her away. Justice seemed to know I was hurt, wanted to comfort me, and was smart enough to know not to hurt me more. She was such an intuitive puppy.

"What d-d-did you do, Georgi?" Willa fluttered around me. There was a reason Willa wanted to be an apothecary, and it was apparent at this very moment. She needed to take care of people, especially if they needed to be "fixed." She had made Pippa a wonderful wound cream for all the times Pippa burnt herself working. Now that I was injured, I was sure I was also going to end up with something special for my leg. Willa couldn't help herself. She wanted everyone to feel like their best self.

"There was a minor mishap on the dirigible, and I'm afraid my leg is the worse for it. I'm sure it will get better soon though. At least, I hope so," I said, trying to make light of it. There were other more exciting things to discuss than my own near plummet to death.

"Georgi, I need t-t-to know what happened to treat you properly and to make sure you don't need a doctor." Willa stood over me, hands on her hips, brow furrowed. She was worse than my mother.

"I guess we are going to discuss it, anyway. The important thing to remember is I am fine." I glanced around the room. Mads and Willa were both staring at me with intent, waiting for me to speak. "My leg is injured because I was pushed off the side of the death trap known as a dirigible. I thought I was a goner, but my foot got stuck in the rope and stopped me, hence all the pain in my right leg." As I finished, I shrugged. I knew it was serious, but I didn't want it to feel serious right this instant.

"D-d-d-definitely a cream for the pain. I'll do something with cayenne pepper, arnica, St. John's Wort, and some other ingredients you probably aren't interested in. I'll try to make it smell nice for you as well." Willa was creating a miracle rub for my leg in her head already. I was sure it would be better than anything I would get from a doctor.

"Thank you, Willa. I'm sure whatever you make will have me feeling like dancing in no time at all. Now that you know what happened to me, how are you doing? I know the other day was rough. I'm so sorry that those horrible rumors have spread so far and are affecting our lives here. The gossip about us needs to be stopped. No one really believes it, but that's not stopping misogynistic professors from using the rumors as an excuse to kick us out of class. I'm so sorry you had to go through that ordeal. I wish I could have prevented it. I should have prevented it."

"It's not your f-f-fault, Georgi. I know I w-w-was out of sorts the last time we talked. But I don't blame you for any of what is happening. The person who's spreading these rumors, that's whose fault it is. The good news is there's a visiting botany and apothecary professor coming after the new year. He specializes in herbal remedies. At least I'll have the opportunity to study with someone then. And he might not be as pigheaded as my current botany professor. He's such a misogynist." Willa's cheeks were red, the reddest I had ever seen her turn. "This could be an opportunity to really advance my studies and actually be able to open my own shop."

"What good news! I'm sure he will see your brilliance and then you will have someone to work with regularly. I'm thrilled that things are looking up. At least one of us will have a chance at some learning here soon." I sighed, lying down on the settee. It might have been dramatic, but I was tired of things feeling like they were falling apart, held together by a thread that someone insisted on pulling.

"I'm sorry there isn't someone for you to t-t-take lessons with. I'm sure there will be soon." Willa tried to get me to perk up and see the positive side of things. I wasn't ready to, though. Not yet.

"Willa, have you told Georgi about meeting with the apothecary yet?" Mads asked. It looked like she was doing some complicated math, or maybe even some cryptography.

"N-n-not yet. Thank you for the reminder. I would have forgotten until much later when I saw the bottles in the lab. I haven't been able to test the bottles, but after talking to Mr. Benson, I will definitely have to." Willa seemed to meander her way through the information without really giving us any information.

"Why do you need to test the bottles, Willa?" I asked, curious and confused.

"Mr. B-B-B-Benson uses a curing agent on his bottles so they won't smudge. Both bottles you found, Georgi, the labels were smudged. He believes it is negligent to allow labels to smudge or erase because what is a cure for some people could be poisonous to others. So those bottles weren't his," Willa explained.

"So that wasn't medicine for the earl?" Pippa asked.

"It m-m-might have been. But if it was, it didn't come from our local apothecary; it came from somewhere else completely."

"I wonder if the earl would have noticed the difference between the bottles?" I said, thinking aloud.

"That's th-th-the thing. The bottles themselves were identical to what Mr. Benson has. It was just a different label."

"So unless the earl looked at the label, he would have no reason to think that the bottle did not contain the medicine he needed for his heart?" I asked.

"I'm not sure if he would have noticed if he had looked at the bottle," Mads said. "I didn't know that apothecaries took steps to ensure the labels did not smear. Now that Willa said it, I think it makes perfect sense. I just didn't know it was something that was done, or even could be done."

"I agree, Mads, I wouldn't think twice about taking a medicine with a smeared label. Well, I wouldn't have before today. Now I'm going to be very aware of the labels on any medicine I take," Pippa said.

I wanted to get up and walk around. It helped me think, but my leg was still throbbing. I didn't think anyone in this room would let me pace at the moment. Justice must have felt me getting antsy to move because she laid her head on my good leg and nuzzled under my hand. Petting her gave me something to do other than pace.

"Is there any other information about the medicine?" I

asked. Not expecting anything, because what else could there really be?

"Not yet. I pl-pl-plan to test the contents of the bottle tonight or tomorrow." Willa paused. "However, this isn't related to the case, but Mr. Benson has offered to take me on as an apprentice."

"Willa, that's splendid!" I clapped my hands, startling Justice with my excitement. "I'm so happy for you. This is going to be so much better than working with that stodgy old botany professor. Just think of all the things you'll learn working with an apothecary! So much better than studying with a botanist."

"It is, and there is m-m-more. If we get along, he will let me run the shop on days he wants a break. This is a proper step towards my goals. Mr. Benson is older and has been thinking about retiring. He didn't want to retire until he knew there was another trustworthy apothecary here in town. He thinks that could be me." Willa blushed as she spoke. She wasn't used to being the center of attention, and now she not only had all of our attention, but she had some of the best news that any of us had heard for quite a while. It was exciting, to say the least.

"Oh, that's wonderful! You are going to be the best apothecary ever. A real benefit to Grantabridge and the

University," I said.

Pippa and Mads both were up and giving Willa enormous hugs. I wanted to be in on the hugging, but my leg was not up for it. As much as I wanted to concentrate on celebrating Willa's good news, my brain was ticking through everything I knew about Lotte's case, and it still felt like so much was missing.

Chapter Nineteen

Willa forced me to rest for an entire two days, making me rub the cream on my ankle, knee, and hip at regular intervals. If she had told me I had to stay in today, I would have screamed. Thankfully, she saw me walk down the stairs with relative ease. I wasn't about to tell her that every other step hurt like fiery daggers were being jabbed into my hip. Even with the pain, I needed to get out, and I needed to continue working on this case. I knew I was missing information, and I had a feeling I needed to talk to someone outside of the case to determine what I was missing. Which was going to require an introduction.

"Pippa," I said, walking into the parlor. I really walked in, as much as I would have preferred to have limped into the room. "I need a favor."

"As long as I don't have to watch you fall off a

dirigible, I can probably help," Pippa said, her usual somewhat irreverent humor back. I appreciated it. Everyone had been so serious since the . . . I'll just call it an accident.

"I can promise you I have no intention of my feet leaving the ground by more than a few feet any time soon. If I never go back up in a dirigible again, it will be too soon." I had probably burst Pippa's plans to take me up in the one she was building with Colin, but I'm sure she understood. "Actually, I was wondering if we could call on Lady Adelaide today. I have a feeling she will know something about the Tavershams from her debut. So much happens during the season that ends up forgotten as the years pass by," I said. "I know she had her season with your Aunt Honoria. I believe Lady Taversham is around the same age and should have been on the marriage market at the same time."

"I'm sure she would be delighted to meet you. Give me a moment, I should go change my outfit," Pippa said, rushing up the stairs, calling for Hannah as she ran.

I sat down on the settee. I thought I might as well stay off my leg as much as possible, even if I refused to actually rest in bed any longer.

"Lady Spencer, there's a Mr. Bailey here to see you. Should I let him in?" Mr. Pendrake sniffed.

"Of course, we should probably send for Lotte as well.

I'm sure he is here to discuss her case."

Mr. Pendrake gave a slight bow and turned on his heel, heading back to the foyer. Moments later, Mr. Bailey entered with his hat in one hand, the other hand was behind his back looking somewhat awkward. Strange, Mr. Pendrake should have taken his hat. Maybe he wasn't planning on staying long. He looked quite nice today in a deep blue frock coat and matching cravat. His cravat pin was the exact same color as his eyes. I wondered if he knew that or if it was a happy accident. He was looking very smart today, but his constantly shifting hands conveyed nerves I believed he was attempting to hide. It was almost like he didn't know what to do with his hands, a predicament I understood all too well.

"Good day, Lady Spencer, how are you?" Mr. Bailey asked, his tone so formal it made me want to laugh.

"Mr. Bailey, I'm quite well, other than my leg, but I'm keeping that a secret from Willa, so I don't lose my mind being stuck in this house. Lotte should be here in a moment. I assumed you wanted to see her about her case." For probably the first time ever, I was nice to him.

"Actually, I came to see how you were doing after your fall. I hope you do not mind. I wanted to make sure you weren't suffering any ill effects from the incident. But, as you just admitted to me, it would seem that you are. I think I should go talk to your friend Willa and see if we can tie you down," Mr. Bailey paused briefly, his face turning an interesting shade of red. "To make sure you get enough rest, of course."

"I can't have you doing that. I'm on my way out, anyway. Miss Stanhope and I are off to see Lady Wetherly," I said, smiling because it was rather nice of him to be concerned and annoying that he thought he could make me do anything. But he had saved my life, so I should be nice to him.

"Any reason you are visiting Lady Wetherly?"

"She is a fountain of information, especially regarding those that had their season with her. I feel like I'm missing something about the Tavershams that would make this all come together, and I'm hoping Lady Wetherly can give a little insight that will help."

"Interesting and potentially an effective process. I would love to discuss any information you get today, or may already have. If you are willing." Mr. Bailey unclasped his hands from behind his back. Doing so allowed me to see he was carrying a lovely bouquet of colorful flowers. He looked down at them as if he had forgotten he was carrying them. "Ah, I almost forgot. These are for you. I wanted you to have something bright and cheerful in your room while you recovered."

"How thoughtful. I'll have Mr. Pendrake put them in a vase for me," I said.

"I should probably speak to Lotte while I'm here. I have little to update her with, but it's always good to stay in touch with clients." Mr. Bailey looked around as if he was unsure what to do next.

"I'm sure she will appreciate seeing you. I can take you to her if you would like." My leg protested as I pushed myself off the settee with a wince.

"Absolutely not. I'm sure Mr. Pendrake will assist me. Is Thursday a good day for me to stop by?"

"That would be lovely. I'll be sure to let the others know as well."

Mr. Bailey nodded and left.

At that moment, Pippa walked through the other door to the parlor. "Who was that?"

"Mr. Bailey. He wanted to catch up on the case."

"It seems he's seeing things a little clearer now," Pippa said with a laugh. "Are you ready to go?"

It took all the willpower I had not to groan when I stood up, pain shooting down my leg from my hip to my toes. Maybe I was pushing myself too hard, too fast. Too late to change my mind now.

"By the way, Georgi, I sent a note to Kaiden. He's

bringing the steam carriage around. I wouldn't want you to be in any more pain than you are already in. And yes, I can tell you are in pain. But I won't say anything as long as you promise this is the only thing that you are doing today." Pippa looked me in the eye until I nodded my agreement. Little did she know, I had already decided this was the only thing I was going to do today.

It was nice to have good friends even if they were a little officious at times.

"Of course, I'll rest for the remainder of the day and some of tomorrow too."

*　　　　　*　　　　　*

Kaiden dropped Pippa and me off in front of Lady Adelaide's townhome. It was like we had our own personal chauffeur, something I definitely could get used to. He opened the carriage door for Pippa and me, allowing us both to alight from the fancy steam carriage. I turned and looked at Lady Adelaide's townhome. It was a lovely home made of brick, trimmed in black and white. It would have been an imposing exterior, but the lovely garden softened the appearance to an almost homey look. Pippa knocked on the bright blue door. In moments, the butler opened the door for us. I don't think I had ever seen a butler who embodied the expected snobbish ways so well.

"Pippa Stanhope and Lady Georgiana Spencer to see Lady Wetherly," Pippa said, holding out her card. It impressed me that Pippa remembered to bring a calling card.

"I will see if she is available. Please come into the foyer. I will return momentarily." The butler turned and walked away, leaving us alone in the entryway.

"He was like that last time as well. Thankfully, Lady Adelaide is nothing like her butler," Pippa said while looking at the paintings that hung on the walls, mostly landscapes of local countrysides.

"He was quite supercilious," I said.

"That he is, Georgi, that he is."

"Lady Wetherly will see you now. If you will follow me to the morning room," the butler said, leading the way to his employer. He opened the door and stepped aside, directing us to enter the most cheerful yellow room I had ever seen. Yellow was one of my favorite colors because it reminded me of sunny days and spring flowers.

"Hello, Pippa! It's been too long. You must come to visit more often. And, of course, you must be Lady Georgiana." Lady Adelaide was as welcoming as the room she was sitting in. She looked delightful in a frothy mauve confection of an ensemble, all lace and ruffles.

"Please, call me Georgi."

"Of course. While I would love this to be just a social call, I have a feeling you are here on a mission. Pippa, you're like your Aunt Honoria in that way, always trying to figure out the next steps," Lady Adelaide said, gesturing for us to have a seat on some lovely white-and-yellow chairs. She turned to the door, her butler still standing there, waiting for her next request. "Can you please send for some tea with those lovely sandwiches that Cook makes? I have a feeling this is going to be a long visit."

"Yes, ma'am." The butler gave a curt bow and headed off to the kitchen to get the tea and sandwiches.

"I wish I could say this was purely social. I've been meaning to visit more often, but working with Mr. Finnigan has kept me busy. As has pursuing my studies with Professor Gates. It's not the same, though, since I'm not actually learning about steam engineering. I hope the University finds a new professor soon. Not that anyone could truly replace Professor Aneurin, but one can hope for a close second," Pippa said in her rambling way. I could tell she was uncomfortable mentioning Professor Aneurin. She was worried about Lady Adelaide's feelings, or at least that's what I assumed.

"I'm sure when you have time, you will come by more often. I've heard the rumors going around, and I think it's about time you ladies tried to make more friends in Grantabridge. Something to combat the ugliness of the rumors," Lady Adelaide said. "In fact, please let me know if you want my help with that. I believe you need more supporters, and not just those amongst the servant class. I know some of my girls love your salons, but they don't have enough clout to help you in the way that you need."

"You're quite right; we really do need to combat the rumors. I'm not sure what path to take since Lady Corinne St. Gramflurri is the one spreading them. It's like trying to fight the devil. This is something I would love to discuss with you, but it's still not why we are here," I said.

"Oh, I had assumed that was the reason for your visit and have been trying to think of some last-minute ideas. What are you here to discuss, if not that?"

"I'm not sure if you've heard about the maid Lotte Lane? Lady Taversham accused her of Lord Taversham's murder, after the earl, ah, after he had assaulted her and Lady Taversham fired her," I said. "I was hoping you might know something about Lady Taversham from your time in Fintan. There is so much I'm missing. It feels like I am unaware of everything related to Lady Taversham and her relationship with the earl. I feel like there should have been some gossip, but I haven't heard any of it."

"Let me think for a moment. I believe she was Miss Augusta Winters at the time. She wasn't anyone of consequence. In fact, I don't think anyone thought about her at all until she caught the eye of Lord Taversham," Lady Adelaide said, her mind still flipping through everything she could remember about that particular year.

"Is there anything else you can remember about her?" Pippa asked.

"I believe she made her debut the year your aunt decided to turn the *ton* on its ear and left the country. If only I had listened to her instead of Lady Corinne, my life would have been quite different." Lady Adelaide paused and shook her head like she was shaking away memories. "Ah yes, Augusta. If I remember correctly, she was the niece of someone well established in society at the time. I can't remember who. Although it must have been someone with an impeccable reputation because she did marry quite well. Even if the earl turned out to be a philanderer, he was considered a catch. I think Duke Farrington was the only other titled gentlemen looking for a wife that year."

"Do you know where Lady Taversham's family is located?" I asked. Maybe knowing more about her family would help me fill out the story about her and her relationship with the earl. I can't imagine it was a good one, with everything I knew about his habits.

"No, which is quite strange. It's been a long time since I've even thought about any of this, but Augusta went out of her way to keep where she was from a secret. Eventually, everyone gave up and stopped asking. She would evade questions on anything related to where she was from and if she had any family. My guess is she came from a rather humble family, and the only reason she had a season was because of her aunt. It wouldn't surprise me if she married way above her station." Lady Adelaide picked up her teacup and took a sip.

"Do you think the earl knew of her background? Or do you think he found out later on, after he married her?" I asked. It wouldn't provide a motive for her to murder anyone, but it just might speak to some family drama, which in turn could suggest a reason to kill.

"I don't know if he knew, but I'm sure he found out. Especially when the only money he got from the marriage was a meager dowry. The earl was well known, even then, for his gambling habits. I can't imagine he was too happy with the outcome of being found with her alone in an orangery of all places. She was quite ruined unless he did the proper thing. And no one else would have him if he didn't."

"Why is that?" Pippa asked.

"It's my understanding everyone believed he was after

a fortune. And you know how members of the *ton* can be. They weren't willing to ostracize him, but they didn't really want him to succeed and marry an heiress. Instead, it appeared he had found his heiress and was sorely disappointed when he found out that the only thing she had was a meager dowry."

"I would imagine he was unhappy about her lack of dowry when he found out. Was there anything that happened because of it?" I asked. I learned from gothic novels that men could become quite irrational when they didn't get what they wanted. And this had the beginnings of a gothic novel.

"I don't think so. It was interesting though; she all but disappeared for two years. No one saw her about town, at any balls, or anything, really. Unless she came with the earl. But that wasn't very often, and they normally left the event early. Then one day we all heard that the Tavershams had a new butler, even though the man he replaced had been with the earl and his family for decades. Suddenly, Augusta was at all the events, balls, and everything else. Something happened in that household, but I don't have any idea what it was." Lady Adelaide set her teacup down on the tray. I looked at the tray and discovered all the sandwiches were gone. Pippa and I had stayed rather a long time and should now be on our way.

I stood up. "Thank you so much for taking the time to talk to us. You've been a font of information," I said.

"You're welcome. Don't hesitate to stop by. It was nice to see you, even if it's not under the most pleasant circumstances." Lady Adelaide stood so we could say our farewells.

"We will set aside time for a visit in the future. For now, Pippa and I will be on our way. Thank you so much for letting us take up so much of your time," I said. Pippa and I took our leave of Lady Adelaide, no closer to discovering who had murdered the earl.

Chapter Twenty

It had been a week since Professor Smythe had kicked me out of his class. Now here I was, setting up an area in the park to discuss politics and theory with a handful of gentlemen that wanted to hear from me and not the professor. It surprised me that anyone wanted to listen to me.

I had brought Justice with me. She needed to stretch her legs, and I was hoping having her around would have a calming effect, if, at any point, I needed to calm down. I pulled out her blanket from my carpet bag and laid it on the ground for her, tying her leather lead to the wrought-iron fence running along the edge of the small square I had picked for this meeting. As soon as the blanket was on the ground, Justice stepped on it, circled a few times, and curled into her adorable cinnamon-bun sleeping position for a nap. I smiled, thinking how nice it would be to be able to nap whenever and wherever.

I ran my gloved hands down over the front of my bodice. My goal was to feel confident and in charge today, so I was decked out in a bold blue-and-gold striped ensemble trimmed in matching blue velvet. I loved how the bodice itself looked like a blue velvet jacket over a gold-trimmed blouse, with a wide blue-and-gold belted waist. The bustled apron was the same blue velvet as the jacket, with hidden ties underneath making the fabric tuck and fold over the blue-and-gold bustled skirt in the most delectable way. I was also sporting a jaunty blue velvet hat and matching boots. The Grantabridge modiste had outdone herself with this ensemble and had worked extensively with the milliner and cobbler to produce such perfection.

I was interested in who would show up to this meeting, and I was nervous as well. I was not an expert. In fact, I was far from an expert. The reality was I was just vocal when it came to my ideas of a better world, especially a better world for women. Which was why today I wanted to talk about the Married Woman's Property Act. The proposed law was constantly being discussed and should be put in front of the House of Lords for a vote. However, there was always something that caused a delay in calling for the vote. So, the proposed law sat there, neither signed nor dismissed. It was instead ignored as if ignoring the proposed legislation would somehow make it disappear.

I was curious to know what the gentlemen who wanted me to speak were going to say about the topic. It was the first step towards women's suffrage, even if they didn't realize it. Ironically, prior to 1830, it was technically legal for women to vote. Not that many women did, but they would have been allowed to if they had tried. I have yet to figure out why Brythion's government changed the law to specifically ban women from voting around 1830, but that's exactly what happened. My best guess was that a group of women voted, unable to be turned away, and caused an upset in the election. Either it was too close for the leading party's comfort, or there was a switch in parties that lasted for a blink of an eye. Long enough that when the other party took control, they did everything they could to prevent a similar occurrence from happening, including outlawing women's right to vote.

I felt like I had been standing around the square for an eternity when Kaiden showed up. It was calming to see a familiar, friendly face. It was like Kaiden showing up opened the way for others to arrive. As soon as he stepped into the small circle I had set up, others gathered around. They all stood there, this titled group of gentlemen, looking at me expectantly.

"I thought today we could discuss the proposed Married Woman's Property Act. I'm sure you all realize that when a woman marries, her property becomes her husband's property. It's why heiresses are so popular nowadays." I looked at all the titled gentlemen standing around, all of them except Kaiden hoping to marry an heiress, or so I presumed. I wondered if they would be here if they didn't believe I was an heiress. Could their interest in my politics just be a way to convince me to marry them? "What would be the reason for marrying an heiress if the property didn't revert to the husband?"

"Why would women want to keep their property when they're married? Once they are married, their husbands are responsible for taking care of them," a newcomer asked as he approached my political salon, for lack of a better word. Although salons were so decidedly female, I doubted the men would approve.

I looked up to chastise the newcomer, only to see Declan Bailey joining the group. Surely, he could not be serious? The man I spoke to the other day would not posture such inane questions.

"While it might be their responsibility to take care of their wife, not all men rise to the task. I'm sure you have seen such failures in your work as a barrister. Or maybe you haven't, as it is still legal to beat one's wife as she isn't thought of as much more than property."

"So now we are to let property own property? That doesn't seem to make any sense," I heard someone say. Hearing something so ignorant had me on the edge of losing my temper. I rolled my shoulders back and took a deep breath. It wouldn't do any good to yell at the men who came to hear me speak within minutes of starting.

"No, that is not what anyone is saying, especially not me. I do not think anyone should ever consider women property. The men in our family, whether it is our father or husband, should not own us. We are, in fact, humans and should have the rights that go along with being human, which includes being able to keep what we own even if we are married. Why do you think women would want to own property? Things like earned wages from work the woman did, or any gifts given to her, including, but not limited to, gifts of land."

Most of the gentlemen looked at each other, at a loss as to why a woman would want to own property. Only two people in my small crowd weren't shuffling in confusion: Kaiden and Mr. Bailey. I looked back and forth between them, raising an eyebrow, daring one of them to answer my question. I was curious to see who would break first.

"Escape," Kaiden said. Just the one word, and while it was what I was looking for, I was really hoping for a bit more than one word.

"What do you mean by that, Lord Fremont? What could women want to escape from?" I tried to pull more from him.

"More like who?" he responded but did not go any further. I didn't know if he was being difficult or trying to get others in this weird mix of people to speak up.

"*Who* is definitely more accurate than *what*," Mr. Bailey said. "As you have already alluded, women are seen as property of their husbands and have very little rights concerning how their husband treats them. Which can, although it does not always, lead to an untenable position where now the woman has lost all access to her money as it belongs to her husband and does not have the means to set up an account or anything else for herself without her husband's permission. Thus, she ends up trapped. The system does not benefit women, at least not in this regard," Mr. Bailey said.

His comments directly opposed his earlier questions. I could not get a read on him. He went from spouting nonsense that made me want to practice Pippa's boxing lessons on his face, to moments like this where it was clear that he understood not only what I was saying but why I was saying it.

"Exactly. That is exactly why this act is so important. It is the first step in giving women the power to protect themselves both financially and politically." I wanted to clap my hands with excitement; instead, I pressed my hands into my sides, doing what I could to maintain my composure.

"But will it really make a difference? Are the meager wages women earn enough to prevent them from being trapped? I think the law is a waste," Mr. Bailey said.

"What?" My mouth dropped open. I couldn't believe what Mr. Bailey had just said. Again, it didn't match with anything he had said before. "How can it be a waste? It's finally doing something to protect women."

"Do you really consider letting women keep their meager earnings protecting them? Stop and think for a moment," Mr. Bailey said.

I heard Kaiden mutter something like, "Uh, you're in for it now," under his breath.

"Did you really just tell me to stop and think?" I glared at him, my hands on my hips.

"I did. If you've read the proposed act, you would see how senseless it really is. It does nothing but allow women to think they are gaining an advantage."

"Do you really think that we are so easily fooled? Pat

us on the head and send us off with a treat, and we're as content as can be? We are not house pets. Is the proposed law perfect? Not even close. That it uses words like 'meager earnings' is insulting and ridiculous. And I'm concerned it would limit someone in my position from keeping any inheritance my parents left me. But right now, the alternative is nothing. When those are your choices, sometimes you have to work on chipping away at the solid rock instead of blowing it up with dynamite." I stood there, hands on my hips, inches away from Declan Bailey. I stared into his whiskey-colored eyes, daring him to say something.

"Maybe you should get a stick of dynamite. It could lead to better results," Mr. Bailey muttered.

"Oh!" I threw my hands up into the air. "It's not like women wouldn't like to try that. I know I would. But at this point, to get anything done in the government, women have to depend on men to do it. And there are those who have our side. Lord Fremont, for one, has done a splendid job taking up the mantle his brother left behind. But he is an oddity when it comes down to it." I started pacing. "As many of you are here right now listening to my thoughts, there are just as many men who do not want to hear what I have to say because I am not feminine enough in my manner. Or if I lose my temper, shed a tear, or show any emotion whatsoever, I am told I'm too emotional, and therefore weak and unable to handle the stress of voting, owning my own property, or working in any field that requires abstract thought. So going into parliament with a stick of dynamite in the form of a law that does everything that we need to be done would lead to nothing. It's taken two years and numerous revisions, each one taking more away from the women the law was set to protect to get to the point of something passing. So excuse me for seeing some benefit in an act that is rather lackluster."

"I . . ," Mr. Bailey attempted to interrupt my speech, but I wasn't quite done.

"Before telling a woman to stop and think about something that is integral to changing her life, I suggest you stop and contemplate what you are saying. Do you really believe that a day goes by when I'm not analyzing the potential pitfalls of my actions? Here I am, hosting this little tête-à-tête at the potential risk of being asked to leave the university. What I should be doing is working out a compromise of some sort with the individual who started the rumors of my lack of moral character. Instead, I'm here, because a group of gentlemen asked it of me. I'm risking even more being said about my reputation. But many of you will take your seat in the House of Lords, and maybe you'll remember the things I talked about and it will influence your decisions, which will then influence my actual life. So here I am, risking a lot for something that may not even chip away at the rock."

Chapter Twenty-One

"I should apologize, but I won't. You enjoy having someone to argue with you, I can tell. It makes you analyze your arguments more, look at them even harder. I doubt there are very many people who dare to question you. I will always question everything, even if deep down I agree with you," Mr. Bailey said. In that moment, like so many others before, Mr. Bailey reminded me of someone. It was the color of the eyes. I had seen them before, but I could not place them.

"I'm not sure I would go quite that far. It is nice to think of things in different ways, but it makes more sense if one really does see things in the way they argue them to others. It makes for more impassioned arguments." I glanced back at Mr. Bailey to see what he thought about my statement. I grabbed Justice's lead, picked up her blanket, and tossed it into my carpet bag. With all of my things with me, I started the short walk back to the Octagon House.

"More impassioned, yes, but more thought out, more logical, highly unlikely. It takes being able to see a proposition from all angles to truly be able to present the best arguments that fit your desired outcome." Mr. Bailey fell into step beside me.

"An argument that has feeling behind it does not make it illogical. And to believe so is to dismiss some of the most well-thought-out opinions on a subject because those opinions are coming from the perspective of someone who has to live with the decisions based on their arguments." I looked at Mr. Bailey; his eyes were focused on me, taking in every word I said. "For example, the act we were just discussing could affect me greatly. I am the only child of my father, and the vast majority of his wealth has been made from personal investments, not from his properties as a marquess. While the property itself will go to some gentleman that we do not know at all, my father has the opportunity to leave me with a substantial fortune, ensuring that I will never want for anything. Unless, of course, I marry. Then my fortune will go to my husband, who can do what he will with it. He need not have any regard for my wishes as to how the money is spent at all. Do you not think I've thought about the current law in parliament from all angles? What each change does to my ability to reach any of my goals, not to mention what it does to my ability to protect myself in this world?" I sighed because I thought about these things all the time. It weighed on me to want things for the future, my future, that were denied to me because of my gender.

Mr. Bailey walked alongside me for a while without saying anything. The silence was heavy. It wasn't awkward, but it was not comfortable. I could feel him analyzing my words, looking at them from different angles. I wanted him to say something after what had turned into a monologue. However, he was silent, his eyes focused on the horizon. His brow was pinched and his hands were clasped behind his back.

Finally, Mr. Bailey spoke. "What are your goals? Rather, what would your goals be if you could do anything you wanted?" He turned to me, stopping. His dark piercing gaze looked straight into my soul, or so it seemed. Why were his eyes so familiar to me?

"I . . ." I blinked once, twice, standing there, the words not coming together in my head. Justice barked and tugged on the lead. Breaking away from his stare, I shook my head and rolled my shoulders back. "Okay, okay Justice, we will start walking again. I'm sorry our stop interrupted your walk." Justice looked at me with her blue eyes until I stopped speaking and started moving again. "What I want more than anything is to be a barrister, like you. I see no reason why I shouldn't be allowed to be. Other than fear, of course."

"There really is not a reason for you or any other woman who wants to be a solicitor or a barrister not to be allowed to be one. The so-called science that is used to validate men's desire to limit women from working in any position at all is based on medieval ideas of how the body worked. Why do you want to become a barrister, though? You are not in need of funds." Mr. Bailey glanced over at me, his eyes thoughtful but questioning.

"It isn't about needing financial stability. It's about needing a purpose. I have a tendency to take in strays. At least that's what my friends call them." I gestured to Justice as I talked. "Justice is an example. I found her in a bush, covered in mud, whining for help. I hired Lotte when she ran into me, crying after Lady Taversham fired her. Our butler, Mr. Pendrake, came to us through Hannah because his employer accused him of stealing a painting, despite the fact his employer knew exactly where the painting was the entire time."

"I don't see how . . ."

I looked at Mr. Bailey, holding my hand up to indicate I wasn't done yet. "Each of them needed a person in their corner. Justice needed to be loved, cuddled, and fed. Lotte needed an employer who believed her. Now she needs a barrister who believes in her. Lady Taversham didn't just let her go with no references. She accused her of seducing her husband and then murdering him. Mr. Pendrake was another that needed a place where he could flourish and have someone look out for him as much as he looks out for others. I can only do so much when it comes to saving people by finding them a place. But as a barrister, I could do so much more." I looked ahead as we continued down the path, Justice trotting along in front of us, happy to be out for a walk.

Once again, we walked in silence. I had expected a response. However, Mr. Bailey liked to mull over what I said to him. At least, I assumed that's what he was doing during these long gaps of silence after I spoke.

"Have you thought about another way you can have a purpose?" Mr. Bailey asked, his crisp accent and clipped tones cutting through the silence.

"I have not. Right now, I'm studying here. Or I was until rumors that I am a whore started flying around town, getting me kicked out of my political theory course."

Justice led the way, pulling us down the street. The Octagon House rose up in front of us at the end of the street.

"There are other things you can do. It won't be the same as being a barrister, but you could create a charity of some sort," Mr. Bailey suggested. "Or you could organize a group of women, fight for suffrage."

I looked over at him. I was surprised by his suggestions. This did not sound like the man who had dismissed me when we first met. It sounded like he understood my need to do something. He didn't brush it off or suggest that my purpose in life was to raise a family. I contemplated this revelation as Mr. Pendrake opened the door to my home.

"Ah, Mr. Pendrake, if you don't mind, can you see that Justice has her lunch with a giant bowl of water? We were out for quite a while today, and I'm sure she is parched," I said, handing Mr. Pendrake Justice's lead. "And have tea sent to the parlor. Mr. Bailey is here and might need to speak with Lotte when she has a chance."

He nodded his head, then, with a slight gesture, motioned for our footman to take Justice.

"Of course, Lady Spencer, only the very best for our Justice here." Mr. Pendrake was working on covering his bit of accent, focusing on mimicking the sounds of the aristocracy. No matter how many times I told him it did not matter to any of us here, he insisted that a butler must sound proper, and the rest of elite society did not consider his accent proper.

I handed my gloves to Mr. Pendrake. "Thank you. I'll

escort Mr. Bailey into the parlor. Please bring Justice around when she is done with her lunch." I turned on my heel and walked towards the parlor, assuming Mr. Bailey was following me since he must want something. There was no other reason for him to show up to my lecture or walk me home.

I heard the click of his shoes on the floor behind me. I sat on the settee, nodding my head towards one of the chairs, indicating he should take a seat.

"Are you here to see Lotte and discuss her case?" I smoothed my hands over my skirts as I sat.

"I do want to discuss Lotte's case. However, I was hoping to discuss it with you and your friends if they are around." Once again, I found myself to be the subject of Mr. Bailey's intense gaze.

"Why would you want to speak to any of us?" I asked, glancing down at my hands resting in my lap. I then watched him through my lashes. It felt like my attempts at looking demure were working. I had a feeling he wouldn't be happy with me if he knew just how much investigating I had done.

"Don't try to look sweet and innocent." Mr. Bailey never took his eyes off me. It was all I could do not to fidget under his stare.

"You're right. We have information on various

subjects related to the murder. Not that any of it really has helped, or makes any sense at the moment. There's something missing that's going to pull this all together, I just know it." I drummed my fingers on the armrest of the settee. Any attempt at looking demure flew out the window as I thought about Lotte's case and my lack of progress. My mind churned through the information that my friends and I had discovered so far. I worked through what Lady Adelaide had told Pippa and me, forgetting that Mr. Bailey was in the room. Lady Taversham's lack of fortune and mention of a new butler circled around in my head. I don't know what, if anything, it had to do with the murder. Just more information I didn't know what to do with.

"Lady Spencer?" Mr. Bailey questioned, drawing me back to the present and the discussion happening in the parlor.

"Please, call me Georgi. Every time I hear Lady Spencer, I think my mother is around. Which wouldn't be a bad thing. I would rather like to see her; it's been way too long," I responded, not thinking of my words, as the case had taken over my mind.

"Um . . . Georgi . . . are you quite well?" Mr. Bailey asked. Concern was etched on his face as he leaned towards me without leaving his seat.

Startled, I shook my head slightly. "I'm fine, just lost

in thought for a moment." I focus on Mr. Bailey. "What is it you want?"

Both of us stopped speaking as tea and Justice were brought into the room. Justice hopped onto the settee, curling up next to me. Leaning forward and trying to not disturb my dog, I poured two cups of tea like a proper hostess and handed one to Mr. Bailey.

"I was hoping to work together. I'm afraid I've run into a wall. While there is nothing to prove Lotte's guilt, I haven't been able to find anything to prove her innocence. I would like to prove she couldn't be the culprit and have the case dismissed." He ran his hand through his hair, disheveling it beyond repair. There was something alluring about a disheveled man asking for a woman's assistance, or at least I found something about it attractive.

"You want my help now? But you were so quick to disregard it before." I was going to work with him. Working with him meant helping Lotte, which was a priority of mine. That didn't mean I wasn't above making him sweat. It was important he learned from his mistakes. Dismissing me was never a good idea. "If I'm going to work with you, I'm going to need you to answer two questions."

He raked his hand through his hair again, ruining any sense of order. His whiskey eyes glared at me. "At this point, you have the upper hand. What do you want to know?"

I continued to pet Justice, so I didn't clap my hands in glee. "The first thing I want to know is why did you dismiss me when we first met? The second question is, why did you become a barrister?"

Chapter Twenty-Two

"You do not play nicely, do you, Georgi?" Mr. Bailey said. "I'll answer the second question first. I'm the third son of Lord Bailey. My two older brothers followed the paths my father laid out for them. Asher will be the future Lord Bailey and Liam went into the military like a good second son. My father had planned for me to go into the church. But I had no interest, no calling as it were." Mr. Bailey tapped the floor with his foot in an incessant rhythm. Did answering my question put him on edge? And if it did put him on edge, why? "How could I help lead others in their faith when it did not call to me? When I started my theological studies, I felt like a fraud. I needed something else in my life, so I started taking classes on law, and there I found my passion. My family is wealthy enough that I can take cases other solicitors and barristers would ignore because there is no money in them.

Lotte's predicament is an example of such a case."

"Has your father come to terms with your decision?" Curiosity got the better of me. I couldn't imagine his father being upset over his passion for the law. It was still a noble calling. But some considered it too close to trade, something high society would never be involved in. I clearly had no such qualms as it was what I wanted to do with my life, and my father had dirtied his hands by involving himself in trade long before I was born.

"You said two questions, Georgi, not three. What would you rather me answer? Your first question or this one?" Mr. Bailey said with a slight smirk.

"Mr. Bailey, it's rude to throw my own rules back in my face."

"It's Declan." There was a twinkle in his eye.

"It's still unseemly to throw my own rules back at me, Declan. But if I had to choose, I would like my first question answered. For now, at least." Silence filled the room as I awaited his answer. Justice took the pause in the conversation to readjust her position and rest her head on my lap.

"It was never my intention to dismiss your help. Your entrance threw me off guard and I did not respond well at all. It seemed that neither one of us was ready to listen to what the other person had to say. I know I implied and probably said things that I did not mean or believe the first few times we met."

"Hmm, not willing to listen to someone doesn't sound like me at all," I said with a coy smile. "I guess we should get down to business. How do you want to proceed now that you've admitted you can't do your job without me?" I was not above some gentle teasing now that Mr. Bailey, I mean, Declan and I were seeing eye to eye. Or eye to chin, as was more accurate. He was rather tall, something I was not used to at all. I rather liked that quality of his, though.

"Why don't we start with your conversation with Lady Adelaide? Did she have any useful information to offer? I won't be able to speak to her and interview her without the proper introductions. And I'm lacking in connections in Grantabridge. My family has never spent much time here, being from the borderlands up north."

"Oh, you are one of those Baileys. My family seat is up north as well. Although not a surprise, with my father being a marquess."

"Yes, we are one of those Baileys," Declan deadpanned.

"Anyway, onto my meeting with Lady Adelaide. She didn't have too much to offer as far as I could tell." I told him about Lady Adelaide's recollections about Lady Taversham's debutante season and how she ended up with the fortune-hunting gambler, Lord Taversham. "Of course, society loved the fact he was trapped by someone with next to nothing."

"I assumed the marriage was not smooth for her."

"No one really knows. Lady Taversham disappeared for about two years, only showing up to events when the earl accompanied her. Then suddenly she was everywhere. Attending every party, musical, and ball. The change coincided with the family hiring a new butler, even though the old one had been with the earl since he was a child," I said.

"People commented on the change of house staff?" Declan asked, his eyebrow raised. He looked so perplexed it was all I could do not to laugh at him.

"Of course they did, especially as it overlapped with a significant change in the behavior of the Tavershams. Something must have happened to cause the earl to let his butler go and hire someone new. If you take the new butler and add Lady Taversham suddenly being seen all around town, the two events are going to be gossiped about."

"I see. Do you have any idea what happened to cause such a startling change?" Declan asked.

"Not at all. But it must be something good, or something absolutely terrible."

"Have you thought about asking Lady Taversham?"

"Don't be foolish. If she wanted her circumstances to be known, she would have discussed it a long time ago. She's managed to perfect an impeccable reputation for herself, and she is not going to let anyone ruin that for her. If she discusses what happened back then, it could ruin her, remind people she's not from money, or make them remember some other scandal."

"And you believe the truth would ruin her reputation?"

"Of course it would. If it wouldn't, it would not be a secret. And whatever was going on between her and the earl is such a secret that those lying about it have probably started believing their own lies. It's how society works." I shrugged, taking another sip of tea. I waited for Declan to say something, but he stayed silent with a contemplative expression. "So, Declan, what have you discovered during your investigations?"

"Nothing really of note. The most interesting discovery so far is that Lady Taversham has an older brother. I believe he is about ten years older than her. But I'm not sure where that fits in at all, especially since no one has heard from him in almost two decades." Declan ran his hand through his hair again. I noticed he did so every time we admitted to hitting a dead end.

"Do you know exactly when he disappeared?" I asked.

It felt important to me, even though it seemed quite innocuous.

"I think it was around 1852. Why? Do you think it is important to our investigation?" Declan peppered me with questions, one following the other in rapid succession. I honestly liked that he referred to it as *our* investigation. Why did it take so little to feel validated?

"I don't know if it's important or not. There's just something about the time frame that feels like it could be important. I believe that's the year the new butler showed up and Lady Taversham started socializing again." I shrugged, not dismissing my feeling but putting it aside for now. The reason behind that little niggle saying this was important would come to me eventually. "Have you looked into the gambling debts, or the smuggling operations—oh, or his business dealings with Lord Frankland?"

"What business dealings? And smuggling operations?" Declan looked at me, baffled by my knowlwdge of the earl's activities.

"Oh, Mr. Bailey, what have you been looking into thus far to miss all of this? I assumed you were on the dirigible to talk to Lord Frankland since the earl was embezzling from him. Not that he cared since he is a silent partner in Mr. Milford's gentlemen's club, and the two of them were cheating the earl out of what he had embezzled from Lord

Frankland. Not that any of the information points to one person or another."

"Can you slow down for a minute? I've been trying to get information about the earl's business dealings for what seems like an eternity. Every time I ask questions, people are silent or act like they know nothing about the earl's business dealings."

"I apologize, but you clearly need a better source for gathering information. I'll admit, we discovered most of this by 'borrowing' the earl's financial books. Mads is a mathematical genius. She spotted everything by going through the books herself. But you could have discovered the majority of this if you just asked the right people," I said, twirling a lock of hair that had fallen from my chignon around my finger.

"Who should I be talking to?" Declan stared at me with those eyes. Why did they have such an impact on me?

"Milford, for one. Maybe you can go to Milford's club tomorrow for the prize fight."

"I will see if I can arrange it."

I nodded and continued my pacing. "Some of his employees and associates might be willing to talk too. If they won't talk to you, you need to send someone whom they will talk to."

I should try to contact someone in the smuggling enterprise to see if I could get a bottle of whiskey for the house. Or have Mr. Pendrake do it.

I nodded. Yes, I'll see what Mr. Pendrake can figure out and get his hands on.

"It's just me. I can't pay anyone right now, especially when taking on cases for free," Declan said, exasperated.

"You're going to have to figure out something to be successful. People won't just answer your questions because you're handsome. Well, most people won't."

"Did you just say that you think I'm handsome?"

"No, I said people won't answer your questions just because you're handsome. There is a difference. One view is subjective, the other is objective. I don't think anyone would deny you have an appealing countenance." I smiled, a slight blush warming my cheeks. "Now, back to the task at hand. The easiest and most well-known information is that the earl was an avid gambler. His debts were substantial."

"I had heard he was in debt but not to the extreme that you say."

"He was in so much debt that he was embezzling from Lord Frankland, his partner in the dirigible business, to pay back Mr. Milford for all of his losses at the gaming tables. I assumed Frankland had a solid motive. Turns out that

Frankland is Milford's silent partner in the gentlemen's club."

"How did you figure that out?" Declan asked.

"I asked him, not intentionally. But when we spoke on the dirigible, I put it together. Kaiden had spoken to Milford and confirmed he was a silent partner. I was able to get Lord Frankland to admit to being that partner in a roundabout way. He also admitted to cheating Lord Taversham at the club until he got the money the earl had embezzled from him back. Unfortunately for the earl, he continued to lose whether or not he was being cheated. The earl had a serious gambling problem." Justice decided she was done on the settee at that moment, jumped off, and stretched. This worked for me. I always found it easier to think things through while moving. So I stood. Declan went to stand as well, but I shooed him back to his seat. No one else needed to stand with me.

I started pacing the length of the room. As had become her normal, Justice started pacing with me. It really was the cutest thing I had ever seen a dog do, but at the moment, I was focused on the case. I could not say the same for Declan. He was watching Justice follow me back and forth with both wonder and amusement. I could see his lips twitching and creases forming around his eyes. He was doing everything he could not to laugh at Justice and me as we worked through the conundrum that was Lotte's case.

"There must be more from the way that you are pacing," Declan said.

"There is. There seems to be so much information, but no one has an apparent motive. Frankland met with the earl the night of the masquerade. He's probably the last person to see the earl alive, other than the killer. If the killer actually saw the earl die." I turned and started walking back the other way, the heels of my boot marking each one of my steps, Justice padding alongside me.

"What do you mean, if the killer actually saw the earl die? He was stabbed. The killer must have seen him."

"The earl was already dead when he was stabbed. That's why there wasn't any blood," I said.

"How do you know that?"

"I was the one that found the body. And when I described what I saw to Willa, she mentioned that he must have already been dead for there to be no blood. Especially since he was stabbed in the heart." I stop walking. "I assumed the coroner or the police would have informed you of that little bit of information."

"Apparently not. This is the first I'm hearing of it, and it could be crucial to Lotte's case. It means he could have died of natural causes."

"He could have. He did have a heart condition, after

all," I said with a wave of my hand.

"The earl had a *heart condition*?"

"Yes, Willa is testing his tonic bottles to see if they actually had something that would help him or if it was something other than his medicine."

"How did you get a bottle of his medicine?"

"The same way we got his account books. After the police had finished their thorough investigation"—I rolled my eyes at the thought of Detective Radcliffe being thorough about anything—"I broke into the study and took anything I thought would be of importance to the case."

"Were you ever going to come to me with any of this information?" Declan was angry. He was no longer sitting; instead, he had taken to pacing the other side of the room, running his hand through his hair and muttering to himself. Justice and I both stood there, watching him walk back and forth across the length of the room.

"Of course, I was planning on telling you once I had confirmed the information. The coroner's report should have included the information that the earl was aready dead when he was stabbed. I hadn't realized the police needed us for every aspect of their investigation. As for the heart condition, I figured the coroner would have been able to figure that out as well, or I would have told you when Willa was done with her tests." I stood there, hands planted on my hips.

Declan stopped and stared at me. It was like he could not believe the words that I was saying. But really, none of this information was hard to find, and it all could have been in the police evidence room if they had the forethought to take it. Instead, they left it for us to find.

"You think that you and your friends are necessary to the investigation?" His hand went through his hair and then to his temples.

"Are you implying that we are not? Look at the facts: the police did not gather any of this evidence despite having the opportunity to do so. They did not inform you of anything strange about the earl's stab wound. And you haven't been able to gather even the most basic of information because the police are so negligent in their job. I ask you, how are we *not* necessary to this investigation?" I wanted to stomp my foot for emphasis, but I was sure that would come off childish.

"You are interfering. Stealing evidence."

"Evidence that had been left behind, deemed unimportant. But to me, it seemed important, and by your reaction, it is crucial to the case. Let me ask you this, have the police gone back to the Tavershams' home to collect any more evidence, or at least look at the scene in broad daylight? No, they never did. I wasn't intentionally keeping anything from you."

"This is all information I wish I had known about long before now." Declan glared at me from the other side of the room.

"All you had to do was come by and ask. I may not have been polite, but I would never have kept something that would help Lotte's case from you out of spite, no matter how much I would have wanted to." I stared at him, holding my ground. I had shared everything I knew about the case as soon as Declan had taken the time to discuss it with me. It was not my fault he hadn't listened to me until now. Was it?

"Lady Spencer, you are insufferable." Declan pushed his hand through his hair.

"As are you, Mr. Bailey," I said to his back, as he had already made it out of the parlor and was gathering his belongings in the entryway. "His pharmacist was Rupert Benson if you want to ask him about the earl's condition."

Chapter Twenty-Three

"I cannot believe we are doing this. Pippa, do you really think this is a good idea?" I said as I tried to tuck my hair into the cap Pippa had found for me. I felt totally exposed despite having layers of clothing on. Hannah and Pippa had worked together to find everyone the perfect male clothing to wear for this evening. Well, almost everyone. Willa had opted out of watching the fight. She abhorred violence and was still struggling with all the rumors that were going around town. Willa was going to stay home and run some tests on the medicine bottles to make sure the results were as conclusive as they could be. Mads, Pippa, and I were planning on going to Milford's to watch the fight and hopefully gather some more relevant information. I really wanted this crazy adventure to pan out and to maybe even narrow down the suspects.

"You look fantastic, Georgi. Your height really helps. While I wouldn't say you look like a man on close inspection, you definitely would fool anyone at a glance. On closer inspection, your features are too feminine, but no one should look that closely," Mads said. "I, on the other hand, look like a woman in men's clothing. There's no hiding it. Even binding my breasts did nothing to make my shape more masculine."

I looked over at her, and she looked stunning in the black pants and waistcoat Hannah and Pippa had procured for her. She was right, though; the outfit did little to hide her curves. But I was jealous of the black brocade of her waistcoat. It was so elegant. She pulled on the frock coat, which helped because it hung down from her shoulders and didn't cut in at her waist, giving her a boxier look.

"You'll be fine. Just don't take off the frock coat," Pippa said.

I'm not sure if I should take Mads's compliment as such. But she was right. Hannah and Pippa had worked together to bind my breasts, which hid the majority of my curves right there. I had always been described as tall and willowy, so it wasn't a surprise that hiding my feminine form was easy. I looked in the mirror at the grey wool pants I was wearing. They fit me quite well and were surprisingly comfortable. The waistcoat was a grey-and-blue plaid, the shirt a crisp white, with a coordinating blue cravat. I had not put on the frock coat yet, but it was the same deep blue that was in the plaid waistcoat. They were right. I looked sharp. Even without the coat, I would wear this out regularly if it was something society would tolerate. Maybe I should have my modiste make a bustle dress out of similar fabrics. I could already picture wearing a bustled day dress with these fabrics to class or maybe a suffragette meeting.

"Pippa, I think you're going to have to pretend to be someone's son coming out to watch the fight for the first time. You're so short, no one is ever going to believe that you are an adult." I looked over at her to see her reaction. I was not disappointed. She threw her shoe at me, which I caught easily, and then she stuck her tongue out. I laughed at her antics, handing her shoe back to her. "Even your shoe looks like a child's shoe. You're definitely going to have to pretend someone is your father."

"Have your fun, Georgi. I'll just get you back at our next boxing lesson. I may be small, but my punch is mighty." Even Pippa couldn't help but laugh at her own ridiculousness and the absurdity of the situation. She wasn't wrong, though. I had watched her right hook take down a man twice her size. I wasn't sure how she managed it.

"I'm sure, next thing you know you'll be dragged into

the ring to fight." I saw a gleam enter Pippa's eyes. "Do not even think of it. We have two tasks tonight: cheer Kaiden on during his fight and find out more about Mr. Milford and the Tavershams. Do not let yourself get distracted by trying to fight someone. It will only draw attention to the rest of us. Attention we do not want tonight."

"Fine, go ahead and take the fun out of tonight." Pippa flopped into the chair by my writing desk, and proceeded to put her feet on said writing desk while crossing her arms, pouting.

It wasn't long before Kaiden showed up in his steam carriage to pick us up. I'm not sure what he was expecting, but the look of shock on his face as the three of us came down the stairs was worth tonight's escapades, even if nothing else came of it. We piled into the car and waved goodbye to Willa, who stood in the doorway looking like a proud but concerned mother, and we all waved back at her as we left, exactly like we were her children.

Kaiden carefully drove through town, Pippa by his side, while Mads and I sat in the back of the steam carriage. I watched the buildings and the trees fly by as we went from one street to another until we stopped in front of the gentlemen's club. It was at that moment my hands began to sweat. There was no way we were going to pull this off. Three women dressed as men. It was asking for trouble. Actually, it was asking to get caught. I wanted to turn back, figure out another way to get in tonight or another way to talk to Milford. Instead, I leapt from the steam carriage along with my friends and followed Kaiden towards the club's entrance. While my head filled with every way things could go wrong tonight, I tried to push through those thoughts as we approached the entrance.

The doorman nodded at us briefly, barely looking at any of us individually. If the night continued like this, my concern was pointless. Kaiden walked off to the right, the rest of us following him. Double doors opened in front of him. Smoke billowed out of the room, and I almost turned around and ran after all the fires in the dormitory when the four of us arrived. But the smoke was not a fire, just trapped cigar smoke that was looking for an escape. Together, we entered the hazy room. It was one of the fullest rooms I'd ever seen, except for the empty square that was roped off in the middle. Men took up every inch of space available to them. Ladies of the *ton* might think their balls were a crush, but they had nothing on fight night at Milford's. There were men everywhere; all of them were yelling and some of them were waving money around. Servers somehow snaked their way through the crowd, handing out whiskey and cigars and taking money and small papers from the men's hands. It was unlike anything I had ever experienced in my life.

Afraid I was going to lose my friends, it was all I could do not to grab onto their clothing or arm. If we were at a ball, my friends and I would walk arm in arm to ensure we stayed together. I didn't do that here because it would look out of place and decidedly not masculine behavior. Somehow, my friends and I successfully stayed together. The three of us waited patiently next to Kaiden as he greeted an older, brawny black man. He looked like a fighter, with muscles straining to pop out of the confines of his jacket. Kaiden greeted him with exuberance, shaking hands and moving in for that one-arm hug men do. I assumed the man Kaiden was talking to was Milford. I recalled he used to be a boxer and had opened this club when he retired, funded by his winnings and a silent partner. Unfortunately, that's all I'd heard about him. Kaiden had told me so much about Milford, but I learned just as much about his club listening to the gentlemen in my class. In their mind, the club and activities that occurred there were not a subject for a ladies' ears. But my presence only stopped them when they were reminded of it. Think how appalled they would be if they knew ladies were amongst them tonight.

Kaiden pointed over at the three of us. Milford's gaze

followed. I attempted to do one of those head nods men give each other. It's like a jutting out of the chin and a slight jerk back. It must have sufficed because Milford turned back to Kaiden. He opened a door, gesturing for Kaiden to go through. It seemed this was the moment we would be separated. After shutting the door behind Kaiden, Milford approached us. He looked us up and down and shook his head in what I could only describe as bemusement. Clearly, we did not pass as men on closer inspection.

"Follow me," Milford said, his gravelly voice somehow cutting through the cacophony of the room. The three of us followed him to a set of benches raised up near the ring. Ah, a spot Kaiden must have assumed we would be safe sitting. It was nice to have a bit of space around us away from the mob that inhabited the rest of the room. I wasn't sure how long I would have lasted if I had stayed down there. It felt like everyone stood so much closer than I was used to. I was used to my bustle giving me more personal space. Even sitting away from the press of bodies, the noise was overwhelming.

"I want to place a bet. Can I place a bet?" Pippa was practically hopping from one foot to another.

Milford looked at her, taking in her stature. "You must be young Pip. Kaiden mentioned you would most likely want to bet. And join a fight. He hinted I should keep an eye on you, said you were a wily one."

"Did he now? Hmm, makes me wonder if I should be on my best behavior or show him just how wily I can be," Pippa said, rubbing her chin, mischief gleaming in her eyes.

"Pip . . . please don't start any trouble. Just place your bet," Mads said with a sternness I wasn't aware she possessed. I guess having three younger sisters taught a person to be stern when she needed to be.

"Oh Mads, you're no fun." Pippa sat, crossing her arms. She really looked like one of our children out to see their first fight.

"I take it you want to bet on the mystery gentleman tonight?" Milford asked.

"Of course, here's our bet. Also, Milford, I would love to have a word with you afterwards, if you don't mind." I handed him a few bills and a betting slip I had pocketed while we waited to be escorted to our seats.

"Of course, Georgi. Kaiden warned me about the three of you. I've set aside time. Come to the back office after the fight and we can have a chat." Milford took our bet and walked away, handing the money to one of the servers as he worked the crowd before the fight.

Suddenly, the crowd was silent. A door on either end of the room opened up, and the men stepped aside, creating paths leading straight to the ring in the center. On one side of the room, the biggest man I have ever seen in my life entered. The man must have been almost seven feet tall. He wasn't wearing a shirt, and his skin was dirty but also had a sheen to it. From where I was sitting, it looked like his muscles had muscles. I gulped, afraid for Kaiden who, I'll admit, was a fine specimen of a man, but he looked like a gangly teenager next to the behemoth that had just walked into the room.

I heard a low whistle from Pippa, causing me to turn to the other door. There was Kaiden, or at least I assumed it was him. He wore a mask that hid a decent amount of his face and covered his hair. It actually made him look like a pirate. The billowing white shirt tucked into tight leather pants didn't disabuse anyone of the notion that he was, in fact, a pirate. All he needed was an eye patch and a parrot. I couldn't help myself and giggled at the thought.

I sat back and watched as the ever proper and reserved future duke sauntered, yes, sauntered across the room. He played to the crowd as he made his way to the ring, encouraging their cheers and mocking their jeers. He climbed into the ring, bowed to the crowd, making direct eye contact with Pippa before he pulled his shirt off. I looked over at Pippa, who had her fingers in her mouth, whistling and cheering with the rest of the crowd. Clearly, she was enjoying the show, where I wasn't sure if I had it in me to enjoy what was about to happen. I held my hands in my lap to prevent anyone from seeing how much they were shaking. Gathering information for the case wasn't worth a good friend of mine getting pummeled, maybe to death, while everyone watched for enjoyment. This was a scene I was clearly not cut out for. I attempted to do what I always did when I felt out of place: channel my mother, but I realized she would never be in this situation, so I had no idea how she would act. It was up to me to remain calm and trust that Kaiden knew what he was doing.

Somewhere I heard someone, probably Milford, announce the fight. I'm sure he made up dastardly names for each opponent. Whatever they were, the roar in my ears drowned out all the sounds around me. Everything sounded so far away from me, like I was in a tunnel or underwater. I felt Mads grab my hands, but I could not acknowledge her. I remember moments like this growing up, when everything around me was so overwhelming I could not breathe. Mads grabbed my chin and turned it towards her. I saw her lips move, forming the words "breathe in." So I did. She nodded her head and patted my hand. The roaring was still too loud for me to hear her, but she mouthed "breathe out," and the air burst from my lungs. She kept my focus on her, helping me regulate my breathing until I could hear again and take in what was around me.

"Are you okay, Georgi?" she asked, concern showing in her deep brown eyes.

"I am. Thank you. It was all a bit much for a moment there. The crowd and my concern for our friend took over," I said, turning back to the ring, still gripping her hand. I'm sure we looked odd if anyone was paying attention, but I needed the physical touch to center me.

The men were circling each other in the ring when I finally looked towards it and allowed myself to focus on it. I don't know how much time had lapsed, but it must not have been much, as neither man seemed to have taken any hits.

The big man swung at Kaiden. I flinched, but no contact was made. Kaiden countered with a quick jab cross and moved away quickly, looking for his next opening. It shocked me to see that the punches actually registered on Kaiden's opponent. He looked more like a solid wall than a man. This pattern continued for a while, the big man slow and lumbering in his movements, Kaiden sharp and fast, but he always backed off instead of going in for the knockout shot. The crowd was getting restless because it looked like Kaiden was toying with his opponent, which I guess that's exactly what he was doing. Then, out of nowhere, the lumbering giant darted one direction, then the other, and wrapped his big forearm around Kaiden's neck.

My breath caught in my throat.

It was over.

I was going to watch my friend die.

But somehow Kaiden flipped himself over his burly competitor. Then Kaiden ended up on the other guy's back, his arm around the thick neck of his opponent. Kaiden released the lumbering giant, moving in front of his opponent, and threw a sequence of punches, one right after the other. Kaiden finished the guy off with an uppercut to the jaw. The burly man fell to the ground as if every bone and muscle in his body had disappeared.

Milford walked to the center of the ring and held Kaiden's hand high over his head, declaring him the winner. The crowd was louder than it had been all night, a few people cheering because they had won, making a mint because the odds were so far against Kaiden. Pippa yelled something like "that's my man" next to me. Thankfully, the crowd was so loud I seriously doubted anyone else would hear her or attribute it to her.

I stood up, signaling to the others that we should all do so, then made my way through the crowd to the room Milford had pointed to earlier. Now that the fight was over, it was time to see if Milford was the person he presented to us tonight, or if he was actually a killer.

Chapter Twenty-Four

"Ah, Lady Spencer, Miss Stanhope, and Miss Cavendish. It didn't take long for you to make your way to my office. Your man put on a show for the crowd. I would love to have him here again." Milford looked around his office as he entered. The three of us had made ourselves comfortable in the chairs the room provided. I had left his desk alone, not wanting to get caught rifling through his things when he was kind enough to talk with me. It had been hard to restrain myself.

"We didn't want to take up any more of your time than necessary. Time is money, after all," Mads said with a wink.

"Right you are, right you are. Lord Fremont informed me that you wanted to know more about my dealings with Lord Taversham," Milford said, taking a seat behind his desk. He kept glancing over at Mads as he made himself comfortable.

"Yes sir, one of our maids has been accused of murdering him. We know she didn't do it but haven't figured out how to prove her innocence. I was hoping you could help," I said.

"Why me?" Milford asked, his eyebrows drawn up in surprise.

"In part because you had business dealings with him. He supplied the spirits you serve here, I believe. And he owed you a considerable sum of money since he had a knack for losing whenever he gambled. It seems of the people who knew the earl, you experienced more parts of his life than most," I explained carefully. I didn't want to offend him or for him to assume I was accusing him. This really was an information-gathering mission. As far as I could tell, Milford was better off with the earl alive. That being said, everything I knew was convoluted. None of it led to any answers. Only a lot more questions.

"Did the earl have any enemies?" Pippa asked.

Milford laughed. "Taversham was liked by few and respected by even less. But enemies, none that I knew of. Somehow, he always paid his debts here. And he brought in the finest spirits. It made it hard to turn him away."

"You turned him away?" I asked.

"Not precisely, although I wish I could have. When he

was in his cups and gambling more than he should, the Tavershams' butler and I had a system to get him out of here before he lost everything."

"Why? Why would you do that?" Mads asked quietly.

Milford turned and looked at Mads. The direct eye contact was almost disconcerting to those of us that had become mere bystanders in that moment. "It was mostly self-interest. If Taversham got in too deep, he would never be able to pay off his debts. I was concerned he would sell his smuggling contacts to someone else, which, it turns out, he was going to do anyway. If someone took over the local smuggling business, it would be a struggle to continue to use them. Taversham cut me a deal on the price of spirits here. Because he did so, I made sure he always left while he could still pay his debts. At least as far as I knew." Milford leaned up against his desk and sighed.

"Would Lord Frankland really raise the price of whiskey and rum he sold to you, which is basically selling to himself since he's the silent partner everyone talks about?" I asked.

Milford's eyebrows shot up, his eyes wide. "How do you know about our partnership?"

"He inadvertently told me when I questioned him on our dirigible ride. He mentioned you helped him get back the money Taversham was embezzling from their company with some fixed games," I said. "I figured you wouldn't do that unless you had some ties to Lord Frankland."

"Frankland's partnership in this club is not common knowledge, and I want to buy him out. But now that he's got the smugglers, I'm not sure I will be able to. I'm worried he's going to try and push me out and move most of the business up in the air to his dirigibles, which would make for an interesting gentlemen's club."

"Sure, until you fall over the railing," I muttered. "I'm sure there are people who wouldn't go up in one of those contraptions. You need a business here on the ground." Granted, I might be a bit biased. "Do you think Lord Frankland could have murdered the earl? He appears to have benefited from his death."

"It's doubtful. Everything that happened was already in the works. Taversham was bringing him into the smuggling business. They were supposed to meet the night of the masquerade to discuss it," Milford said.

"You knew about that meeting?" I asked.

"Yes, I'm pretty sure Frankland figured out I was trying to buy him out. He was warning me that he was going to control the smuggled-in spirits. Implying that if I push him out, I'll regret it."

I can't believe Milford had to explain that to me in such basic terms for it to finally click in my head what he was getting at. There's no way Milford wanted the earl dead. The earl was his safety net from Lord Frankland's machinations. Now, Lord Frankland, he could have wanted the earl dead just to hurry the process. Or maybe the earl was backing out of the deal. There was no way to know unless the earl had left some sort of record. With the way this investigation was going, there was no chance of something that convenient happening.

"How long had you known the earl?" I asked.

"Not that long. I was still boxing two years ago. I won a large purse and decided to open a club here in Grantabridge with it. There was nothing like it in town, with Fintan being so close. But there are so many young gentlemen here it seemed the perfect opportunity."

"It appears you are doing quite well for yourself if tonight's crowd is any indication," Mads said.

"Having a mysterious new fighter helped with that. Lord Fremont fought well, better than I expected," Milford said, looking at Mads. It was like once he was reminded Mads was there, Milford couldn't help but focus all of his attention on her.

"You thought he was going to lose, and you sent that giant oaf out there. He could have been seriously injured or killed." Pippa crossed her arms and glared at Milford.

"I knew he would be able to hold his own. I just didn't think he would win so soundly. It made for a good show at the end. And the house won tonight." Milford smiled at Pippa, but his eyes kept darting back to Mads as he spoke.

"Can I ask one more question?" I looked at Milford, hoping this question wouldn't ruin whatever rapport the four of us had created.

"One more question, then I have to get back to work." He nodded to the door and the room beyond it.

"Of course. Where were you the night of the Tavershams' masquerade party?" I asked, cringing a little on the inside.

"I've been waiting for this question. The one that implies you think I did it." Milford shook his head slightly and smiled. "I was here, hosting a fight night. There were tons of witnesses who saw me. I don't know all of their names, but I can point them out in a crowd."

Mr. Milford did not do it. He had no reason to murder the earl. In fact, he was worse off now that the earl was dead, and I didn't feel like I was any closer to finding the earl's killer. I had more information, but nothing that connected it with anything I already knew. I was at my wit's end. It felt like I was running out of options.

*   *   *

It was a quiet ride back to the Octagon House. I was running out of ideas, and it felt like I was also running out of time. The more I investigated, the more complicated and confusing the case became. Solving Professor Aneurin's murder seemed like a walk in the park compared to the earl's murder. It had to be because I was not talking to the right people. Or maybe I was talking to the right people and they weren't telling me the truth. It really could be either scenario, or maybe it was a combination of both. I had no clue.

I mean, look at the Taversham–Frankland–Milford relationship. I didn't think I'd ever heard of anything so complicated. The earl was in business with both Frankland as a partner in the dirigible company, and with Milford as a supplier of the spirits needed to operate the club. I couldn't forget that Milford and Frankland were partners in the club. Frankland was a secret partner and wanted to stay secret. These three and their relationship got even more complicated as one started thinking about the duplicity between them. Taversham was embezzling money from the dirigible company, which Frankland knew about, so he decided to get his money back by cheating Taversham when he gambled at the club. Frankland and Milford only cheated enough to break even. Then the earl continued to lose at the club until Milford would send him home for the night. The cycle would start all over again with no real resolution because it seemed these men had found a balance that made their relationship work.

Until one threw in who had what amount of power. Taversham and Frankland were changing the balance of power with their negotiations over the smuggling crew. They were also leaving Milford out of those negotiations, which was unfortunate for him. It left him lacking in power and gave Frankland the upper hand in every negotiation from there on out. Milford was very accommodating and nice. I felt for him and his situation with his business partner. He didn't seem like a murderer. Frankland, on the other hand, was not as nice. His friendliness seemed like plating on jewelry. Nice on the outside, but not so pretty on the inside. In fact, part of me wondered if he arranged to have me pushed over the edge of the airship. He had said, twice, that I was going to get myself into trouble the one time we had talked.

My thoughts circled the entire drive back. The drive itself was a blur. I remembered leaving the club, and then suddenly we were parked in front of our house.

"Thank you, Kaiden," I said as he held the door open for Mads and me to get out of his steam carriage.

"Was the night a success?" he asked.

"It was for you. You definitely showed some superb

fighting skills tonight." I smiled at him as Mr. Pendrake opened the door. Kaiden nodded as if the compliment was due course, but at the same time, he shuffled his feet back and forth like he didn't know how to accept it.

"But did you get the information you were hoping for?" Kaiden asked.

"No, and yes. None of the information I have on the Tavershams is really making any sense or leading me in any particular direction." I was dismayed, at a loss for what to do next. I didn't like the feeling one bit. It was not one I felt very often.

"I know you and the others will figure it out, Georgi." Kaiden squeezed my shoulder before going to Pippa to tell her goodbye.

I walked into the house, handing Mr. Pendrake my hat and coat. "Thank you so much, Mr. Pendrake. You always go above and beyond. We could have let ourselves in on our own tonight."

"That would not have been proper, Lady Spencer. Do not worry about the hour. It is part of the job, and not a hardship when you let me know ahead of time, like tonight."

"Thank you, Mr. Pendrake. I have a feeling the four of us will be up for some time. Please don't wait for us."

"Of course." Mr. Pendrake bowed, turning to the

others to take their things before he pretended to take off for the night. I knew he would wait up until we were done for the night, no matter what I told him to do. The thought that Mr. Pendrake would lose a good night's rest because of my friends and me was concerning. It made me think that the conversation should be cut short, at least for tonight.

I sprawled out on the settee, waiting for the rest of the ladies to make their way in to talk. Wearing men's clothing certainly allowed for much better sprawling. Out of the corner of my eye, I saw a ball of golden fluff dart into the room. I moved just in time for Justice to hurtle towards me. I caught her midleap and set her down on the settee. She circled a few times and curled up next to me, laying her head on my lap. Hannah must have waited up as well and was nice enough to let Justice out, knowing I would be up for a while. Hannah knew me well, having listened to me work through theories while she was working way too many times.

"Okay, Georgi, what do you need to talk through tonight?" Mads asked.

"Everything. I'm so lost on this case. What should my next steps be? I know this is different in a lot of ways than researching political theories and putting together arguments based on facts and theories, but the process is kinda similar. It's like solving a puzzle. I'm not used to not knowing what to do next. I don't like this feeling at all," I said, squirming in my seat, trying to find a comfortable spot and not disturb Justice. I failed at that as well. Justice moved, finding her new spot and resting her head on my lap.

"It's f-f-fine to be lost," Willa said. She must have come into the room as I was talking.

"I feel like I'm running out of time, and Lotte is counting on me. But I don't know where to look next." I sighed.

"Why do you feel like you aren't getting anywhere?" Mads asked.

"I'm just confused because it looks like no one really wanted the earl dead. None of his business partners really had a motive, unless it was Lord Frankland, and he was just tired of waiting for the earl to hand over the smuggling business. On top of that, I have weird information on the earl's relationship with his wife. She was almost a recluse for two years, then she was seen at every event in town. And then there's the brother and a new butler."

"Miss."

I turned to the voice, surprised to see Hannah and Mr. Pendrake standing in the doorway.

"Yes, Hannah."

"It sounds like you are forgetting about servants,

miss," Hannah said.

"What do you mean?" I asked.

"Well miss, you should try to find someone who worked for the Tavershams back when everything changed if you want to know why things changed. If you think it's important, that is."

"Even if it's not important, it couldn't hurt to have the information. However, I feel do like this information is the missing piece." I wanted to get up off the settee and start walking the length of the room, but Justice had snuggled up on my lap, trapping me.

"I took the time today to see if there were any servants either still working for the Tavershams or that lived in the area. Lady Taversham's former personal maid is here in town. Her name is Mrs. Benton."

"Hannah, that's fantastic thinking. Thank you. I'll have to talk to her tomorrow. Maybe she can shed some light on this case." I grabbed Justice and made my way towards the stairs. "Let's get some rest. I feel better knowing I have some sort of plan in the works."

Chapter Twenty-Five

"Hannah, I need you to tell me everything you know about Mrs. Benton," I hollered as I went through my clothes, trying to determine what outfit would be best for today's visit. It couldn't be anything too fancy; I wasn't going somewhere that required showing off my status. I would rather come off as approachable and kind than part of the judgmental and stuffy aristocracy. At least that was the plan for today. But everything I had just looked so posh and fancy. Ugh, I had absolutely nothing to wear, even as I stood in front of a veritable mountain of clothing.

"Miss Georgi, stop. Your room looks like an absolute disaster. What are you trying to accomplish today?" Hannah asked, going around the room to collect all my dresses. It was a herculean task, and watching her made me feel guilty for what I could only describe as a tantrum.

I stood there in the middle of the mess in nothing but my underthings. I had torn off my dressing gown at some point this morning in my need to find the perfect armor for my goals for today.

Hannah held up my dressing gown, helping me shrug it on over my chemise, corset, and pantaloons. I sat on the bed as she worked her magic in my room, undoing the havoc I had created.

"Mrs. Benton was Lady Taversham's personal maid from the time she married the earl until a few years ago when Mrs. Benton decided it was time for her to spend more time at home with Mr. Benton. When I spoke to her, she was chatty, but very loyal to Lady Taversham. She did not think highly of the earl though, despite being in his employ before he married."

"Thank you, Hannah. So I need to be nice when talking about Lady Taversham, even though she's one of the awful women spreading rumors about my friends and me. But I do not need to control myself when talking about the earl." I nodded, forming a plan for my meeting with Mrs. Benton.

"Here you go, miss. I think this blue ensemble will do the trick for today," Hannah said, gesturing for me to come over so she could help me dress.

In moments, the bustle dress was on. As always,

Hannah picked out the perfect look for the task. It was a lovely bright blue dress with three-quarter sleeves, a high neck, and pleated ruffles along the bottom of the skirt. Simple, but flattering, perfect for today's plans. I wondered where she had found it.

"It's like you're a magician, Hannah; I had forgotten all about this dress. And it's just right for today. I think I'll wear my straw boater hat with it—oh! And my ivory gloves and boots."

"Thank you, miss. I do my best." Hannah bobbed her head and left the room. I wouldn't be surprised if she was off to find Mr. Pendrake. The two of them have spent a lot of time together ever since she asked me to hire him.

I looked around the room. Justice watched me from the bed, yawning. "Well, Justice, it looks like you're ready for your nap. I'll be back later to take you for a stroll," I said, patting her head as I left.

Making my way down the stairs, I saw Hannah had gone looking for Mr. Pendrake, and they were whispering something in the foyer. How adorable would it be if they made a connection? I wondered what I could do to encourage it.

"Mr. Pendrake, I'm off for today. I don't know exactly how long I'll be gone. Hopefully, it will be a good, productive day, and I'll come home with information that will help Lotte.

Justice is still in my bed. If someone can get her and let her out, I would much appreciate it."

"Of course, miss." He nodded.

"Thank you, Mr. Pendrake. Why don't you and Hannah take the afternoon off after that? Both of you work so hard, I'm sure you can use a break." I winked at Hannah before walking out the door.

Outside, I took in a deep breath of the crisp, cold air. What a pleasant day for a walk. It's like there was a hint of spring in the air. However, that was probably all in my imagination. It was my second favorite season, and I had a tendency to see signs of it way before it was actually springtime.

I took my time walking to the outskirts of Grantabridge, thankful the university town wasn't too large, and followed the directions Hannah had given to me to get to Mrs. Benton's home. It wasn't long before I came upon a cute little cottage. This must be Mrs. Benton's home. The garden was lovely, with tea roses lining the path to the door. There was a cute wraparound porch with a swing on it. The windows all had window boxes filled with plants. I bet if it was actually spring, those boxes would house the prettiest, most colorful flower assortment. I was charmed by the home. It was easy to tell it was well loved.

I took a deep breath before walking up the path to the door. I was good with people, but meeting new people always made me nervous, especially in situations like this. Hannah had tried to prepare me so I would get the information I wanted, but I was never sure if it would be enough.

I knocked on the door, reminding myself to breathe as I waited for someone to answer. After a brief moment, the door swung open. Standing in the open doorway was a frazzled woman. Her curly brown hair did not want to stay put in her topknot. She was out of breath, her chest heaving and drenched. I questioned what I saw, taken aback by her disarray.

"I'm so sorry. You look busy, and I don't want to interrupt you if you need to be doing something else," I said.

"Nonsense. I was just scrubbing the wash and then tripped over the bucket when I was walking to answer the door. I've always been a clumsy one." She wiped her hands on her apron, rolling her eyes when she realized it wouldn't do any good.

"Hi, I'm Georgiana Spencer. I believe my maid Hannah mentioned I might stop by," I said, still not sure what I should do. Walking away seemed like a good option, but I wouldn't get any information that way. So I just watched her. It was like she was scurrying about, but also not really moving because she hadn't stepped away from the door yet.

"Well, what are you doing standing there? Come in. I need to do something to dry off before we chat. Please make yourself comfortable. I'll be right back." She walked towards the stairs. She stopped. "Can I get you anything? Maybe some tea."

"No, thank you, I don't want to be any trouble," I said, looking around the sitting room. I made my way to an armchair and sat. Mrs. Benton left the room to clean herself up, leaving me quite alone. The room was bright, with light streaming in through the windows. There was a mismatch of fabrics, wood tones, and pottery, but the decor still made me smile. The room showed that the woman living here liked what she liked and wasn't afraid to show others, even if it was a random assortment of items.

"Much better, if I do say so," Mrs. Benton said, interrupting my perusal. "Hannah said you had some questions about the Tavershams. Not sure if I'll be able to help. But I'm more than willing to listen to you ask your questions." Mrs. Benton sat down in the other armchair in the room. The furniture was all very sturdy, almost like her husband made it. It definitely did not look like the popular delicate styles of the day.

"Thank you. It is kind of you to take time out of your

day to talk to me. I'll jump right in, no use delaying right now," I said, doing almost the opposite of my words. "Were you with Lady Taversham before she married the earl?"

"I wish I was. I might have convinced her not to marry that horrendous man. I was actually an employee of the earl's. He promoted me to her personal maid when they married."

"I see. You don't seem to have liked the earl very much. Any particular reason?"

"Let's see, I could always say it was the groping in the hallways anytime he passed one of us maids while we were just trying to get our work done. Or maybe it was the fact that at some point, it went from groping in the halls to things that were much worse, and no one did anything about it."

"He was like that back then? The maid I'm trying to help was fired after the earl tried to, well, it seems you know what he was trying to do. He was caught, but Lotte was let go without references, and then when he was murdered, she was accused of his murder."

"Poor thing. The earl has been like that for as long as I can remember. And I know you should never speak ill of the dead, but that man was rotten to the core. He used to beat on Lady Taversham something fierce until she found a way to protect herself."

"That's horrible. I don't understand why, as a society,

we let men get away with this awful behavior. What stopped the earl? It must have been something drastic," I said.

"I probably shouldn't say anything. It's been a secret for so long." Mrs. Benton paused and shook her head, the movement so small I barely saw it. "About eighteen years ago, I helped Lady Taversham pack to leave the earl. She had just found out she was pregnant, and she was terrified the earl would hurt her baby. He caught her leaving with her valise. She tried to pass it off as needing fresh air at the country estate. But the earl got mad, said he didn't believe a word she said, all the while manhandling her at the top of the stairs. When he let go, she slipped. She caught herself before falling down the stairs. That's when he struck her. She tumbled down the stairs like a ragdoll. When she got to the bottom, she didn't move at all. I thought for sure she was dead. She might have been happier if she was. The fall caused her to lose the babe." Mrs. Benton wiped her eyes, still upset over the actions of a horrible man.

"And she stayed with him? Even after that?" I asked, baffled. Why would anyone stay after being hit like that?

"What was she supposed to do? He had almost killed her when she tried to leave. She wasn't about to try again. But she did bargain for a new butler. When he showed up, everything changed for Lady Taversham," Mrs. Benton said.

"What do you mean? How could a new butler change everything?" I didn't understand how a new servant could change anything. Why would she want a new butler? How would he make her life better? Was he someone she had loved in the past?

"He was always there, lurking in the background, especially when the earl had been drinking or lost at cards. It was like he had a sixth sense of when the earl would get violent, and he would separate the two of them. I don't know how or even why, but it worked." Mrs. Benton smiled a slight, wistful smile. "He had such kind eyes, just like Lady Taversham's. I was always surprised how much their eyes were alike."

"That's interesting," I said. Especially the part about his eyes. "Did the earl and Lady Taversham ever reconcile? I would think they would still try to have a child. He is an earl, after all. The estate is going to his nephew now that he is dead, isn't it?"

"Not even close. From that day forward, not only did they keep separate rooms, but they were at opposite ends of wherever they were living. She never let him touch her again. And that new butler, he made sure that if Lady Taversham didn't want to be touched, she was not to be touched. I wish I could say the same for the maids. But his protection only seemed to go so far. Just another thing I never understood."

"It had to have been a terrible place to work as a woman," I said.

"It was. I'm not going to lie: I was almost thankful when I got my first grey hairs. It meant I was too old for the earl and his roving hands. I was as safe as Lady Taversham was once that happened."

"Thank you, Mrs. Benton. You've helped me understand some things that were confusing me. I'm not sure how it will help Lotte, but I hope it will." With that, I stood, letting her lead me out of her lovely home.

Chapter Twenty-Six

After the visit with Mrs. Benton, I made my way back to the Octagon House. The visit had been informative, but it hadn't really answered my questions about the earl's death. Other than the fact the earl had always been a terrible person, worse than anyone had actually known. I actually felt bad for Lady Taversham for having to live with such a terrible person for such a long time.

"I'm sorry it t-t-took such a long time for me to test the tonic. I finally finished this morning," Willa said, running into the room, her lavender skirts floating around her. She came to a sudden stop and stood there, bent over, hands on her knees, panting. Clearly, Willa wasn't the type of person who normally ran anywhere. I'm sure the corset she was wearing wasn't helping her catch her breath.

"Willa, why don't you sit down? Where did you run

from?" I patted the seat next to me on the settee. I had never seen Willa in such a hurry.

"I w-w-went to Mr. Benson's, you know, the apothecary. I wanted to see what the earl was supposed to be taking for his heart. Mr. Benson had prescribed the earl digitalis for his heart. Mr. Benson added sugar and mint to the tonic because the earl didn't like the taste of the actual medication. However, what was in the bottle was not the earl's heart medication," Willa said.

"What was it?" I asked. Willa had definitely piqued my curiosity. Maybe this would be the information that broke the case wide open, and I could bring it to Declan to clear Lotte's name.

"It was a pl-pl-placebo of sorts. Mostly sugar water with a hint of mint and ginger. My guess is that it tasted just like the digitalis he was used to taking. It almost was something I would give someone suffering from indigestion. It wouldn't help anyone with a heart condition, though," Willa explained. "It is interesting that it would help with indigestion. Sometimes people confuse indigestion with heart problems. The earl might have thought the medicine was working if he thought it was his heart, but it was just an adverse reaction to dinner."

"What does that mean? Someone stole his medication?

He decided he didn't want to take it anymore? Does it tell us anything at all?" I sighed with frustration. Everything about this investigation left me feeling annoyed. I felt like I was failing Lotte, and I hadn't done anything about the rumors Lady Corinne was spreading, so I was failing all the Ladies of WACK as well. Not to mention I wasn't allowed to attend classes, so I was basically failing at being a university student. I wasn't used to this feeling, and I definitely didn't like it.

"This is what I think happened b-b-based on the information we have. Someone wanted the earl dead but wasn't in a hurry. That person found a place, or maybe even the place, that makes bottles like the ones the apothecary uses. Whoever this is has to be somewhat close to the earl, right?" Willa was sitting, but she was on the edge of her seat, her hands flitting about as she spoke. "They would have to know about his condition, the tonic, where he keeps the tonic, and all of the details that go along with this condition. The person replaced the tonic with the placebo. And then they just wait and wait and wait. The earl is basically living on borrowed time at this point. He's basically one attack away from death. He just didn't know it. I don't know how someone could do that to another person."

"I'm almost sad for the earl. This seems so diabolical. At the same time, he was so awful to so many people—not people, he was awful to women," I said.

"I know it is v-v-very sad. He lived with someone who was taking steps to end his life for an unknown amount of time. I wonder how long this was going on?"

"I don't know if this helps Lotte or not. It does really limit who could have killed him by changing the tonic. But not who could have stabbed him after he died. I'm just tired of all the questions, and whenever I think I get an answer, like the fact the tonic wasn't the right medicine, or even medicine at all, it just leaves me with more questions."

"At least you kn-kn-know it's someone who knew the earl very well and had access to him. It should limit the suspects." Willa was so practical and trying so hard to cheer me up, but I was in a mood.

"I'm sorry, Willa. You're being so helpful, and the information is useful. I really thought Lord Frankland was the killer, but I can't see him having the access needed to switch the tonic out. So now I'm in a mood because I feel like I've been going in the wrong direction in the investigation and everything else." I sighed.

"C-c-could he have hired someone who worked in the house to do it for him? Maybe he is the one you're looking for," Willa asked.

"That is a possibility, and not a bad theory." I leaned

back, thinking about what Willa just said. "You know what, Willa, I think I'm going to see if I can rest before afternoon tea. Maybe a little nap will help me see things with fresh eyes." I got up from the settee, brushing my skirts down. Justice, who had been lying in her bed in the corner of the room, got up and followed me out of the room and up the stairs. I loved how she followed me around all the time.

I went to my room, the patter of Justice's paws right behind me. Throwing myself on my bed, I waited for inspiration to strike. It didn't; however, there was an adorable furry creature curled up next to me, content as can be. I had the thought that I should call Hannah to have her help me out of my clothes, but it never happened. Instead, I drifted off into sleep.

Chapter Twenty-Seven

Falling asleep yesterday with Justice curled up against me had felt like the right thing to do at the time. However, upon waking up, it was clear I had made a mistake. I didn't know what time it was, my rib cage and waist hurt from the pressure of the corset, and Justice was no longer in the bed with me. Glancing over at the window, I noticed light trickling through the curtains. I wasn't sure if it was dawn or dusk, but if there was light out, I'm pretty sure Hannah would be up at the very least.

The quiet in the house implied it was morning, and I had slept a good portion of yesterday away. It wasn't my intention to spend the day that way, but at this point, there was nothing I could do about it. I tiptoed up to Hannah's room, which was difficult in my boots. I can't believe I slept for so long in a corset and boots. I would never have thought that was possible.

I lightly tapped on Hannah's door. "Hannah, are you awake?"

"What is it, miss?"

Did she sound groggy? I hope I hadn't just awoken her, that would make me feel awful.

"I fell asleep in everything yesterday and need help to get out of it. Unfortunately, sleeping in my corset has made most of my body ache today," I said, whining just a little.

"Of course, miss, give me a second and I'll be right down." She did sound groggy. I felt so bad for waking her.

"Thank you, Hannah. I don't know what I would do without you." I turned and tried to quietly make my way back downstairs.

Back in my room, I sat on the edge of my bed. I twisted and turned my body, trying to reach the back of the bodice to start the arduous process of unbuttoning it. My endeavors were not successful. I had to wait for Hannah to come down to help me. It was really quite ridiculous how modern fashion insisted women depend on others for the very basics, like getting dressed and undressed. This was especially true if a woman wanted to be fashionable, which I did, very much so. I loved clothes; I loved how I could use clothing to manipulate people, how wearing certain clothing made me feel. As I told Pippa when she first moved in, clothing was women's armor, and to ignore it as pointless was like ignoring a weapon in one's arsenal.

"I was surprised when you didn't call me last night, miss. I checked in on you, but you were sound asleep, and I didn't want to disturb you. You've been working so hard on clearing Lotte, I figured you could use the sleep," Hannah said as she walked into the room. "Then Willa told me you weren't your usual positive self. You told her you were in a mood. I thought maybe some sleep would help you with everything." She had me stand and took care of the line of buttons running down my back in moments. After that, she removed the corset off. I was finally able to fill my lungs with air, and it felt so good.

"Thank you, Hannah, I was really in a mood yesterday. I feel like every time a question is answered, new ones come up. And the thoughts are just circling around and around. I'm worried I'm going to fail Lotte, and she's counting on me." I plopped down onto my bed.

"You have to take a moment to breathe. You have the information you need to stop worrying so much and allow your brain to put the information together. I've seen you put together some complicated theories before. This is just like that." Hannah continued to help me undress, then dress for the day. "Maybe you just need to take a step back."

"Not the traditional corset, please. I can't after sleeping in one. It was too much; my ribs and hips are killing me. Let's find something that will fit over one of Pippa's short corsets. I can't handle being constrained after last night." I shook my head. My request was very out of character. Hannah didn't even glance over at me when I made the request, though. She just went with it. "This seems so different from my theories and arguments. Someone's life will be affected by what I manage to put together, or not put together, as the case may be."

"You will figure it out, miss. I know you, and you always accomplish what you set your mind to doing. Lotte and I both know there is nothing to worry about. What do you plan on doing next?"

"I don't know. That's the problem, Hannah. I don't know where to go next." I sighed, trying not to fidget as Hannah finished up my outfit.

"Maybe you should go back to the Tavershams," Hannah said.

"Ha, like she's going to talk to me. She's best friends with Lady Corinne, the one who started all the rumors. I'm sure Lady Taversham didn't mind sharing them with others to help her friend's vendetta."

Hannah grabbed a pale grey ensemble trimmed with burgundy pleated ruffles and a burgundy ascot. She laid it out next to me on my bed. It was one of my favorite outfits because it complimented my burgundy leather boots.

"Talk to someone else, if you can. Surely someone will talk to you," Hannah suggested.

"I don't know. Do you think the servants will talk to me?" I tapped my fingers on the bed.

"They might. It's worth a shot. Especially if you're stuck."

*   *   *

I decided to follow Hannah's suggestion and was making my way to the Tavershams' home. It was the perfect day to be outside walking. I wish I could have brought Justice with me, but it wasn't polite to show up at someone's house uninvited with a dog. I was already taking a chance in trying to gain entrance to the home.

Instead of walking to the front door and gaining entry through the imposing double doors, I slipped around the back of the house, staying as close to the house as I could rather than heading towards the stables like I had done when I spoke with Benjamin. I hugged the building, trying to find an open window or door that would allow me to overhear anything happening in the house.

I made it all the way to the back doors before I found anything that was open. It happened to be the wood-and-glass doors that led outside were open. The problem: no one was in the room. I leaned up against the house with a sigh. Everything I did led me to another dead end. I didn't even have someone to eavesdrop on at the moment.

I turned to leave. Why stay if there's no one to listen to or talk to at the home? But then I heard the unmistakable clicking of boot heels on hardwood floors. It sounded like Lady Taversham had just come home, or at least come down the stairs. I stayed out of sight. No one in the house wanted to see or speak to me based on the rumors Lady Taversham helped spread. It was imperative that I stay quiet.

"Really, Lord Frankland, it behooves you to sit down and speak with me. I promise you will not regret it." I heard Lady Taversham walk across the room, then the click of a door shutting. "Shall I ring for tea?"

"I don't have all day. Get on with it. You summoned me here, and I'm here. I've wasted enough time as is." I couldn't imagine any reason Lady Taversham would have for requesting Lord Frankland's presence. My back up against the wall, I tried to peek into the room without being seen. Unfortunately, I couldn't see in the room from my current position.

"Fine, if that's the way you want to handle this. I want to be a partner in the dirigible business and the lesser-known spirit-smuggling trade," Lady Taversham explained. Her gown rustled. I could picture her walking across the room and sitting down primly in one of the fragile-looking chairs so popular today.

"No. Why would I want to take you on as a partner? I finally don't have to deal with your husband's involvement in my business. I have what I need to get my liquor for both the dirigible business and the club. Milford is stuck with me as a partner, no matter what he actually wants. What could you possibly offer to convince me to take on another partner, and a woman partner at that?" There was a scuffling sound, probably Lord Frankland standing to take his leave. I doubted he would stick around to hear more without an excellent reason.

"Don't you find it just a little odd that I know about the smuggling ring?" Lady Taversham asked. I heard a chair scuff against the floor as Lord Frankland sat back down. Like me, he was probably curious to know how she knew about the criminal activity. It was not like she was close to Lord Taversham, even though he was her husband. The earl wasn't the type of man to share his business exploits with his wife. He was much more inclined to share his bad temper.

"I will humor you, Lady Taversham. How do you know about the smuggling ring?" Lord Frankland asked. I could just imagine him crossing his arms and leaning back in his chair, a smug look on his face.

"Did you really think the earl was capable of making any sort of decent business decisions? He was a gambling addict. He would have been arrested and transported to a labor camp or debtor's prison if it weren't for me. I made all his business decisions. I found all of his contacts and kept those relationships intact. How do you think we were able to live this way, let alone throw extravagant balls, with the earl's gambling problem?"

I clasped my hands over my mouth to keep myself from gasping. Lady Taversham was embezzling from the smuggling business! Mads would be thrilled to have that mystery solved. I knew it had been bothering her since she found the bookkeeping discrepancy.

"What are you trying to say?" Lord Frankland's confusion was apparent without even seeing his face. The fact he was confused surprised me. I thought Lady Taversham had made it quite clear. She was the brains behind everything the earl supposedly had done; at least, every successful business the earl had ever been involved in.

"Let me spell it out for you, then. I'm not asking to be

a partner. I'm telling you, if you want your businesses to succeed, you will make me a partner. One word from me, and you won't have any liquor to serve. If you don't have fine spirits, who's going to come to the club or fly on your precious airships?" Lady Taversham explained herself slowly, enunciating every single word. I wish I could have seen the look on Lord Frankland's face once he realized he was being blackmailed. "If you decide that you still don't want a partner in this business, one word from me either to my smugglers or the police, and all this dries up."

"Is that a threat?" I heard the chair move, and I imagined Lord Frankland leaning forward.

"Of course not, Lord Frankland. I'm a lady. I would never resort to something so vulgar," Lady Taversham said.

I wanted to see the smile on Lady Taversham's face, so I leaned forward, knocking into a potted orange tree. The whole thing scooched forward, making the most heinous noise I have ever heard in my life. I didn't hesitate—I turned and ran out of the yard, unwilling to be caught by anyone in the Taversham house.

Chapter Twenty-Eight

As soon as I was off the Taversham property, I stopped
running. Thankfully, they hadn't called for the butler to come
after me. I wasn't in the mood to see him again. There was just
something about him that made me uncomfortable whenever
he was near. It was a good thing he hadn't been at the front
door; they would have caught me for sure. Catching my breath
as I walked down the street, I modulated my steps to a stroll,
attempting to look like everyone else out for a walk. I
exchanged greetings as I passed other Grantabridge residents
taking their perambulatory exercises on this lovely Brythionite
day.

I couldn't believe what I had heard. In almost all my
interactions with Lady Taversham, and I'll admit that there
haven't been many, I had assumed she was a bit flighty. How
could I have underestimated her so much? The only

explanation I found even slightly reasonable was every interaction until now had also involved Lady Corinne St. Gramflurri. I thought Lady Taversham was just a lackey of Lady Corinne because Lady Corinne had a way of overshadowing her companions. And I had let her character leave me unaware of the cunning and intelligence that was Lady Taversham.

Lost in thought, I let my feet meander along the sidewalks of Grantabridge, turning here and there at random. At least, I thought it was at random, but my subconscious had other ideas, I realized, as I stood in front of Lady Corinne's home. It was time. I needed to talk with Lady Corinne and get her to stop spreading those awful rumors about the Ladies of WACK. As much as I wanted to brush it off, I couldn't anymore. The rumors were hurting my friends. I couldn't stand around and let that continue without a fight. It was time to put up the fight.

I squared my shoulders and knocked on the massive wood door in front of me. It was mere moments before Lady Corinne's butler answered the door. He attempted to stare down his nose at me, but I had a good couple of inches on him, plus the rage of the wronged burning inside me.

"Hello, can you please inform Lady St. Gramflurri, Lady Spencer is here to see her? Oh, and if she has the thought of claiming not being home, I will be quite offended, and I'm in no mood for that." I handed the butler my calling card. Doing everything I could to channel my mother's natural authority.

"Of course, do come in." The man held the door open for me, stepping to the side as I swept past him. "If you will wait in the parlor, someone will be with you momentarily." He bowed his head as I made my way into the parlor.

The room was best described as ostentatious. There was an excessive amount of gilding on the walls and furniture, at least in my opinion. It looked nice with the burgundy silk paper on the walls and burgundy velvet cushions on the furniture. I had just expected Lady Corinne to have a much more subtle taste. The room did not look like someone raised with money designed it. Instead, it looked like a room with the only goal of letting anyone that entered know how wealthy the owner was.

"Lady Spencer, what is it you want from me?" Lady Corinne said as she breezed into the room. She looked back at the butler, giving him a brief nod. He closed the French doors, leaving the two of us alone, both tense in our dislike of each other.

"You need to stop spreading falsehoods about my friends and me. I do not understand why you are out to hurt us, but I can no longer allow it," I said. I might have been standing in her home, but I was done letting her intimidate us.

"What falsehoods?" She had the audacity to ask.

"It's no use claiming false ignorance or innocence. I've heard you tell others that my friends and I are running a brothel. Which we are not. There is no reason for you to be spreading such falsehoods." I refused to let this woman continue to bully the Ladies of WACK.

"I do not know that they are falsehoods, as you say. I've seen Lord Fremont and some other gentleman coming and going. What else am I supposed to think?" She sat primly on one of her ornate chairs as she spoke.

I took a deep breath and squared my shoulders. I refused to lose my temper with this woman. "Are you willing to go so far as to accuse a future duke of such behavior? Not to mention, what you are saying about his future duchess? Instead of making assumptions and spreading lies, you could have asked. Lord Fremont is engaged to Miss Stanhope, and Mr. Finnigan is a family friend."

"Is that supposed to mean nothing scandalous is going on in your house?" Lady Corinne asked.

"It means just that. There is nothing untoward happening. And for you to assume so says more about you than it does us." I sat on the velvet-covered settee, my hands folded across my lap.

"How dare you insinuate such a thing!" Lady Corinne's face flushed an unbecoming shade of red.

"Why not? It's exactly what you have done to us. Except you decided to say such things around town, doing your best to destroy our reputations." I smirked. I couldn't help myself. Lady Corinne was losing the battle to stay calm. "I have only said something to you in the privacy of your own home, allowing you to keep your reputation intact."

"The least you could do is hire a chaperone," she spluttered.

"Is that what it will take to get you to stop? Will any chaperone do?" I asked.

"Yes, I'll stop if you have a chaperone in that home. But I will choose who it is. In fact, why don't you have Miss Pierce as your chaperone again? The four of you are familiar with her." Lady Corinne looked smug. It's like she didn't think my friends and I would realize Miss Pierce would be spying for her.

"I believe that can be arranged. I want the rumors to stop, and Wilhelmina Schulz must be allowed back in her botany class."

"I don't have control over anything at the University."

"Of course you do. Don't bother trying to lie to me. I

know you can fix the damage you've caused. Not only do I know you can do it, I expect it done. I know you won't disappoint me."

With that, I stood and left Lady Corinne sitting in her parlor all alone.

The walk back to the Octagon House was short. For once, I didn't let my mind wander as I made my way over the cobblestone streets of the city. I had news for the Ladies of WACK. Back home, I stood outside for a moment. I was excited to tell my friends that the rumors were going to stop and things would return to normal. Whatever normal was; life had been pretty abnormal since the four of us had started our lives here.

"Hello, Mr. Pendrake," I said as he opened the door for me. I took off my hat and gloves, handing them to Mr. Pendrake. "Are the ladies home?"

"They have gathered in the parlor."

"Thank you," I said as I made my way into the parlor.

It was nice to see all of my friends gathered in one place. I felt like I hadn't been around them in forever, even though Willa and I had just talked yesterday. I had spent so much time thinking about the investigation that the four of us hadn't just sat together doing the things we all loved for a while. Yet here they were, doing just that. Pippa was sitting on the floor in her leather leggings, all of her gears and tools spread out over the coffee table. She was clearly making something mechanical. Willa stood in the corner, arranging a gorgeous array of flowers. One of them was a beautiful, unique flower with variegated colors. I had never seen anything like it. I hoped she had more of them; they were beautiful. Then there was Mads, her nose buried in budget books or working on breaking some code, I couldn't tell which it was.

"I have news, ladies." I always loved making a bit of an entrance. "I just left Lady Corinne's . . ."

"I don't know how you were able to be in the same room with her. She's awful," Pippa said.

"She frightens m-m-me. I wouldn't have been able to speak to her at all," Willa said, still arranging the flowers.

"The real question is, did it make a difference?" Mads said, looking up from her books.

"Lady Corinne has agreed to stop the rumors," I said.

"What did you have to give up for her to agree?" Mads was to the point, as always.

"You are, of course, correct. I had to agree to something she wanted to get her to stop the awful rumors." I sighed, flopping onto the settee. Justice jumped up and crawled into my lap. Well, she was half in my lap. She was too big now. But the way she rested half her body in my lap was adorable. "She insisted that we have a chaperone of her choosing."

"A spy. She just wants someone in our home reporting back to her." Pippa rolled her eyes in disgust.

"It won't be the first time she's had someone in our home reporting back to her. Her pick for a chaperone is Miss Pierce," I said.

"I bet she was the one causing all the havoc in our dormitory. I don't want to have to deal with that all over again," Pippa said as she continued to piece together whatever she was working on. It looked so small and delicate, not like her normal inventions.

"Hopefully, since we know they are connected, there won't be any new sabotage here, at least not from Miss Pierce. We can keep an eye on her, make sure she doesn't do anything to harm us or our home," I said. If that woman did something to this house, I would lose my mind. It wouldn't be pretty.

"At l-l-least the rumors will stop." Willa moved the vase she was working on to a side table. "What do you think?"

"It's so gorgeous and unique," I said, leaning in to take a whiff. The flowers smelled both sweet and citrusy. "It even smells good. Where did you find it?"

"It's a hybrid I cr-cr-created. I was thinking about entering it into the horticulture competition next month, but I don't know."

"You have to do it. I've never seen anything like it." I wanted to encourage Willa to break out of her shell and do the things she wanted to do, especially after all the negatives that have affected her this year. I wanted to do something to remove that burden from her and my other friends here.

Chapter Twenty-Nine

"Lotte, have you heard from Mr. Bailey lately?" I asked, pinning my hat into place. The dusty blue wool hat brought out the caramel tones in my hair. It also matched the blue trim on my dove-grey wool bustled gown to perfection.

"It's been a few days, miss. I rather expect to hear from him soon. He's been good at checking in every few days," Lotte said. "I'm not worried. He has seemed in control of everything."

"I would love to go to his office, see what his progress is, if you don't mind. It is your case, after all." I took the gloves Mr. Pendrake offered me. Hannah must have brought down the dusty blue leather gloves earlier this morning so they would be ready for me when I left for the day. I had a bit of an obsession when it came to matching my accessories; hat, gloves, and shoes. All had to be the same color, hopefully a color that accented my ensemble.

"Of course not, miss. Everything you've done for me has been so helpful. If you think it's a good idea, I'm sure you're right." Lotte continued about her work as she spoke. She seemed so at ease. I would have been a nervous wreck if I were in her place. I couldn't believe how much she trusted Declan and me to get her out of this situation.

"Thank you, Lotte. I want to see if I can help him in any way." I waved as I walked out the door Mr. Pendrake had opened for me. Mr. Pendrake impressed me more and more every day. He had taken on the role of butler with great aplomb and was excellent at anticipating each of our needs.

I made my way to the center of town, shivering slightly from the damp cold. The mist had settled over the river; the banks were empty because of the cold weather. It was strange not to see children running around and their nannies trying desperately to keep them out of the water. Even at this time of year, it seemed like at least one child ended up in the river every morning. If it wasn't a child, it was a dog. Every time I saw it happen, it made me laugh.

I crossed over the bridge and followed the cobblestone street until I was standing in front of Mr. Bailey's office. I looked in through the window, and there was Declan Bailey asleep at his desk. It looked like he had spent the night sitting in a wingback chair. I checked the door; it was open. I pushed it open slowly, trying to be quiet. Instead, a bell rang, waking up Declan.

"What, where, what?" Declan looked around like he was lost. His eyes fell on me. "Georgiana . . . I mean, Lady Spencer . . . Georgi. How can I help you?" He stood, smoothing his hands over his waistcoat. Not that his actions made him look any less rumpled. I guess it was to be expected when you slept in your clothes.

"Hello, I was wondering how Lotte's case was going? And if there was anything that I could do to help." I made my way into the room, noting how elegant it looked with the wainscotting on the walls and the walnut desk with leather insets.

"Actually, I would love for you to help me go through these notes, and if you have any new information to share, I could use the help. The last time we met, I didn't leave things on the best of terms. I'm sorry about that. I know Lotte didn't do it, but it would be nice to be able to show the court another suspect, or even better, have someone else arrested and her case dismissed." He swiped his hand through his hair, messing it up more than it already was. "I can't let her stand trial for this. The young woman doesn't deserve to go through that.

And in trials, there's no guarantee that a jury will reach the right result."

"It's okay. We can work on this together. We should have been working together from the beginning." I walked farther into the room. "We both have things to apologize for. Why don't we start over?"

"You know, we could have been working together this entire time if you had given me a chance." The burr of an accent came through stronger than it ever had before. Declan looked up at me with those eyes. I also wanted a snifter of whiskey suddenly.

That's when it struck me. I really did recognize those eyes and the soft burr of his voice. "You're Vrondias!"

"Honestly, Georgi, I thought you would have figured that out a long time ago. Here you are acting like a detective and you're just now figuring out we've met before." He laughed as he teased me, once again running his hand through his hair.

"Why didn't you tell me earlier?"

"I assumed it didn't matter to you. Either you weren't interested in the man you danced with or you knew who I was, and you weren't interested. So, I didn't think it was worth saying anything."

"Oh." I stared down at my hands, suddenly finding the

blue of my gloves to be the most interesting thing in the world. I didn't know what to say. It wasn't that I hadn't been interested. There was just so much going on with Lotte and Lady Corinne; I was so preoccupied that I hadn't even thought about the dance we shared.

"Let's start by going through your notes." I sat down in front of his desk, grabbing a stack of papers. "What are you looking for?"

"Anything to connect the facts in a way that points to anyone but Lotte. I haven't been able to piece it all together," Declan said, sitting back down in his chair.

We worked in silence for hours. I set up a board on one side of the room. I wrote out all the things the two of us knew and pinned them to the board. It didn't take long for the board to look like a mess. It was a visual representation of what was going on in my head. I grabbed the next paper on the stack. It was a second autopsy report. It confirmed all the things Willa had said about the earl's death, which I had never told Declan about. There was actually a lot I hadn't told him.

"I have some information that I don't think you know about yet," I said.

"Oh," Declan looked up. "What information do you have?"

I rolled my shoulders back, taking a seat on the edge of

Declan's desk. "The earl died of a heart attack. Someone replaced his medication with sugar water, well, a little more than sugar water. It also had mint and ginger in it, but it wasn't the digitalis that the apothecary prescribed. I believe something happened during the conversation with Lord Frankland that triggered the heart attack. But the lack of medication meant there was nothing to stop the heart attack."

"I have a coroner's report that says something similar. I was surprised when I received a second report. Someone at the department knows what they are doing."

"I'm actually looking at the report right here. I wonder what made them update the report. After the last murder, I'm surprised there's anyone that knows what they are doing there. My friend tested one of his medicine bottles, and as I said, it was basically sugar water. We also talked to the earl's apothecary. The bottles the fake medicine was in were not from the apothecary. Even though the bottles were the same, the fake bottles had smudged labels, and the apothecary's labels do not smudge. He does something to ensure that for safety reasons." I leaned towards Declan, using my hand to keep my balance.

"That's something. Looks like the murder was a well--thought-out job done by someone in the household. It does still leave the question of why he was stabbed." Declan put his hand on top of mine. I looked down at where we touched, then up at Declan, unspoken questions in my eyes. I blushed and looked away, but I left my hand there.

"I have an idea about that as well. I think someone in the household decided they were tired of the abuse going on. There was one person who had taken it upon themselves to protect all the women there. At first, he only protected Lady Taversham, but after a while, things changed," I said, pushing myself off the desk. I started pacing. "Wait, didn't you say her brother disappeared eighteen years ago? That's right around the same time Lady Taversham fell down the stairs and convinced her husband to hire a new butler." I stopped and looked over to Declan at his desk.

"Lotte mentioned the butler was always there whenever the earl tried something. Do you think . . .?" Declan raised an eyebrow as he looked at me.

"I do. And I think I know exactly how the murder happened." It was time to get the Ladies of WACK involved.

Declan stood, maneuvering around his desk. He picked me up and swung me around. When he set me down, our eyes locked. I licked my lips; my eyes fell to his mouth. Slowly, Declan lowered his head to mine, giving me plenty of time to back away. Our lips met in the briefest of kisses. His hand came up, cupping my face. The kiss deepened. His tongue caressed my mouth, causing me to gasp. Declan took that moment to invade. Our tongues danced. My knees went weak. I felt Declan's arm around my waist, his other hand behind my neck. My hands splayed on his chest. It was solid beneath my fingers. I grabbed the lapels of his frock coat. I pulled Declan closer, tugging on the lapels.

My breath came in quick gasps as I broke away. There didn't seem to be enough air in the room for me to catch my breath. I pushed Declan away. "I can't . . . I can't do this."

"I'm sorry, I . . ."

"No . . . I have to go."

I ran out of Declan's office as fast as my heeled boots would let me. I made my way back through town and over the river in record time. It felt like only a few moments had passed between my leaving and standing on the porch of the Octagon House. I needed . . . I wasn't sure exactly what I needed, but talking to my friends would be a good place to start.

"Hello, Lady Spencer. I hope your day was fruitful," Mr. Pendrake said as he took my hat and gloves.

"It was Mr. Pendrake, it was. Are the other ladies home?"

"Miss Stanhope is in her room. I believe Miss Schulz will be home soon. She's working with the apothecary today.

As for Miss Cavendish, she left a while ago but did not apprise me of where she was going. Is there anything else?" Mr. Pendrake waited for my instructions.

"When they do get home, can you send them to Pippa's room? I could use their counsel." I made my way upstairs to Pippa's room. It had been a while since we had all gathered in one of our bedrooms now that we lived in a house that was actually pleasant to spend time in. I tapped on Pippa's door, hesitant to disturb her if she was experimenting.

"Come in." Pippa hollered through the door.

I pulled the wood door open, surprised it didn't creak or groan as our last home had. Pippa looked up at me in surprise, her green eyes made even larger by the goggles she was wearing, dropping whatever she was working on in the process. I glanced at her solid granite-topped desk, ensuring nothing was going to catch on fire before turning to her. Not surprisingly, Pippa was sitting there in her leather leggings and teal blouse, her hair in the two long braids she was constantly flipping back over her shoulders.

"Georgi, you're back. Did you figure it out? How did it go with Mr. Bailey? Did he accept your help?" Pippa rattled off question after question like only she could. She went back to inspecting whatever it was she was working on at her desk.

"Do you ever ask just one question at a time, Pippa?" I

asked as I flopped onto her bed. Her room was shades of aqua; it reminded me of the ocean. Pippa's family lived near the sea. I'm sure that's why she painted her room this way. I lifted myself up on my elbows so I could still see her as we talked.

"Why would I ever do that? It's more fun to watch people try to remember what I asked and in what order." Pippa flipped down another magnifying glass in front of each of her eyes.

"In that case, I think I've figured it out. I want to gather all the suspects and the detective to clear Lotte's name. And yes, Mr. Bailey accepted my help. As for how it went—that's what I want to talk about." I sighed.

"Oooh, what happened? Something happened, right?" Pippa turned in her chair towards me. She looked like some sort of weird owl in her goggles. I laughed. She looked at me quizzically. I pointed to my eyes. She removed her goggles as fast as she could, causing me to laugh even more.

"Knock, knock," Mads said as she walked into the room with Willa. "Mr. Pendrake told us to come up here. Sounds like you need to talk, Georgi. Is it about Lotte's case?"

"No, it's not about Lotte's case. It's about Declan, I mean Mr. Bailey." I fell back onto the bed.

"Wh-wh-what happened?" Willa asked.

"We kissed. I don't know how it happened. We barely

like each other." I grabbed Pippa's pillow to hide my face underneath it.

Pippa took the pillow from me. "It's been clear for a while now that you two like each other. I don't see what the problem is."

"I don't either, Georgi. He's tall and handsome. He comes from an excellent family. And he has been working diligently on Lotte's case, which shows he has a good character. I don't see any issues." Mads said.

"Although those things are true, how do I know all those things will stay true? I don't have the best judgment when it comes to men. At least, not when it comes to men for *me*. I'm superb at matching my friends," I said.

"Are you talking about the tutor? Please tell me we finally get the story of your last tutor?" Pippa asked, scooting forward on her seat. I looked around the room; all eyes were on me. I guess I had mentioned the tutor before.

"I am talking about him. I thought we were in love. We spent so much time together. He was patient and thoughtful. He seemed to support me and my ideas. One thing led to another. The lessons and discussions turned to poems of love and kisses and more. I . . . I planned on running away with him." Tears filled my eyes. "I was so naive. He wasn't in love with me; he had never been in love with me. All he wanted was access to my fortune. I don't know what happened. He must have gone to my parents. I've never asked, but the day we were supposed to leave together, he was gone. Disappeared, no note, nothing. I saw him ride away from my window. He didn't even look back. After that, how can I trust myself? I've felt things like this before and it almost ruined me."

"Do you want me to kill him for you? Since living here, I've learned a lot more about death," Pippa asked. "I'm sure together we could plan something and avoid getting caught."

"Oh, Georgi, come here," Mads said as she sat on the bed with me. I pushed myself up to sit beside her. "So you fell in love with a scoundrel. It happens to the best of us. But look at your track record with your friends here. Pippa is happy with Kaiden. You were spot on with his character, and you like Colin, who is another upstanding man. What would you say to one of us if we were interested in Mr. Bailey?"

"I would push whoever it was into his arms. He's kind, brave, intelligent, and handsome. Who wouldn't want a man with all those qualities?" I sniffed.

"You should take your own advice. Concentrate on the qualities you know he has and stop expecting the bad ones to come through." Mads patted my skirts.

"Maybe I'll do that the next time we see each other."

Chapter Thirty

"I want to gather all the suspects together—and the detective, of course. Lotte, Benjamin, Lord Frankland, Lady Taversham, and her butler all need to be there," I said. The Ladies of WACK were gathered in the parlor, but I was talking to myself more than I was talking to any of them. "Oh, and Mr. Bailey, of course. He will want to know how this turns out. Lotte is his client, after all."

"I thought you had ruled out a lot of the people on the list?" Mads asked.

"I have, but it seems right to gather everyone that could be involved."

Willa raised an eyebrow, questioning me. "It will b-b-be dramatic, at the very least. Are you sure it w-w-will be safe? You are outing a killer."

Willa's questions surprised me. Maybe I wasn't doing

the right thing. Should I just tell the detective inspector everything and let them handle it?

"It should be fine, especially with the police there."

"We're just concerned about your safety. What can we do to help?" Pippa asked, setting aside whatever she had been tinkering with.

"Getting everyone together, convincing Lady Taversham to let us into her home—although maybe Detective Radcliffe will be better suited for that job—and transporting the evidence over to the Taversham house or the Station House. Do we have a list of everyone we talked to and how to find them? That would be helpful as well. At least for the police. They are going to have an upward battle, as are the barristers." I rattled off all the things that needed to be done to end this investigation and save Lotte.

"I c-c-can gather the evidence," Willa offered.

"I'll get the detective. I don't think he will want to see Pippa after the last time," Mads said. She was right. Detective Inspector Radcliffe was not a fan of Pippa—or me, for that matter.

"Good idea. Pippa, why don't you and Kaiden gather up the suspects that aren't already at the Tavershams' home? Let's meet there in three hours," I said.

"Are you going to tell us who it is first?" Pippa asked.

"If you really want me to, I will," I said. The three nodded that they wanted to know. So, I sat down on the settee and explained it all to them. Each of them had their questions. I had the answers. It was a nice rehearsal for what was to come.

*   *   *

All the suspects were just on the other side of these double doors. It was time to end this once and for all. Taking a deep breath, I rubbed my hands down the front of my deep-aqua bustle gown. The skirt was trimmed with coral pleated ruffles and matching embroidery. I wanted to wear something that boosted my confidence. I rolled my shoulders back and took a deep breath before walking into the library at the Tavershams' townhome.

Glancing around as I entered, I saw Detective Inspector Radcliffe standing in the corner, surrounded by bookshelves filled with books. Lotte and Benjamin stood as far from the detective as they could while staying out of Lady Taversham's line of sight. Lady Taversham sat on the leather sofa next to Lord Frankland; the tension between the two of them permeated the room. Mr. Butler stood just inside the doorway like he was waiting for orders to serve the rest of us. My friends and Mr. Bailey were scattered about the room.

"Why are you imposing on my time and in my house?

This is absurd. I need you all to leave." Lady Taversham stood.

"I'm sorry, Lady Taversham, but that's not possible. Now please sit. Lady Spencer, can you please explain why we are all here?" Detective Inspector Radcliffe asked.

Lady Taversham sat back down with a huff. It was clear she wanted nothing to do with me or what was going on. She glared at me as she sat there. "Well then, get on with it. I don't have all day."

Declan looked at me and nodded, encouraging me to start. I took a deep breath, rolling my shoulders back. I started recounting the investigation. "I met Miss Lane the day she was let go from the Tavershams. It was after an unfortunate incident with the earl."

"I couldn't have her here after that. Once the earl set his sights on a girl, he never stopped. I let her go to protect her," Lady Taversham interrupted.

"But you refused to give me references. You acted like it was my fault. Then you accused me of murder!" Lotte cried out. "How was that protecting me?"

"It's okay, Lotte. We know you didn't do it. It was unfortunate timing that you were at the masquerade when the earl died. I did think it was possible that your beau, Benjamin, could have killed the earl." I looked over at Benjamin.

"I would never . . ."

I held up my hand, interrupting Benjamin midthought.

"I mean, he did have motive. The earl had tried to take advantage of the girl he loved. The problem is he didn't have the opportunity. He was busy the night of the masquerade. There was a constant influx of carriages with horses to care fot." I paused. "With those two dismissed as suspects, it left very few people with both a reason to kill the earl and the opportunity."

Lady Taversham stood and stomped her foot. "Are you implying I'm a suspect in my husband's murder? Mr. Butler, can you escort these interlopers out?"

"I'm afraid I must insist you take a seat, Lady Taversham," Detective Inspector Radcliffe said. She huffed as she sat back down, waving her butler back to his position by the door.

"Where was I? Oh yes, only a few people left. First, there's Lord Frankland. Now, you might be wondering why the earl's business partner would want to kill the earl."

"How dare you! I would never kill anyone," Lord Frankland interrupted.

"You wouldn't?" Declan raised an eyebrow, glancing over at Lord Frankland.

"What are you implying?" Lord Frankland turned an

unbecoming shade of red, clearly angry at Declan and at what he was implying.

"I think it's pretty obvious," Declan muttered under his breath.

I cleared my throat to gain the room's attention. "From what I've gathered, the earl was embezzling money from the dirigible business. This was a business where the earl and Lord Frankland were partners." I reached into my bag and pulled out the two sets of books the earl kept. "Here are the set of books that show the embezzlement. Definitely a reason to take out the earl, but Lord Frankland also has business with Mr. Milford, and together, the two of them cheated the earl out of the money he owed Lord Frankland, not any more than the earl stole, though. In addition, the earl and Lord Frankland met the night of the masquerade right before I found the dead body. The earl had allegedly given Lord Frankland all of the contacts for his smuggling ring. Those smugglers provide all the spirits for both the dirigibles and Mr. Milford's club. So, the question remains, did Lord Frankland really have a motive? Or was it someone else?"

I paced the room because this is where it got complicated, more complicated than it already was. "While I do believe the conversation between the earl and Lord Frankland was heated and led to the earl's heart attack, I do not believe Lord Frankland killed the earl, at least not intentionally."

"Can I leave if I'm not a suspect?" Lord Frankland asked.

"Just stay seated, Lord Frankland. This will all be over soon enough," the detective inspector said.

"I talked to someone while trying to find the actual murderer. She told me a story about a woman she worked for. The woman had come from humble beginnings, raised on a farm with her parents and her much older brother. The woman wanted more. Luckily, she had an aunt who was well connected to society. She had her season and caught the eye of a titled man who was looking for an heiress. Instead, he found and married this woman who grew up on a farm."

Lady Taversham stared at me, hate in her eyes. This was not information she wanted her friends to hear. However, she did nothing more than stare at me.

"The man was angry, and for two years, barely anyone saw her. The person I talked to mentioned bruises, broken bones, and a miscarriage from being pushed down the stairs. Then, one day, a new butler showed up. The butler was able to keep the woman safe. She went to teas, balls, and soirées. She was happy for a short while. Until her husband started abusing the female staff. The butler prevented as much as he could, but he couldn't be everywhere all at once. And some staff, like Lotte, didn't escape the man's notice."

"Well, I never . . .," Lady Taversham interrupted, but I continued, ignoring her irritation.

"There's more though. This man—I'll stop with the pretense that we don't know who I'm talking about now—the earl, in addition to thinking every woman owed him, had a gambling addiction. He lost every dollar he earned or stole. Some of it was because of the cheating of his partner, but in reality, the earl couldn't hold onto money. If he had money in his pocket, he needed to place a bet. Remember all those years ago, he was looking for a fortune? He just didn't get one. Thankfully, his wife had a head for business. She organized the smuggling ring. They were her contacts, her crew, and the earl had given them to Lord Frankland without even talking to his wife. And if you've met Lord Frankland, you know he isn't the type of man to believe a woman could run a business or do him harm. He was very wrong about that, though."

"There's a smuggling ring here?" the detective inspector asked under his breath.

"Why are we sitting and listening to this?" Lord Frankland stood, taking a step towards the door.

"Sit down, Lord Frankland. We're going to talk later. Don't plan on leaving town any time soon," the detective inspector said.

"Clearly, Lady Taversham has had an interesting and difficult life, but did she kill her husband? And if she did, how did she do it? One of the things that my friends and I learned during this investigation is that the earl had a heart condition and was on medication, digitalis to be exact. In fact, the earl died of a heart attack. One that could have been prevented if he had his medication. But . . ." I pulled the medicine bottles out of my bag and set them on the table. "We tested the contents of the bottles and they were nothing more than sugar water, not the medication that was supposed to be in there. It was the labels that really gave it away; the ones on these bottles are smudged. The apothecary in town uses a special process that prevents the smudging of his labels. The bottles may have looked the same, but they weren't from the apothecary. Someone had switched out the bottles, but who knew how long the earl hadn't had access to his medication. The switch also implied someone in the household was responsible. But who?"

"I don't like what I'm hearing," Lady Taversham said.

"You are not going to like what I say next, then. I believe that you've been swapping the earl's medicine for sugar water, which was the reason the earl had the heart attack that killed him."

"How dare you!" Lady Taversham stood, outraged at my accusation.

"I dare because it's the truth, and I understand why you did it. But it doesn't make it right, especially since you accused someone who doesn't have the money or the status to get herself out of a murder charge. That was cruel."

"I . . .," Lady Taversham began.

"Don't bother, Lady Taversham. The most interesting thing about this case is the fact that there are actually two murderers. One was just a bit late to the party. See, the earl was stabbed after he had a heart attack. Which had me confused for a long time. But it really all came down to the butler, or should I say your brother, Lady Taversham. He disappeared eighteen years ago, right when Lady Taversham suddenly had a new butler. It just took me a while to figure out why, after all these years, he would kill the earl." I looked at Mr. Butler, stopping him from leaving now that all our attention was on him.

"I couldn't stand it anymore. I may have been able to stop the earl most of the time. But all those times I failed—I can't forget them. Each one weighs on me. I knew the earl would never stop, so I had to stop him. I saw the tray sitting outside the study door from the meeting the earl had with Lord Frankland. The knife was just there on the tray. I grabbed it and went into the study. The earl was asleep on the sofa. He was sleeping when he should have been getting ready for the masquerade. Without even thinking, I walked over and plunged the knife into his chest, getting rid of a problem I had been dealing with for way too long. I didn't realize my sister had already taken care of her problem."

I nodded to the detective inspector. He took Mr. Butler away while one of his officers escorted Lady Taversham out. It was done. Lotte's name was cleared.

Chapter Thirty-One

The rest of us filed out of the Taversham home, a place I would happily never go into again. I was so happy to be done with this investigation. The real culprits were found, and Lotte's name was cleared. I was also ready for a celebration, which was exactly what I told my friends.

"A celebration! Does this mean ices? It's been forever since we've gone to Jarrin's. I've been dying for lemon ice." Pippa clapped her hands in excitement.

"Lemon, Miss Stanhope? Lady Spencer bought me chocolate when we first met. I was having such a horrible day, and suddenly I had a new job and someone who believed me. She got chocolate. And I can't think anything could taste better than a chocolate ice," Lotte said.

"Oh, Lotte, you have to try all the flavors. How else are you going to decide which one is your favorite? Get your young man to take you there more often. Each one of us likes a different flavor best. I'm sure you'll find one that's perfect for you." Pippa grabbed Lotte by the arm, leading her towards the ice parlor.

It appeared there would not be a choice in how we celebrated. Not that I was complaining. I never turned down chocolate in any form, especially not a delicious frozen treat. Even if it was a little too cold out to enjoy an ice to the fullest.

"Lady Spencer, I don't want to ruin the celebration. But with both Tavershams gone, I'm out of a job. Do you know of anyone that needs someone to work the stables?" Benjamin asked.

"I will find someone. Are you sure the earl's nephew won't keep you on?" I asked.

"I don't think he will spend any time here in Grantabridge, and I want to stay close to Lotte."

"We can't have Lotte's beau worrying about funds. You're going to have to treat her to Jarrin's regularly now if Pippa has anything to say about it. I'll do what I can to make sure it happens. Now go get Lotte before Pippa talks her ear off." I smiled, waving him along.

Mads and Willa were walking together arm in arm, deep in conversation. My curiosity would force me to ask them about their conversation later. I looked back towards the house and saw Lord Frankland standing in front of it. I wish I could prove he was involved with something more nefarious than cheating at cards and smuggling in spirits. Right now, I couldn't, so he got to walk off free of any charges this time unless the detective inspector decided to break up the smuggling ring.

Declan stepped beside me, clearing his throat, which interrupted my thoughts. He offered his arm to me. "Can I escort you to our place of celebration?"

"Why yes, I do believe you can." I took his arm, and we walked in silence for a moment.

"Georgi . . ."

"Look, Declan . . ."

We both spoke at the same time.

"You first, Georgi."

"I wanted to apologize for running off the other day. I don't have the best record when it comes to judging a man's character. Things have happened in the past that cause me to question, well, everything," I explained, but was interrupted.

"Georgi, you do not need to apologize. I crossed a line, and I should have never kissed you. I'm sorry for doing so."

"You're sorry? Does that mean you regret kissing me? That you don't want to kiss me?" Had I interpreted everything wrong again?

"No, I mean, yes. Wait . . . what I'm trying to say is I want to kiss you, but only if you want me to. And the other day, you clearly did not want me to." He swiped his hand through his hair, messing up his constantly messy hair.

"I wanted you to kiss me, but then doubts came crashing through my thoughts. What if you were like . . . That's neither here nor there, as I was saying. I don't always have the best judgment when it comes to men, and I've made mistakes in the past that could have cost my family and me dearly. I was afraid I was once again making the same mistake."

"How about we keep things slow for now? As long as you know I like you and my intentions are honorable, we can see where the road takes us." Declan looked at me. I looked at his mouth, then up at his eyes. "Unless you want me to kiss you now."

"I think I would like that . . . I mean taking things slow, at least for now. Not the other . . . not in the middle of the street." I looked away, suddenly feeling even more out of my depths than I had moments before.

"I have another proposition for you," Declan said. My head snapped back to face him, our eyes meeting.

"Oh, what is it?" I asked, not sure I was ready for whatever he was about to say.

"I think you—and your friends, of course—should work for my firm as investigators. Since you've moved to town, the four of you have solved two murders."

"Actually, three murders, if you're counting," I interrupted.

"That is true. How could I have miscounted? You also found out more than I ever would have and found the information quicker. I'm pretty sure you already have all the servants in Grantabridge spying for you. I want to put you, your friends, and your network of spies to work."

I stopped walking. His proposition shocked me completely. I don't know what I had expected him to say, but this, this was definitely not it. I threw my arms around his neck and kissed him on the cheek.

"Can I take that as a yes?" Declan asked.

"I would love to, but I do have to talk to the other Ladies of WACK. This is the type of decision we have to make as a team. I'm positive they will be thrilled by the idea, though."

"Ladies of WACK?" Declan raised an eyebrow at me.

"Have you not heard? We are the Women Adventurers' Consortium of Knowledge. So far, we have hosted salons to help other women, especially those in service, to learn new skills to better themselves, as well as self-defense classes. Mads hosted a budgeting salon, and we are trying to convince Willa to host one on herbology. We just have to boost her confidence a little."

"That's fascinating. I wouldn't be surprised if one day you and your friends take over the world. I hope I'm there by your side when you do."

*   *   *

After a wonderful celebration at Jarrin's, I called my friends into the parlor. I needed to tell them about Declan's offer. And while it could wait, I was way too excited.

"I'm sure you saw me talking to Declan," I said.

"So it's finally *Declan*. About time." Mads winked at me.

"Yes, so it is. Anyway, he wants to hire us as investigators for his law office. Turns out, I was wrong, and he sees how good we are at solving crimes." I clapped my hands in excitement.

"Wait, did I just hear you correctly? Did Georgiana Spencer admit to being wrong? I must not have heard right," Pippa teased.

"Oh, do shut it, Pippa. I can admit when I'm wrong, but can you?" I glared at her briefly before addressing all my friends. "What do you think? Do you want to form an investigative agency and work for him? We have solved three murders in a relatively short amount of time. And think of the good we could do with the backing of a person who believes in us."

Willa looked over at me. She looked dazzling in a bright purple gown. I loved that her wardrobe was more colorful than it had been before. She was organizing flowers in the different vases we had around the room once again. I think the flowers were even more unique than the last ones she had brought in.

"I c-c-can tell you want to do this. But do you really think there's going to be any more need? Hopefully, there won't be any more murders here," Willa said.

"It would be nice if the murders stopped, but there will always be crime. And to use our skills to do some good—I want to be a part of that. It's rare that I feel like I'm acknowledged for my actual skills rather than my looks. I want to take advantage of any opportunity that wants me for my talents," Mads said. Her statement resonated with me and made me wonder what else she had dealt with here and before coming to Grantabridge.

"Can I make more gadgets for our investigations? I loved making the grappling gun. And it was even more exciting to see it being used and working," Pippa said.

I looked over at Pippa, my eyebrow raised. "What do

you mean 'working'? Did you have me use your invention to scale a building without testing it first?"

"I mean, I tested it, but you never know what will happen until you really need the tool. And it worked like a charm." Pippa clapped her hands. She was always so excited about everything.

"So, Willa, what do you think? I don't want to do this without your agreement. You are a crucial part of our team," I said.

Willa's hands stopped midarrangement "You th-th-think I'm crucial to the team?"

"Of course I do. We all do. Do you think we could have solved any of these murders without your help? Each time you determined what exactly killed the victims. Without your skill and knowledge, I don't think we would have reached a satisfactory result at all."

"If everyone w-w-wants to do it, and you think I truly help, I'm in. I wouldn't want to hold us, the only women at the University, back from anything."

"It's settled then. We are now the Ladies of WACK Investigative Services. We should have cards made." I grabbed a paper and pencil and started writing down all the things needed to start this enterprise.

"Lady Spencer, I was hoping to have a word with all of

you, actually."

Chapter Thirty-Two

"Sit down, Hannah, what is it you want to discuss with us?" I
was worried she was going to quit, my perpetual need to save
everyone and everything overwhelming her. I mean, I was
always adding to her daily work.

Hannah sat, wringing her hands as she did so. "I've
been toying with the idea of taking cases on my own. While
you were working on getting this lovely house, I actually
solved the theft of the painting."

"Yes, I remember. That's how we ended up with Mr.
Pendrake," I said.

"You remember?" Hannah asked, surprised.

"Of course, I remember. I know how amazing you are.
I remember everything you do," I said.

"Was it exciting tracking down the clues?" Pippa
asked.

"It was, but more importantly, I felt like I really got to help someone. There are so many servants accused of the wrongdoings of those they work for. It felt good to help one of them. And I know we can help more people," Hannah said.

"I think this is a wonderful idea. I don't know if you heard, but Mr. Bailey asked if we would offer our investigative services to his firm. The four of us just decided that we would. You know we can't do it without you and your network," I said.

"You can't? I mean, of course, you can't. My friends and I have been calling ourselves 'shadows.' I even took notes on the one case that I did if you would like to see them." Hannah was buzzing with excitement, as was I. I had been so worried she was leaving me that this seemed fortuitous. It was like our plans were aligning. This was perfect if I do say so.

"We can call you the Sisterhood of Shadows. S.O.S. It's perfect because the people who need you require your help. We can work together on cases, but you're free to take on your own cases as well. Hopefully, some that don't have me hiring more staff. Eventually, we will have too many people working here." I would hire everyone done wrong if I could, which would be a problem.

"What I think we need is a way for people to contact us anonymously. I don't want anyone to be afraid they will get fired for reaching out. And you know how things can be. I mean, look at what happened to Lotte. If you weren't around, she would have ended up out on the street, or in prison," Hannah said.

"You are so thorough in everything that you do, Hannah, truly a gem to have around. What if we put in a mailbox, or a tip box? We can label it S.O.S. and spread the word through our salons and your network that it is there," Mads said, joining in with her own inventive ideas. I loved how we all worked together.

"What a fantastic idea, Mads. I wouldn't have ever thought of it. But now that you mention it, I can work on something to have the notes automatically sent to the house," Pippa said.

"If w-w-we make it truly anonymous, we could also get help on cases we are working on through the mailbox. I read this story that used the personal ads in the newspaper to relay information through code. Mads could set up a code and we could do the same thing when we have cases. And then the shadows can help us out without risking their employment." Willa sat, joining in on our plotting.

"I love it, Willa. This is going to be so much fun, using our skills to help others. I can't wait to get started," I said.

*   *   *

It took a few days to get organized and find the supplies we needed to build the mailbox. It really wasn't a typical mailbox. Pippa had explained the science behind it, but I was not a steam engineer, or any type of engineer, so almost all of it went in one ear and out the other. Colin and Pippa had worked together to create this mailbox that first lowered the letter on a platform using a series of weights, pulleys, and gears until it got to a certain level. It then encapsulated the letter in this tubular-shaped casing, which protected the letter as it was sucked through a series of tubes until it was dropped into a basket in the room all of us decided was best used as the headquarters of our investigative services. Pippa had talked about vacuums and so much more when she was putting it together. I tried so hard to pay attention and understand her. Instead, I learned that building things was never going to be my specialty. However, I was excited that we had such an advanced way to get requests for help and potential tips into the privacy of our office. It was very clandestine, in the best of ways, because it felt like those who needed us would definitely stay safe.

"Gather round, everyone," Pippa called out to all of us. It really was all of us. The Ladies of WACK were all present, as were Hannah, Mr. Pendrake, Lotte, and Benjamin. Also there to support us and this new venture were Colin, Kaiden, and

Declan. While I had always had the support of my parents, it was overwhelming to see so many others that we had all just met here supporting us. Especially when it constantly seemed like we were fighting an uphill battle here in Grantabridge. I felt myself tear up, but there was no way I would let actual tears fall. I attempted to wipe them away without anyone seeing. But as I glanced up, I saw Declan watching me, a knowing smile on his lips. He would find out how much of a sentimental fool I was if we kept courting.

"This is how letters will get to our office." Pippa held up a letter and put it in the mailbox with dramatic flair. She closed the box. Suddenly, I could hear the sounds of gears moving. "Right now, the letter is being taken down to the transport level." There was a louder, abrupt noise, and then it sounded like a breeze had picked up. But there was no breeze.

"The loud noise is the letter being encased, and what you hear now is the vacuum transporting it from this box here to our office, where it should land in the basket Mads labeled 'incoming.' We let Mads set up the office because I don't think any of us can top her organization skills," Pippa continued.

"Especially not you," I teased.

"Like you're one to talk, especially when you can't decide what you want to wear for an event." Pippa teased right back, and rightly so. After sharing a room at our dorms for a couple months, it was apparent that we fed off each other's messiness. If it wasn't for Hannah, we probably would have suffocated under a mound of our things.

"Can we go see if the letter made it to the office?" Lotte asked.

"Of course. Let's go see if our contraption was a success," Pippa said.

Chapter Thirty-Three

The group of us made our way to the front door, excited to see if all the hard work Pippa and Colin had done actually worked. I'm sure they were confident it had, but it was new to the rest of us.

As we approached the porch, I saw a well-dressed man wearing a bowler hat walking away. Curious, I thought. I wondered what he wanted. I couldn't see his face, but I felt like I knew him from somewhere.

"Oh, n-n-no!" Willa's hand covered her mouth as she looked at the door. Colin reached up and pulled her closer to him. She hid her face in his chest. I couldn't see what she saw, but it was clearly distressing. Colin was doing an exceptional job of comforting Willa. I hoped they became something more in the future.

"Georgi, you should come look at this," Pippa said.

"Apparently, things aren't over with whoever is sabotaging us." Pippa inspected the door.

I made my way through my friends until I stood before the door to our home. In the center of the door was a note held up by a sword buried deep into the wood. My hand trembled as I took the note down, ripping it off as I could not remove the sword.

"Red ink. Isn't that cliché?" I laughed, trying to dismiss the fear that had my heart racing. It was either laugh or cry, and I really didn't want to cry right now. I read the note, unable to control my shaking hands.

"What does it say, Georgi?" Mads asked.

" 'You've been here long enough. Leave or your fate will match the professor's.' "

The four of us stood in front of our home, surrounded by our friends, trying to comprehend why someone would threaten our lives.

Acknowledgments

Thank you to my parents for their constant support. I couldn't do this without them. I also have to thank my cover designer and writing friend Jamie Dalton for listening to me babble as I attempt to figure out what I want to write and market. I also appreciate the constant support of my editor Sarah Hawkins that encourages me by commenting on my growth as a writer. The feedback is really appreciated especially when imposter syndrome sets in. And finally, my dear friends Kat Cross and Charlotte Lehman who are two of the best cheerleaders to have in your corner.

About the Author

Stephanie K. Clemens is known for many things: an author, photographer, dog mom, instagrammer, adventurer, teacher, lawyer, and more. When she's not sitting behind her laptop she can be found on some adventure. Most of the time it's a road trip with her two doggos, but recently it has been in the pages of a book.

You can find her on Instagram and TikTok under the username @bookishstephaniek

Also by Stephanie K. Clemens

Available on Vella

The Daring Adventures of Honoria Porter: Part One

The Daring Adventures of Honoria Porter: Part Two

Stripped Away

The Adventures of Alex Granger

Novellas

The Adventures of Alex Granger

Ladies of WACK series

A Study in Steam

A Practicum in Perjury

A History in Horticulture … Coming Soon